The Pursuit

Also by Lisa Herrington

The Renaissance Lake Series

The Fix

Fall Again

Million Reasons

Mistletoe in Maisonville

The Pursuit

Sunny Paradise

Standalone Books

One Starry Night

The Pursuit

Lisa Herrington

Writerly House Publishing

THE PURSUIT

Published by Writerly House Publishing
www.WriterlyHouse.com
www.LisaHerrington.com
This is a work of fiction. Characters, names, places, and events are products of the author's imagination. Any similarity to events or places, or real persons, living or dead is purely coincidental.

First Published January 2023

ISBN: 978-0-9990626-5-4

10 9 8 7 6 5 4 3 2 1

For James

Prologue

Tenille only had one chance to leave. She was in the most romantic place she had ever been, The Four Seasons Resort in Lanai City, Hawaii, and approximately 3, 857 miles from her home in Texas.

Arriving only two days ago, Peter had reminded her no less than eight times how ungrateful she was and how he was a sucker to spoil her. Tenille didn't make his coffee the way he wanted, and she didn't wear the clothes he expected even though he'd picked out every single item in her suitcase, including the shoes. The list of things she wasn't went on and on.

She'd met him after her aunt died and moved in with him after only one week. The rest had been unbearable. Learning who he really was and how he made his money, she understood her life would never be the same.

Peter was in the middle of telling an inappropriate joke as she quietly excused herself from the large dining table. Six Middle Eastern men stood when she did, but Peter just stared at her.

"Going to the ladies' room," she whispered as his jaw

clenched. He was angry. Mad at her for interrupting his story or because she took attention off him. Honestly, it could have been because she was human and needed to use the facilities. She had no idea what went on inside his crazy head. She just knew this was her only opportunity, and she needed to act as casually as possible if she was going to make it out alive.

She smiled at the guests surrounding the table and smoothed down her blue silk dress before she strolled across the opulent room. Softly clicking her four-inch heels like she didn't have a care in the world, she gently pushed open the door and stepped inside to where their waitress stood anxiously.

The waitress, Nalani, waiting on their table, had been in the parking lot when Tenille and Peter had arrived. Nalani saw when Peter grabbed Tenille's face, slammed her head against a window, crushing the daisy she wore in her hair, and threatened her before they walked inside the restaurant.

Tenille caught Nalani's concerned eyes as she wiped tears from her face, careful not to smudge her makeup and upset him again. The slight nod and understanding in her expression were almost more than Tenille could take.

While the men at the table talked, Nalani signaled Tenille to meet her in the restroom. She waited there with a pair of flip-flop sandals and then hugged Tenille harder than she'd been hugged in a long time.

Nalani led her outside to a pickup truck and introduced Tenille to her cousins, a young woman and a man who were twins. "I'll refill the drinks at the table and when he notices you're still gone, I'll stall him by saying you're not well, but will be out of the restroom soon. Good luck."

Tenille reached for Nalani's arm. "You can't let him know you helped me. Understand?"

The look in Nalani's eyes told her that she did.

"Mahala," Tenille whispered before she hurried out of there with the cousins and onto a two-lane road. In fifteen minutes, Tenille was on a small boat and heading away from the town of Lanai and the scariest person she'd ever known.

Chapter One

Daisy Jones sat on her made bed at Mrs. Bower's Boarding House in Maisonville and stared at the unopened letter on her dresser. She'd sent it two weeks ago to her friend, Nalani, in Lahaina, Hawaii, and last night when she returned to the boarding house after work, the letter stamped with red letters *Return to Sender* was waiting for her.

It didn't necessarily mean that something was wrong. Perhaps there was an issue with the postal service, or perhaps she needed more postage for the birthday card, since it was a little larger than a regular letter?

Nalani had become her best friend in such a short period of time. "Happy Birthday to you," she'd sang to Daisy back in September. They'd just moved into their own apartment the month before, and Nalani woke her up on her birthday with a cupcake in bed. "I know you have to work all day, but in case you don't get another chance for cake, you should eat one for breakfast." Then she gave Daisy a giant bag of tootsie-pops, which was her favorite candy.

Thinking about how wonderful the large Hawaiian family

had been to her helped cheer Daisy up. They were incredible people. She laid back on her bed and tried not to worry. She thought about calling, but knew she shouldn't. Daisy had left in the middle of the night and understood the stakes.

No contact.

It was the only way to be sure no one could trace their relationship or her new name and location. But what if Peter found out they'd helped her? What if he was there now?

She closed her eyes tightly and tried not to think about it. The Kahale family was resourceful. They could take care of themselves and each other. They'd taken care of her. Saved her life. She owed them by keeping safe and following the rules.

No phone calls.

She checked the clock and saw it was almost time for work. Waiting tables at the local diner, Main Street Grocery had helped her get back on her feet. Locals called it Miss Lynn's Diner after the owner, and she wondered where the name Main Street Grocery came from since it wasn't a grocery and wasn't on Main Street.

It was just one of many quirky things she'd found in the quaint little water town. She couldn't explain why she immediately felt comfortable in Maisonville, but there was something sweet in the air and comforting to her nervous soul.

Daisy had always been fidgety and her Aunt Sue would smile and say, "You are just like me and a wanderer at heart."

They'd spent a lot of time traveling together after her Uncle Ed passed away, trying to ease that antsy feeling. However, the more they traveled, the more it was obvious that her Aunt Sue was everything that Daisy wasn't.

Sue Langley was fearless, never met a stranger, and loved adventure. Daisy was scared of her own shadow, rarely talked to strangers which she had learned the hard way was a rule that shouldn't be broken, and thought adventure was overrated.

Despite that, she traveled with her aunt because she adored Sue and secretly wished she could be more like her.

After Daisy graduated high school, Aunt Sue kept them traveling nonstop for several years. While sunning themselves on the Amalfi Coast, Sue announced that she'd been wrong about the whole wanderer's soul thing. "Kiddo, it's true I have a wanderer's soul, but you, dear, are an old soul trapped in a heart-breaker body." Her sweet aunt then added, "And it's my duty to help you find that youthful spirit."

Aunt Sue's best girlfriends had been on that trip too. Mel, Carol, and Amelia flirted shamelessly with any boy close to her age, as if it were their job, trying to get her to go out with one of them. It was the best and most embarrassing trip.

It seemed like just a few weeks ago that they were in Italy, but it had been almost a year. Wiping her eyes, Daisy smiled as she thought again about her sweet aunt's personality. Aunt Sue would be proud of how brave Daisy had been recently. Changing her name and jumping on a flight out of Hawaii just in time to avoid trouble. She'd conjured up just enough of her aunt's ambition, and that was how she found her way to Maisonville. Maisonville wasn't quite her destination, but it was because of her Aunt Sue that she'd ended up there.

While trying to figure out a place to hide, she instantly remembered how fondly Aunt Sue and Uncle Ed used to talk about New Orleans. Sue had gone to college at Loyola University and then lived in a suburb called Metairie when the two of them met. Uncle Ed showed her his version of the city through all his favorite restaurants, and they'd fallen in love almost instantly. It was one of the most romantic stories, and Daisy loved it when they retold it to her as a child.

Sue had promised to take her niece to visit, but hadn't gotten around to it before she suddenly passed away. It made sense to Daisy that she should go there.

The only problem was that she'd booked everything over the internet after she'd escaped on a red-eye flight from Maui. It had been a harrowing night, and she was thankful to have made it out of there before Peter caught her.

Somewhere over the northern Pacific Ocean, she stopped shaking long enough to get on-line, and secured a place. But instead of renting a room in Metairie, she'd rented a room in Maisonville. It was an honest mistake—made purely from the sleep deficit and adrenaline combo she had coursing through her body at the time. But she didn't have enough money to correct it.

So instead, she rode a shuttle van across the lake and settled into the quiet boarding house in Maisonville. That same day, she was interviewed by Miss Lynn, and it felt like divine intervention had put her in the right place at the right time. She couldn't deny that after being scared out of her wits, the calm surrounding her in Maisonville was exactly what she'd needed.

Daisy felt stronger and braver than before and while that still wasn't very strong or brave by most standards, it was a huge mountain that she'd climbed.

Now, as she headed into the diner and saw the handsome large man that had annoyed her a few days ago pulling in, she hoped she could maintain more of that stubbornness.

❧

Reaper parked his truck as he watched the blonde waitress walk into the diner. He was certain she'd seen him and when she looked the other way and then hurriedly went inside—he laughed.

There was something about her that niggled at him, and it wasn't just because she was attractive. He'd stopped in for dinner several days ago and hadn't realized how late it was before he'd ordered a ton of food. It was past closing, and although exhausted, she continued being kind to him. She refilled his tea glass and then coffee cup three times and never rushed him, although the kitchen staff was giving her a hard time.

After a while, she gave in and let the two guys in the kitchen leave. She tried to act like that was something she did all the time, but he could tell she was nervous. "When that little voice inside your head tells you something is wrong, listen to it," he'd told her, and she froze and stared at him. "I can tell you from personal experience it saved me and my team on countless missions while I was in the Navy. I didn't and don't take it lightly."

She seemed to dismiss his comment, and so he made himself clear. "It isn't safe for you to remain in the diner with a stranger. No matter how nice they may appear."

Reaper was certain he'd scared her, but she put her hands on her hips and pointedly asked him if he was a serial killer. He thought that showed a lot of guts and he laughed about it for days afterward.

That night when they walked out of the diner, he saw her walking home and it didn't sit well with him. There were a few gas-style streetlights around the diner but for most of her way, it would be dark as pitch.

What was an attractive woman like her doing there alone, without a car or anyone looking out for her? It wasn't like he hadn't been around people who had a tough upbringing, but she was a bit refined, like she'd been well taken care of for most of her life. It was clear by the way she spoke and all her sweet and delicate mannerisms. Fending for herself wasn't something she'd had to do for very long because she was terrible at it.

"I'll walk you home or drive you home, but either way, you will not do it alone."

The petite waitress rolled her eyes at him and then actually put her hands on his chest as if she were going to shove him away. He had at least a hundred and fifty pounds on her and was more than a foot taller. Most men wouldn't pick a fight with him, but she had.

She definitely hadn't been alone for long.

Absolutely refusing to get into his truck, she stormed off in the direction of the boarding house, where she was renting a room. He gave her space, but walked behind her the entire way. At first, she jogged down the sidewalk, turning around every so often to check and see if he was still there. He could tell when she finally accepted the fact that he was just looking out for her because her shoulders lowered from around her ears, and she stopped clutching her overstuffed book bag.

Reaper stood at the iron gates in front of the boarding house as she climbed the steps of the front porch, watching as she turned around one last time. He smiled at her, but she shook her head at him and rolled her eyes before going inside.

What the hell was she doing in this little town, away from her people?

He'd asked around and heard she'd told Miss Lynn that she was from Hawaii, but there was no mistaking that sweet Texas accent. In his experience, there was no place to go but hell after beginning with a lie.

But he couldn't stop thinking about her. Reaper had a fondness for trouble, which was why he spent most of his adulthood single. His ex-girlfriend had done a number on him, more times than he would like to admit, and he wouldn't welcome that back into his life.

Recently, Reaper and his security team eradicated a serious threat against Alexavier Regalia's girlfriend, Olivia Dufrene, and her seven-year-old son, Lucas, and he owed it to them to keep an eye out. He would keep this sweet little town and its residents safe. In fact, that was why he'd told his friend Cage to meet him at the diner for an early lunch before they headed out to go fishing with their new friend, Ryan Gentry.

Cage could see past a beautiful woman and her story better than most, and he would call it like he saw it when he met the little waitress. But Reaper didn't see Cage's SUV in the parking lot and so he went inside to get them a table and make sure they were seated in her section of the diner.

He was curious, which always sent him into investigative mode. Her name was Daisy, and he'd learned enough about her over the last couple of days to make him interested. He hoped another hour around her would reveal even more.

Chapter Two

Miss Lynn watched as Daisy hurried into the diner like the devil was after her. She nodded her way, but Daisy went straight to the back room to stow her bag and put on her apron.

Completely ready to defend her girl if needed, Lynn smiled when she heard waitress Olivia greet Reaper. He'd been part of the security team in St. Marksville that helped find Olivia's son, Lucas, when he'd been taken. Miss Lynn thought a lot of him and smiled when she realized he was the person who had motivated Daisy to run inside and hide in the back room.

Miss Lynn walked over and gave Reaper a hug before seating him in her largest booth near the window, which was Daisy's station. Daisy may not know how good Reaper would be for her, but Miss Lynn knew he was exactly the person who could help her. Of course, Lynn didn't know what type of predicament Daisy was in, but she certainly was scared of something, and it had happened before she came to their little town.

The young woman had told Miss Lynn that she had lost her social security card and then she explained she was dealing with identity theft. Daisy wasn't very good at not telling the truth, and Miss Lynn knew there was more to her story.

However, she wasn't the first young woman that had walked through the diner door with a bit of trouble on her heels. So, if paying Daisy in cash for a while would help the young woman, then Lynn could do it. Of course, she would also softly guide her toward the handsome man that could protect Daisy if trouble came calling too. And Reaper had more than proven himself by helping Olivia and Lucas. He and Daisy would be a great fit.

Before Reaper could ask, Miss Lynn patted his large forearm with her hand, "Daisy will be right with you in a minute." She winked at him and then headed to the back room to see what was taking her newest waitress so long.

"We're getting busy out there and need you, honey," Miss Lynn said, sounding frantic. She'd missed her calling in theater and used all of her gifts to manage the people who worked for her.

Daisy walked slowly toward the white-haired woman and nodded. "Yes, ma'am."

Miss Lynn could see Daisy wringing her hands on her apron. She reached over to hold her still. "What's wrong, dear?"

Daisy shook her head.

"Does it have anything to do with the handsome man sitting in your section?"

"Oh, Miss Lynn. You didn't?"

"Oh, yes, I did. I know he looks intimidating, but he is truly a sweetheart. Besides, some bad boys are worth it."

Daisy laughed nervously and wrung her hands more. "I-I'm not looking for anything, Miss Lynn."

Miss Lynn guided Daisy toward the front, but before they stepped into view of everyone else, she leaned over and whispered, "Honey, that is when you find the best things."

Daisy shivered when Miss Lynn walked away. Her Aunt Sue

used to tell her the same thing. “You find the best things whenever you aren't really looking.” But Daisy had never found that saying to be true. In fact, someone really awful had found her when she wasn’t looking, and it had changed the course of her life. It would be a very long time, if ever, before she looked for a boyfriend, and it certainly wouldn’t be a bad boy. She'd already done that.

She took a deep breath as she slowly walked over to Reaper's table. "Good afternoon. Are you ready to order?"

Reaper smiled at her, and his light eyes lit up. He was a beautiful man and made her nervous about being around.

"How are you today, Daisy?"

She stood there staring at him until she realized he'd asked her a question. "I'm sorry, what?"

He continued to stare as he repeated his question, and she wondered if he ever blinked and then admired how straight his teeth were. Daisy was distracted checking him out and hadn’t heard him again. She swallowed and lowered her eyes to the ground, unable to ask him to repeat himself a third time.

He seemed amused by her, and she felt her face, neck, and chest heat. She quickly turned around, but then felt his warm hand on her shoulder as he stood up behind her. His body heat surrounded her as he stood too close. It made her feel dizzy.

He lowered his head and whispered into her ear. "You seem a little distracted today. Everything okay?"

She nodded but didn't speak.

He gently turned her around to face him. "I'm waiting on my friend to join me for lunch. I'll wait to order. Can I have a glass of iced tea for now?"

"Sugar?" she asked, suddenly realizing he might meet another woman for lunch and then felt her neck and ears get even hotter.

He liked the way she said *Sugar*, like the r was silent. She was definitely going to be a problem. He shook his head. "Unsweet."

Daisy hurriedly went back behind the counter to get him a glass.

Olivia and Miss Lynn watched the entire show and felt terrible for Daisy. Clearly, Reaper was interested and by all indications, so was little Daisy, but she was so nervous she couldn't handle his attention. Olivia had to help her.

Miss Lynn took the glass of tea from Daisy, and Olivia pulled her into the kitchen to chat.

"Alright, Daisy, let's have a pep talk. I know you're nervous and I'm guessing you haven't had a lot of experience in the guy department? So let me tell you, that hot guy out there, he wants you really, really badly. This is his second time in here in four days and he doesn't even live on this side of the lake. See how he keeps giving you those smoldering bedroom eyes every time he looks at you? That's also how you know. Basically, you can do anything, and he still will want to jump your bones. Got it? Now do you like him because the way I see it, what's not to like? Tall, muscular guy with blue eyes and dark hair, rocking a smoking biker vibe all day long, but more Hollywood biker than creepy unemployed biker dude. Am I right? So, you have to ask yourself what are you going to have to do to pull yourself together and talk to him? And the answer is, not much. You can basically stand there and drool out the side of your mouth and he's still going to be on board. You got it? Now—" Olivia reached over and loosened Daisy's ponytail so her hair flowed around her shoulders and down her back.

"You look great. And he's honest to goodness, a good guy who saved my son and watched over us to make sure we got home safely. When I say a good guy, I mean like one of the best. And if I wasn't head over heels with Alexavier, I might even fight you for Reaper. But I can tell he is completely into you. So, let's get you out there so you can keep his attention. You ready?"

Daisy was pretty sure she'd just swallowed her gum. She

nodded and let Olivia tighten her apron to accentuate her figure and then headed to the diner floor to help another tabletop of six people nearby, so Reaper could stare at her. Olivia's directions, and Daisy followed them to the letter. She moved around the table, smiling at the guests while he looked on.

While putting the order in with the kitchen, she watched Reaper's friend join him at the table. Thank goodness it was another guy. Olivia patted her on the bottom and whispered, "Go get him." And Daisy went straight back over to them like she had steel in her veins. Only when she got there did she realize what she was doing, but it was too late. Both men were staring and smiling at her, and she grinned back like she was directed. That Olivia was cut from the same cloth as Aunt Sue and was going to get her into heaps of situations that Daisy wasn't sure she could get herself out of.

Both men ordered the special, but before she could walk away, Reaper reached out and held her hand. She stopped and looked at him while he cleared his throat. "Daisy, this is my friend Cage. We were in the Navy together."

Daisy smiled at Cage. "Nice to meet you," she said and then finally headed back to the kitchen. Once out of everyone's sight, she fanned herself and tried to catch her breath. The dizziness was back, and she felt like she might even faint. She hadn't done that in a while and was going to be super embarrassed if it happened at the diner at the beginning of her long shift.

One of the kitchen helpers ran and got Miss Lynn and, when she walked into the room, Lynn immediately had the guy grab Daisy a chair. "Put your head between your knees so you won't faint, honey," she said and then grabbed a paper bag for Daisy to breathe into when she sat back up.

Olivia rushed into the room to see what all the commotion was about, and Daisy saw dark spots in her vision. She quickly put her head down between her knees again and tried not to pass out. It made little sense. She'd been through hell escaping Peter in Hawaii. Her life had been in danger almost from the moment she'd met him, actually, before she even knew he existed, but she never once passed out. But now, on a beautiful afternoon at the diner where she was completely safe, her friend gave her a pep talk about a handsome man that may or may not be interested in her, and she almost hit the ground?

Before she could calm herself down with reason, Reaper stepped into the kitchen and knelt in front of her. When she looked up at him, the concern on his face made her want to cry. Maybe from embarrassment or perhaps from the tenderness, but still her eyes watered, and he immediately tried to soothe her.

"Hey, angel. Tell me what's going on? Do you feel dizzy like you're going to pass out or feel you might throw up?" He gently brushed her hair off her face and checked her pulse at the same time.

"B-both."

"What did you eat this morning?"

She shook her head. "I haven't eaten yet."

Miss Lynn stepped up and whispered, "Honey, you didn't eat anything last night either."

Daisy had to think hard through the whooshing sound in her ears to remember. Sometimes she got distracted and forgot to eat properly. Without Aunt Sue around, she simply didn't keep to a schedule, and she certainly didn't eat like she should.

"Did you eat yesterday at all?" Reaper looked concerned.

"I'm sure I did," she said, not entirely sure if she had. She was upset with herself because while she'd gone through a phase of not caring about her health, she wasn't doing that anymore.

Reaper smiled and leaned in closer to her. "Your pulse is slowing back down. Do you feel any better?"

The whooshing sound in her ears had stopped, and she could

hear the dishes clanging around in the kitchen again. She suddenly felt more embarrassed than dizzy.

She nodded and tried to stand, but Reaper stopped her. "Hold on there, little lady." He turned toward Miss Lynn. "She needs to eat something before she goes back out there."

Daisy wanted to protest, but her stomach growled as soon as he mentioned her eating. How could she have been so ridiculous and not eaten anything in over twenty-four hours?

"You're welcome to sit with Cage and me?" he said, and she immediately had to shut that down.

"Thanks, but I'm a waitress here, not a customer." She sat up straight and, despite her low blood sugar, refused to look weaker than she already had in front of everyone. "Thank you for your help, but I'm fine now."

Miss Lynn felt guilty that she and Olivia might have pushed Daisy too hard when she wasn't ready. She looked so tiny sitting there in a chair in the diner kitchen. Lynn stepped over and assured Reaper she was going to feed Daisy before letting her go back to work and then looked at Olivia, who could practically read her mind. Olivia took over and ushered Reaper back to his table and brought both men their hot lunches and then some dessert on the house.

Miss Lynn walked Daisy out back to a small table and chair set she'd bought recently. She'd actually had her former waitress turned home decorator, Sydney Gentry, help her set up the nice little covered area. Sydney found the comfortable chair set and added a rock garden, some privacy lattice barriers, and plants, since all the girls seemed to enjoy going out back when they needed a break.

Miss Lynn handed Daisy a tattered paperback copy of Rebecca by Daphne DeMaurier, and told her it was her favorite book of all time. She insisted the young woman relax and read until she came back with a deluxe sandwich, celery and carrot sticks, chips, and a drink.

Daisy smiled that Miss Lynn was treating her like Olivia's little boy, Lucas, but she appreciated the sweet woman more than she would ever know. She settled into the outdoor chair instantly, noting how comfortable it and the entire space made her feel. This town and its people were charming.

She sipped her Coca-Cola and began reading. The book was amazing and pulled her in from the first sentence. At least that was the excuse that she used, along with the food coma she was in from eating the entire sandwich, when Reaper found her. He said he'd called her name twice, but she hadn't looked up. When she acknowledged him, he swore she looked confused by her own name as she looked around as if he were talking to someone else.

"Sorry, I get like that sometimes when I'm reading. You know, swept away into the story." She tried to look sure of herself, but she knew she wasn't convincing the man who saw too much.

But he was a gentleman and nodded his head as if he believed her. "I just wanted to check on you before I left."

"Thank you. You didn't have to do that, though. I'm fine. I'm always fine."

He stared at her for a moment, looking less convinced than he had before. "Take care of yourself, okay?"

Daisy nodded and then as he turned to leave, she whispered, "You too."

She watched him get into his truck and drive off without looking back. It was exactly what she needed him to do, but absolutely the opposite of what she had wanted. She'd been so sure after she got away from Peter that she would never fall for anyone ever again. Then Reaper walked into the diner and showed her an ounce of kindness.

What was wrong with her? She'd narrowly escaped the most

dangerous man she'd ever met, was scared to death she'd put the precious Hawaiian family that helped her in danger and soon would have to move away from Maisonville before she was discovered. So why was she thinking so much about the handsome man who paid her a bit of attention?

Chapter Three

Daisy took a long look at herself in the mirror on the back of her closet door. She was wearing white jogger pants and a matching zip-front jacket with a black tank top underneath. It was comfortable and sort of cute, maybe even age appropriate.

Her hair was completely back to its natural color, and she added a bit of mascara and tinted lip gloss, feeling a small bit like her old self.

Everything seemed to be either before Peter or after Peter, and she hated he was in her thoughts at all.

She hadn't bought herself a single new item of clothing in ten months. Peter had packed her suitcase for Hawaii with sexy dresses and stiletto heels. She'd felt like a high-priced hooker. He insisted on choosing her undergarments and sometimes demanded she went without. Goosebumps covered her body as she remembered how exposed she'd felt and how he loved when everyone stared at her.

Once she escaped, it was all about concealing her identity. Nalani helped her dye her hair dark brown and gathered secondhand clothes that were baggy and would conceal her figure. She'd lost fifteen pounds that she didn't have to lose, making her look emaciated. The stress induced weight loss added to her disguise, she'd told herself until Nalani's mother sat her down and made her eat regularly. "Skinny is not healthy, girl," she would say. Daisy could see the worry on all their faces as she picked at her food. She didn't mean to cause them more worry and so she tried harder to find her will to live.

She worked with one of Nalani's cousins who had a salon and helped transform her into what she called a goth chick. Darker hair dye, zero makeup, except for some dark lipstick, and a fake nose-ring did the trick. She barely recognized herself.

Mr. Kahale got her a job at one of his friend's restaurants and she washed dishes day in and day out, avoiding speaking to anyone. Through their contacts and enormous family, they could keep close tabs on Peter Miller and his security goons. They scoured the island for weeks until one of Nalani's first cousins faked evidence that she'd caught a flight out of Maui to Dallas, Texas.

It was such a relief to know he was off the island. The entire family celebrated and gathered for a huge family cookout, including freshly caught squid. They were sweet to her, and she could never repay all of their hospitality and care.

As she looked at herself again in the mirror and how much she resembled the girl that her aunt and uncle raised, it made her emotional. Would she ever be that "before Peter" girl again?

It had taken everything she had in her to get away from him. It had been almost ten months, and he still hadn't given up. But he would not find her because she would run as far and as often as necessary until he lost interest. She just had to keep her guard up and always be ready for the next move.

Picking up the returned letter from Hawaii, Daisy held it to her chest. There had to be a logical reason that the letter hadn't made it to its destination. Nalani and her folks had to be okay.

She tucked the returned letter back into her backpack and then slipped on her sneakers.

Olivia and Miss Lynn had insisted that she join them at the Gentry's house for a cookout that afternoon. It was the first day she'd had off in three weeks and a rare event for the three of them to be off at the same time. On these rare Sundays, customers would order and pick up their food at the lunch counter instead of having wait staff. "The kitchen guys can handle it once in a while," Miss Lynn explained.

Daisy would have stayed in bed and reread one of her romance novels or watched television all day if they hadn't pushed her to go. Olivia threatened to pick her up and force her into the car, her piece of garbage car, whether she was dressed or not. Miss Lynn told Daisy she needed to do something fun. She also insisted that the gossip in town would buzz about Daisy if she didn't stop being a hermit.

Daisy already cared about Olivia and Miss Lynn and, even though she would have to run again, she would make the most of the time they had together. If she'd learned anything, it was that time with those you cared about was fleeting. You had to seize the moments and hold on.

She needed to get out of her small room at the boarding house and get her mind off the friends she'd left behind in Hawaii. The idea that she'd put them in danger constantly whispered at the back of her mind and she needed a reprieve from that dark place.

Zipping up her bag and grabbing the bottle of wine she'd bought as a hostess gift, Daisy looked around the room. Satisfied that everything was in order, she headed downstairs to leave a note for Mrs. Bowers that she would be back later.

The screen door on the front of the house creaked as Daisy eased it open. Mrs. Bowers had already had her lunch on the porch and was asleep in her rocking chair as Daisy crept by, trying not to disturb her.

The silver-haired woman was in her eighties but told everyone that she was seventy-nine. She had moved to Maisonville when she'd retired. Initially, Mrs. Bowers had set her house up as a bed-and-breakfast, but decided it tied her down too much. She had a social life after all, so five years ago, she opted to change direction and do short-term rentals instead. Thus, the Bower's Boarding House was born. Daisy was the only tenant at the moment, and it seemed less like a rental property and more like she was visiting with her grandmother.

If she had a grandmother.

Mrs. Bower's story was one of many Daisy had heard since she'd moved to town. The town seemed to woo people to it and once they were there, their lives became wonderful.

In fact, it was hard to find someone that hadn't transplanted their lives to Maisonville and loved everything about living there. They nicknamed the town Renaissance Lake because every type of person got a new start or began their lives over again once they settled down.

Daisy adjusted her bag and crossed the street to the worn path that followed the lake and would lead her to her new friends and the cookout. She didn't know much about the magic of Renaissance Lake or Maisonville, but she loved the stories she'd heard and wished she wasn't just passing through. She could use a little magic in her life and liked to pretend that it was Aunt Sue acting as her guardian angel that had led her there.

She swiped at a stray tear and told herself to get control of her emotions as she neared the giant white house up ahead. It was amazing and easily the most beautiful home in Maisonville. Daisy took a deep breath as she passed several cars parked along the large driveway. Miss Lynn had said there wouldn't be many people at the cookout, and now she was nervous, wondering if that was true. She was fifteen minutes late, but certain Olivia would have kept her promise and dragged her to the party if she hadn't shown up. She wasn't much of a party person and her Aunt Sue would pull her along to every event possible, sort of like Olivia and Miss Lynn.

As she rang the doorbell, she heard some noise from around the back. Before she headed around the house to the side gate, a beautiful redhead answered the door.

"Daisy, right?"

Daisy nodded.

"I'm Sydney. Ryan's wife. We've met at the diner a couple of times. I used to work there before you. Come on in. Everyone is out back."

Daisy handed Sydney the bottle of wine and followed her through the house to the kitchen and then out the back glass doors to the giant deck. They walked across it together toward the pier to an open dock house where they had set up a giant table and an outdoor grill. Olivia walked over and handed Daisy a drink as Miss Lynn waved to her.

Thankfully, it wasn't very crowded as she looked around, noting every person there. Learning to survey her surroundings hadn't come naturally, but another one of Nalani's cousins, Keola, Ke for short, who was a martial arts instructor, helped train her to protect herself.

She saw Olivia's son, Lucas, playing with a couple of older boys in the yard and Olivia's boyfriend, Alexavier, talking to Ryan Gentry, who was cleaning the grill. There weren't too many people there after all, but just as Daisy relaxed, a large splash of water came from behind her, and she jumped quickly to avoid getting drenched. Her shoes got wet, and she looked out to see two boys in a canoe who couldn't have done it.

While she stared at the rippling water, Reaper emerged twenty feet away like a water god sitting up and wiping his thick, dark hair out of his face with both hands. She had a spectacular view of his strong bare arms and chest, and the tattoos that adorned them. She gasped as he locked eyes with her, and she felt her face and neck heat.

"Mercy," she whispered, and Olivia cleared her throat.

Thank goodness for Olivia. Daisy wasn't sure she could have broken the spell of his stare if Olivia hadn't been standing there.

"Bathroom?" Daisy asked and quickly turned to go back into the house to dry off her shoes but mostly to hide until she composed herself.

It was early November and the weather in Maisonville had been tropical, like the weather in Lahaina, until this week. It was too cold to be in the water. Wasn't it? What was Reaper doing in there? She didn't even know he was going to be at the cookout.

Quickly turning around, Daisy ran back inside.

Chapter Four

Reaper climbed onto the pier, and without speaking to anyone, he stalked into the house. Cage had told him that he didn't trust Daisy. They'd quietly argued at lunch over her, and Cage reminded Reaper he'd asked him to check her out and give his opinion. It wasn't the first time Cage had intervened, and he'd been right multiple times about women Reaper went out with.

"Her story doesn't add up, and she's too damsel-in-distress. You and I both know that is your weakness. What woman in her twenties isn't on social media? I haven't even seen her with a phone, brother. Isn't that odd?" Cage had argued his point until Reaper got up and paid the bill for both of them. He nodded his head at Cage, who told him he'd see him later. Then he'd walked behind the diner to say goodbye to Daisy. He watched her curled up in that wicker chair, reading a tattered book, and didn't know why he knew she wasn't faking, but something about her was so different from his ex and any other woman he'd met.

If he was honest, he hadn't known for sure if Daisy would be at the cookout, but he certainly hoped to see her at some point that day. Once Olivia and Lucas and then Miss Lynn arrived, he'd figured Daisy was at the diner. He was going to stay for an hour and then go see her. When he sat up in the water and saw her standing there, he'd thought she was a dream—until she ran.

Inside the restroom, Daisy locked the door behind her and leaned against it. Reaper was the single hottest man she'd ever laid eyes on and completely not for her. She was quiet and unassuming. He was larger than life and people noticed him when he walked into a room or spoke in that deep, gravelly voice. Despite what Olivia had told her, Reaper looked dangerous, especially with those tattoos. She was a good girl, no matter what had happened with Peter, and she tried to always follow the rules. Reaper was a powerhouse, and she was a wimp. Gosh, she'd almost fainted when he was at the diner the last time. She fainted over simple things like when she got her ears pierced or when she had to speak in front of a room full of people. She hadn't been that big of a coward in a long time. So why couldn't she stop thinking about him and quit blushing whenever he was around? She was not interested in him. Besides, his name was Reaper, and that scared the daylights out of her.

After drying her shoes, she splashed cold water on her face and used a napkin to pat it dry. A couple of deep breaths and she'd be fine. She dug in her pocket and pulled out a grape-flavored tootsie pop. It was her only vice and one she refused to give up. Her Aunt Sue loved lollipops and tootsie pops had been her favorite.

With a deep breath and her shoulders pulled back, she turned out the light and headed out of the powder room and right into Reaper.

"Whoa, angel." He reached out and steadied her.

"Sorry." She tried to walk around him, but he still held onto her.

"My fault." He smiled, and she stared at his beautiful teeth. Teeth that perfect weren't natural. Was he the kind of man to have cosmetic work done on his mouth? Daisy was still looking at his mouth when he leaned in closer to her ear to speak. "I didn't mean to startle you. Out there or in here."

She didn't know what to say, so she dashed back outside, leaving him standing there. She couldn't talk to him, or she wouldn't be strong enough to walk away. He had some kind of spell over her, and she felt foolish around him.

Reaper grinned and held the towel around his waist a little tighter as he watched Daisy. He sure liked those white sweatpants she was wearing. Was that a grape lollipop in her mouth?

He laughed as he went into the restroom to dry off and changed back into his clothes. He shouldn't have let his buddy Rex goad him into racing Cage across the lake. They both knew Reaper was faster, but with the young boys chanting him on, he was in the water and heading to the buoy without another thought. It was fun, and he'd beaten Cage by a yard, but when he sat up and saw her staring at him, he'd wished he'd been up there on the dock with her.

Her sandy blonde hair was brighter than before, down and glistening in the afternoon sun. It was like a golden halo surrounding her. He was in a trance, staring into her big brown eyes until she broke and ran back into the house. Damn if he didn't want to catch her. Show her that she never had to be afraid of him.

He swam to the dock faster than he'd swam to the buoy. Without a word to anyone, he had a towel, his clothes, and headed into the house to find her. His pulse slowed when he realized she hadn't gone out the front door.

When she'd stepped out of the restroom and he saw her sucking furiously on that grape lollipop, he used all his willpower to not pull her into his arms. He couldn't remember a woman ever having that kind of effect on him.

After getting dressed, he headed to the kitchen for a couple of bottles of water. He found Sydney there and helped her carry a tray of burgers, hot dogs, and sausages out to Ryan for the grill.

He helped man the fire for a while since he had a perfect view of Daisy sitting across from Olivia and the mayor, but next to Miss Lynn. She didn't talk, but listened to them as she quietly watched the kids playing in the yard. The place was a kid's paradise with a tether ball, badminton net, a soccer area, and a large tree house. She seemed to take it all in, but didn't really take part.

Was she shy or was something on her mind? He wanted to find out. Rex and Cage continued talking to Ryan when Reaper walked over and offered Daisy the extra bottle of water he had and then he took the seat next to her.

"Thanks," she whispered.

"You're welcome." He leaned in. "The burgers are about to come off the grill. Can I get you one?"

"Oh, no, that's okay. I can get it." She stood up, and he stood too, holding his hand out so she could go first. She ducked her head and walked over to make her plate as he followed her.

He watched as she made a cheeseburger and precisely placed each item on it—ketchup, mayo, mustard, onions, pickles, lettuce, and tomatoes. It looked like art when she finished. He followed her lead except his burger was more thrown together and he added a hotdog to his plate too. He sat beside her again, and as she took a huge bite, he grinned. "That's a great-looking burger," he said, and then took a big bite of his own.

Daisy wasn't great at small talk and so she nodded and continued to eat while the rest of the gang sat down and chatted throughout the meal. Rex told a couple of funny stories about their time in Afghanistan, which made the younger boys laugh. Daisy seemed to enjoy it, too.

After eating half her food, she took her plate over to the table and covered it with tinfoil, then she helped clear everything away.

Sydney tried to get her to relax, but Daisy insisted on helping and then stayed inside to wash dishes, too.

It was an hour before she returned, and everyone had gathered around a large fire that Ryan had built. Daisy had a tray of homemade cookies that she and Sydney had baked, and she walked around, making sure everyone got what they wanted before she found a seat on the outside edge of where everyone else was sitting.

Reaper watched as she curled up in an Adirondack chair and listened to the boys telling scary stories and entertaining everyone. She even jumped a few times at some of the punch lines and he enjoyed watching her honest reactions.

Things wrapped up around seven, but it had been dark for a couple of hours, which made it feel even later. Daisy helped clear things again, but Reaper hung back and helped, too.

He watched Daisy decline rides with Olivia and Miss Lynn and there was no way he was going to let her walk home in the dark alone. Had she walked there that afternoon? It had to be a couple of miles to her place from the Gentry's house and it was much colder.

He quietly walked out when she did and then as she headed down the driveway, so did he.

"What are you doing?" she asked, a little startled.

"I think we covered this the other night at the diner."

She stared back at him.

"It's not safe for you to walk back this late at night alone. It's too dark and a driver might not see you on these back roads."

"So, you're going to walk me home and then walk back and get your truck? That's twice as dangerous."

Reaper put his hand over his heart. "Concerned about me, are you?" He laughed. He was 6'4" and 280 pounds of mostly muscle. He'd been a Navy SEAL and put the fear of God into most mortal men, but she was worried about him walking back alone? "Then get in my truck, angel, so I can drive you."

Her eyes watered when he called her angel, and without another word, she turned around and headed to the dirt path toward the boardinghouse. She was stubborn, and he had to admit that he really liked that about her, too. He put his keys in his pocket and followed behind her like before.

Daisy swung her book bag around her shoulders and then began running. He shook his head. She was damned hardheaded, but he could run for miles and so he kept pace behind her. For her size, she was fast and must run regularly to keep that type of speed. Unlike the other night when she slowed down and walked for a while, this time she ran the entire way home.

When she reached the front door, she barely glanced back to see him before hurrying inside. Clearly, she wanted him to understand she wasn't interested. But he was concerned about her and couldn't help himself.

She was hiding some serious secrets. Would that trouble follow her to town? Whatever it was, had to be a doozy because she didn't talk to anyone much. In fact, he was certain he'd never been around a quieter person.

Cage had taunted him about her. "She doesn't really talk much, even to the other women. The situation just gets curiouser and curiouser." Before Cage left the cookout, he leaned in and told Reaper that curiosity killed the cat. Reaper punched him in the chest. He wasn't a damn cat. But he was concerned about that secretive girl. She was self-composed in a way he didn't understand and sweeter than anyone he'd ever met. She called to him in a primal way, and he couldn't shake the feeling he had about her.

Who was Daisy Jones?

Chapter Five

The returned letter Daisy had sent to Hawaii seemed to stare back at her when she woke up. She'd placed it on her nightstand before she went to sleep as if it would tell her what to do or whether The Kahale family was okay. She always kept it with her, and she needed to stop worrying about it.

It haunted her day and night.

Her aunt hadn't liked indecisiveness and Daisy knew if Aunt Sue had been there, she wouldn't approve. Surely the letter had been returned by mistake or for incorrect postage. Nothing else made sense.

Daisy had known better than to send it to Nalani's family home. Instead, she'd sent it to the restaurant where Nalani had worked for most of her life. It was her family's business, specializing in seafood for fifty years and was very popular.

She hadn't addressed it to Nalani for fear the wrong person would intercept it. She hadn't put a return name, only a return address to the boarding house. The Kahale family would know it was from her and that it was a sign that she was okay. But apparently, they didn't get it.

It was one of several things that were weighing on her mind. Like the handsome beast of a man that she ran away from a week ago.

Reaper had been a gentleman the entire time he was at the cookout and besides sitting near her, he never overstepped the boundaries she'd clearly set. But when he offered to drive her home, she panicked.

The only superpower she had was that she could run fast. During self-defense training in Hawaii, Ke told her when all else was lost, just run. Run like your life depended on it. Why that hit her the moment she stepped onto the dirt path that night, she would never know. But apparently, it sent the message that she was not interested because Reaper hadn't been back to the diner. And that was what she had wanted. *Wasn't it?*

Daisy looked at her clock. Miss Lynn had asked her to work a couple of early shifts this week, and she didn't have time to worry over the attentive man that was not her type or the letter any longer. She couldn't take back her previous behavior and she either needed to put the letter into another envelope, add extra postage and mail it again, or forget about it.

No reason to continue fretting over what could have been. But still, she thought about the overprotective man who had followed her home again.

Reaper was a force of nature, and Daisy wasn't sure why he was interested in her. But he sure took up a lot of room in her daydreams and in her head at night. She wasn't available and after running away from him, full tilt, he must have taken the hint.

Still, she considered the first time he'd eaten at the diner. She'd thought she might have made a grave mistake as he lectured her on how dangerous it was to stay there alone with a stranger. But she kept reminding herself that Miss Lynn had told her about Reaper being a hero who helped Olivia. When she refused to let him drive her home and then insisted on walking with her, she'd tried to stop him. He actually laughed when she put her hands on his chest and couldn't budge him. It was like moving a mountain. It knocked the wind out of her, and she'd realized how crazy she must have looked.

She was exhausted, but turned and jogged back to the boarding house. He followed her, but gave her plenty of space. When she slowed down, he did too, never imposing on her territory. That said a lot about the man, and she understood why Olivia always beamed when he came around. Besides, even though he had that imposing hard body, he also had very kind eyes. His blue eyes shined every time he talked to her.

Peter Miller had looked harmless but was a horrible person. His eyes, his eerie blue eyes, were soulless. Daisy wasn't sure she'd ever completely trust anyone again, but Reaper didn't know her past or that she was scared every second of every day because Peter was out there looking for her. Reaper was just trying to help a woman get home safely.

Daisy pulled her hair into a ponytail and took a deep breath as she hurried out the front door and down the steps of Mrs. Bower's House. She would mail her letter again, stop thinking about Reaper, and get to work. Taking control of her day would give her the confidence to take control of her life. Even though she was frightened, she knew taking things one day at a time would be enough to set her in the right direction. Aunt Sue had told her something like that after her parents' accident when she was a young girl.

"Honey, we will take this one day at a time and if that is too much, then we will try one hour at a time or even one minute at a time until we figure things out." It had been one of many significant pieces of advice Aunt Sue had given her over the years. Lord, she missed her aunt.

When she arrived at the diner, she could see the light on in the kitchen. Miss Lynn liked to get in extra early a few days a week to make buttermilk or sweet potato biscuits and, when possible, a few extra pies.

Daisy put her things away and then made the coffee and tea before she set out all the condiments for breakfast. There was a small crowd that came in extra early, and Daisy enjoyed how that crowd was quiet as they drank their coffee and scarfed down their food.

She and Miss Lynn had served about fifteen people by the time Olivia came in. Olivia wasn't scheduled to be there until lunch, but Alexavier had stayed over and they stopped in to have breakfast before taking Lucas to school.

Daisy sighed as she watched them sitting together. They were such a cute little family. She marveled over how much Olivia reminded her of a young Sue Langley, spirited in a way that Daisy wasn't.

There was a storm following Daisy. One that she wasn't sure she could handle on her own. Her aunt would have known what to do, which was probably the reason she felt at home at the diner and close to Olivia over such a short time. She tried to absorb that energy and strength whenever Olivia was nearby.

Olivia's ex was bad news too, but when she needed it most, an entire task force swooped in and helped resolve things. It was the sort of swift resolution her Aunt Sue would have conjured up if ever she'd been in trouble. Daisy didn't have those types of resources internally or externally, but it comforted her being close to someone so much like her aunt who did. Plus, she enjoyed watching Olivia's awesome romance with the mayor.

Goodness. He was almost as beautiful as Olivia and the sweet things he did for her, and she did for him, made Daisy happy. After all, love was all that mattered. Even though she had never had romantic love, she had enjoyed reading about it. Seeing it up close was even more powerful.

It was enough to bolster her for the rest of the breakfast shift and lunch. Things finally slowed down around three that afternoon, and she cleaned out the coffeepot and wiped down the counters. She was officially in her end of shift trance when the little bell on the diner entrance rang. She tried not to look surprised when Reaper walked through the door.

Miss Lynn and Olivia were both suddenly scarce, and she had no choice but to wait on him. She swallowed her smile as she looked up at Reaper. His face was dark, but it made him seem sexier as he smiled back. Just like before, she was locked onto his stare. Internally, she scolded herself for being so attracted to the man. *Was Reaper his last name? First name, Grim?*

She definitely had a type, bad boys.

"What can I get for you today?"

"Good afternoon, Daisy."

She bit her lip but didn't speak. At the cookout, he'd looked at her that same way. As if he could read her mind and it was so unnerving.

He shamelessly continued to stare until she finally answered. "Good afternoon. What can I get you?"

"How about some iced tea?"

Daisy tried not to blush as he watched her fill up his glass. Reaper slid onto a bar stool, and they were almost eye to eye when she turned around.

"Without Sugar? Right?" she asked. When he slowly shook his head, she felt the heat creep up her neck and face again.

What was wrong with her? Sure, she was lonely. It still didn't make sense for her to act like an idiot whenever he came around.

Daisy hadn't even considered going out with anyone in almost a year. Why was this big guy getting under her skin?

She felt Olivia wrap an arm around her as she slid in beside her. "Hey, Reaper," Olivia said.

As soon as he saw Olivia, his dark features lit up. It didn't make Daisy jealous—well, maybe a little, but honestly, Olivia had that effect on most men. "Hi, Olivia."

"Want some pie? Miss Lynn's pies are famous. Get him some pie, Daisy."

Daisy nodded and turned quickly to plate him a large piece of coconut cream pie. He looked younger when she handed it over and he took a large forkful into his mouth. *His hot mouth.* She shook her head.

Olivia smiled slyly at Daisy, and it was all the warning Daisy got. "So, Reaper, what are you back across the lake for? Our girl, Daisy?"

Floor, please, swallow me whole. Right this second, Daisy thought. Olivia didn't flinch as she hugged Daisy's waist tighter.

Reaper didn't miss a beat. "As a matter of fact, I stopped by to ask you out, Daisy. I had to come across the lake to meet Ryan Gentry. He's selling off some old architectural items he removed from a house that I can use in my home in New Orleans."

Reaper had been more machine than man for the last twelve years, but during his downtime, he remodeled his house in New Orleans. It was one of the oldest structures in the French Quarter and when he bought it ten years prior, it was mostly the shell of a building. He found he liked the work and restoring the property. He was a detail guy and not much got past him. Like how he didn't miss the moment it mortified Daisy that Olivia had asked him about her, or the flash of a hopeful glance she gave him when he answered.

Daisy was nervous all the time, and he wanted, rather he needed, to know why. Did he make her feel that way? Or did someone else? He had a protective nature, but there was more to it than his need to protect her. She was beautiful in an old movie star way. Brown eyes with heavy eyelids that made her eyelashes flutter when she blinked. Sandy blond hair with a wave that looked similar to an old Hollywood actress. He was a big fan of those old pin up posters. Of course, the first thing he'd noticed was how her tiny waist accentuated her hips. She was something to hold on to, and he wanted to hold on to her in a way that would make her more than blush.

Yup, trouble.

Olivia cleared her throat. "Well, you're in luck. Daisy's shift ended just a few minutes ago, and she's free for the rest of the day. Day-date, anyone?"

Miss Lynn walked over as if on cue. She had Daisy's book bag and the paperback novel she was reading. "Here you go, honey. I have already clocked you out." She snatched Reaper's plate away before he could get another bite, and Olivia took his fork. He'd never been rushed out of a place so quickly and expertly in his life.

As he tucked Daisy into the passenger seat of his truck and closed the door, he understood they knew her better than he did and if he'd hesitated, she would have run. Instead, she was all his for the afternoon.

Daisy watched him as he strode around the truck and climbed in easier than a man his size should move. How did she get herself into these situations?

Chapter Six

Reaper lowered the sound on the radio and adjusted the air vents in the truck toward Daisy. "Are you hot?" he asked, and she flushed again. He'd never been around a woman that blushed more than Daisy and it did something for him.

"No. I'm fine," she stopped talking and licked her lips.

He stared at the way her lips glistened in the sun, beaming through his truck windows before he forced himself to turn away and pulled out onto the road.

She was quiet for the short drive. When he pulled into the Gentry's driveway and parked in front of their large white house, she finally spoke.

"Why do they call you Reaper?" She swallowed hard before continuing, "Is it short for Grim Reaper? Didn't your parents like you?"

He laughed. "My handle or nickname is Reaper. I'll save that story for later if that's alright by you?"

Daisy nodded.

"My parents named me Michael, Michael Thibodeaux." He

reached his hand out to shake hers. “Nice to meet you, Daisy. Now, what's your real name?”

She froze instantly at the question and removed her hand out of his.

Reaper felt the way her skin went ice cold when he teased her. The other day, she hadn't looked up when he called her name outside, which he filed away as odd, but he’d just been kidding. Instantly, he knew she wasn’t who she said she was.

"M-My name is Daisy."

She was a terrible liar, but he wouldn’t make her more uncomfortable. It would take time to get her to trust him, and he had time.

He grinned at her. "Ready to go inside?"

She nodded, and he rushed to help her down out of the large truck. He slid his warm hand around hers and led her to the giant front doors.

The way he held her hand distracted Daisy. It felt nice. Like they were together and not as if he owned her. Of course, she hadn’t known the difference when she’d first met Peter.

Reaper noticed the far off look in her eyes, but before he could ask what had her distracted, Ryan Gentry answered the door. She leaned into Reaper and he kept hold of her hand as they followed Ryan to his large workshop.

Reaper picked out several doors he wanted and a lot of hardware that he needed in his place. He and Ryan settled on a price for everything and discussed getting together at Reaper's house soon, so Ryan could see Reaper's work.

The guys loaded the salvaged items, and within ten minutes, he and Daisy were on their way again. "I would really like to show you my place, Daisy, if that’s alright with you. We could drop this stuff off and then go grab some dinner or, if that seems like too much, then we could just grab some coffee and park by the lakefront?"

"Your house is in New Orleans?"

"Yes, ma'am. In the French Quarter. I could get you back home at a decent time. Scout's honor."

"Were you actually a boy scout?" she asked without looking at him. She mostly stared at her hands as she twisted them together. The truth was that she didn't feel comfortable with the idea of going to his house alone with him. She wasn't sure if she would ever fully trust any man again.

"I was a boy scout. Worked hard to become an Eagle Scout."

She nodded even though she knew little about the boy scouts except that her Uncle Ed had been a proud Eagle Scout. "I've never been to New Orleans, except for the ride from the airport. But maybe we could save that for another time?"

Her voice quivered when she said that last part, and he could feel the nervousness rolling off her. Reaper gently lifted her hand and kissed the back of it. "Angel. There's no rush. We can go to my place some other time, okay?"

She nodded, and he didn't miss how she turned her face to look out the window to hide her watery eyes. He would give anything to know what had happened to her, but she held that secret tighter than she held onto that book bag she constantly carried around.

So, he tried the next best thing as he pulled up to the small coffee place that had popped up in town a short while ago. It was a mobile food truck and the two best friends that started it made exceptional coffee and pastries. The patio space in the back was still new and gave the place an air of permanence. Espresso to Geaux was a nice little addition in the small town and people loved the coffee, tea, various pastries, and donuts they made.

"What's your favorite kind of donut?"

Daisy grinned, leaned forward, and whispered, "I've never met a donut that I didn't like."

"Me either," he said as he turned off the truck. He held her hand again as they walked up to the window and he placed their order for coffee and a full dozen donuts.

Fifteen minutes later, he drove them to a quiet spot on the lakefront, backing into a space so they would have a clear view. Daisy watched as he opened his glove compartment and pulled out a stack of napkins. Then he reached behind the seat and pulled out a large blanket.

Had he known she would say no to going to his house?

She hopped out of the truck and followed him to the back, where he lowered the tailgate and placed the blanket across it. "Hold on tight," he said, and she gripped the box of donuts and her coffee. Then he picked her up and gently set her down on top of the blanket before having a seat next to her.

Daisy handed over the box and watched as he leaned in so she could smell the aroma when he opened it. They were piping hot, and it was hard to choose, but she finally settled on a chocolate dipped donut, and he grinned as she took a bite.

Coffee was always a good idea. Before he pulled out the blueberry cake donut, he handed her a napkin. He'd already had an entire piece of coconut pie at the diner, but it didn't slow him down. He ate half of the donut in two bites before he offered it to her.

Daisy took a bite and closed her eyes as she ate it. "That is so good," she said and her whole face smiled. For the first time since he'd met her, he got a glimpse of who she really was underneath all those secrets.

They each ate a glazed donut as they watched a small alligator swim up to a sandy area a few hundred feet away. It wiggled around in the sand and then finally rested in the setting sunlight.

Daisy scooted over closer to Reaper and he grinned as he gently bumped her shoulder with his. "You aren't worried about that little thing?"

She shook her head. "No. I'm worried about his mother."

Reaper laughed before explaining that was another good reason for her not to walk along the dirt path by the lake alone at night.

The shocked look on her face made him laugh again. He took his empty coffee cup and used napkins to the trash bin and then took off his jacket and handed it to her.

Her chin dipped down as she accepted it. It seemed the slightest gestures embarrassed her, but it was chilly by the water, and she couldn't hide the goosebumps on her arms.

The jacket swallowed her, but as the sun set, it would get even colder and he wanted to hang out with her as long as possible.

He pointed out three pelicans that were flying above the water, looking for fish. And when the little silver fish started jumping out of the water, she laughed. "It's like they're teasing the birds."

It was the first time he'd heard her genuine laugh, and it took him by surprise. The innocent way she marveled at the surrounding nature was special. She was absolutely the sweetest girl he'd ever met. He explained the fish were mullet. Then they watched as several other birds flew in for the flying fish game.

Next, mother nature put on a spectacular show with the sunset spinning off dark purples and deep blues. He pulled her closer as the wind picked up. It wasn't until the sun slowly dipped down out of sight that she sighed and finally relaxed, leaning into him for the second time that afternoon.

They didn't talk as much as he'd thought they would, but there was comfort in being close. Her body language told a story. One he wanted to get to know well.

Contrasting to the slow setting of the sun, darkness swept in quickly. Reaper helped her hop down as he grabbed the blanket and walked her to her door.

Once she settled into her seat, he draped the blanket over her lap. Reaper had never been around a more feminine and delicate lady, and he caught himself staring more than he should have.

The night was still early, and he wished he could think of a way to spend more time with her, but she didn't make it easy. So, he slowly drove her back to the boarding house.

When he pulled up to the curb. She thanked him for the coffee and donuts and the wonderful time watching the sunset.

"Anytime, angel."

When he expected her to open her door, she hesitated. Was she looking for a way to spend more time with him, too?

He reached over and gently squeezed her hand, and she finally looked into his eyes. It surprised him when she spoke. "Michael? Did you grow up here?"

"About an hour from New Orleans. My parents still live in the house where I grew up."

"Are you close to your family?"

He noticed she didn't look at him when she asked that question, so he intertwined their fingers. "We're very close. But everyone from the neighborhood was close. It's a small working-class town, just a little bigger than Maisonville. Most of the men work out on the oil rigs or at the cabinet factory and most of their wives stay home and manage the kids."

"And your dad?"

"He was a roughneck," Reaper said, and grinned when she looked confused. "That's a manual job on a drilling rig, so oil."

"And you didn't want to do that?"

Reaper grinned. "Nah. That wasn't for me. He was gone a lot and sort of checked out of the family. I saw how hard my mother had to work to take care of the house, the family, and—well, everything. Not that she couldn't handle it. Beth Thibodeaux is stronger than the tide. She not only ruled our household but also kept most of the neighborhood kids on the straight and narrow too.

"No one screwed up around my mother or she would have hung them out to dry on the clothesline where she still hangs out her sheets today. She likes to say she's old school. She believes in a strong work ethic."

He could practically see Daisy's mind processing all the information he was giving her. She crossed her arms and sat back against the door of the truck. "So, there were a lot of kids in your neighborhood?"

Reaper enjoyed watching her settle in before she continued questioning him. He could do this all night. "Define a lot," he said and when she looked at him, he winked. "There were nineteen kids that lived on my street alone. Probably eighty in the entire neighborhood."

"Whoa. Eighty as in eight and zero?"

Reaper nodded. "It was like a giant beehive, and my mother was the queen. She didn't miss a thing."

Daisy figured that was where Michael must have gotten that trait, since he paid such close attention to everything.

"I have great memories of growing up, but it wasn't easy. When I was young, money was tight, and my folks fussed whenever my father was home. He wanted to relax, and my mother was on a mission to fix up our house, yard, and the neighborhood.

"Mom came from a long line of headstrong women, and she wouldn't sit back and take whatever was handed to her. She and my father dated in high school, and he knew her expectations. She said you either had money or time and since we didn't have money, she expected us to spend our spare time fixing things up." He winked at her and she smiled, listening to his every word.

"I could use most tools by the time I was seven and was wielding a power washer, lawn mower, and edger by the time I was eight."

"Eight-years-old?"

Reaper nodded. "My mom took in laundry and saved every penny she made, plus put some of my father's paychecks back. I also gave her everything I made from mowing lawns. By the time I was ten, she bought her first rental property. Then another one each year for five years. She also got three of her girlfriends pooling their money together so they could buy properties too. Eventually, all the kids had to help keep up the houses and the yards. What started out as a little extra income for our family grew into a comfortable life where my father could quit working his dangerous offshore job."

"Your mom sounds incredible."

"She is incredible," he said, and the smile on his face was so genuine it made Daisy smile too.

"My parents finally had financial security and enjoyed being together every day working on their business. Today they are happier than I've ever seen them. Mom swears it's because she has grandkids."

Daisy stared at him. "You have kids?" He watched her take another deep breath before she whispered, "Have you been married before?"

Reaper shook his head and watched as she bit her bottom lip.

"My little sister and her husband have four, all under the age of eight."

"You have a sister?"

"Yes, Abigail is a couple of years younger than me. She and her husband also dated in high school. She lives close to our parents and works in the family real-estate business. Her husband, Mac, works offshore, but unlike my folks, they like that arrangement. She's even bossier than our mom and it's funny watching the next generation of kids in the neighborhood coming up."

"It kind of sounds fun."

"Say the word, Daisy, and I'll take you over there to meet them."

She shook her head and avoided looking at him. "Oh, I wasn't scheming to meet your family."

Reaper stifled a smirk. He was certain Daisy didn't have a conniving bone in her body. No, she was a unique type of trouble.

Suddenly, he watched as she became nervous all over again. She began taking off his jacket and opening the truck door so she could get out. Reaper walked around to her as she folded his jacket to place it on the seat she'd vacated.

When Daisy turned around, she could feel his body heat, and it made her want to lean in close, but she stood still.

Gently, he tilted her chin up so he could look at her. "You didn't ask. I offered. Okay?"

Her eyes darted past him, but she nodded in understanding. Reaper held out his hand for her to hold so he could walk her to the front door of the boarding house.

"Thanks for the conversation," she said, letting go of his hand so she could pull out her keys.

Reaper nodded before slowly reaching out to pull her into a hug. Daisy fit against his body perfectly, but she only leaned into the embrace for a few seconds. It was a lot for her, and he knew it. So, he stepped back onto the porch to give her plenty of room.

"I'll see you soon, Daisy," he said before heading back to his truck.

When he climbed inside and turned around, she was standing in the doorway so she could wave to him.

He waved back and noted that he would have to get a lot quicker if he was going to keep up with that nervous girl.

Chapter Seven

There was a debate between Olivia and her boyfriend when Daisy walked in to work the next afternoon. She ducked behind the counter and into the back room quickly to stow her backpack and then put on her apron so she could get into service mode.

It was getting harder for Daisy to stop getting involved with the people around her. Olivia and Miss Lynn, both treated her like she was a long-lost member of their family. Even Mrs. Bowers was precious trying to grandmother her by leaving sweet notes about the boarding house. She kept tabs on where Daisy went or checked to see if she needed anything from the store.

Of course, she desperately missed her Aunt Sue and Aunt Sue's best friends, Mel, Carol, and Amelia. It had to be the reason this place felt like home. But she'd never really dated anyone before Peter. So why was it so comfortable to hang out with Michael yesterday?

Sure, she loved pastries and coffee, but he didn't know. Going back to the boarding house alone would have been the smart thing to do, but she snuggled in and watched the sunset like she didn't have a care in the world. Then, instead of getting out of his truck, she sat there and asked him questions about himself, as if getting to know him was an option.

Daisy barely slept last night because she couldn't stop thinking about Michael Thibodeaux. Did he know that giving her his jacket to wear would have that effect on her? It felt like a hug as she slid into it while it was still warm from his body heat. It smelled clean and fresh, just like him. The stories about his family made him seem as wonderful as Miss Lynn had said, but Daisy needed to keep her distance. She was supposed to always keep her guard up, and she wasn't doing a very good job of it.

Back in Hawaii, Nalani's cousin, Ke, told her she wasn't a fighter. He couldn't in good conscience let her believe she could fend off an attack. Instead, they focused on a couple of moves that might help her get away, and then they worked on her stamina. She was small and could wriggle in and out of lots of spaces and climb skillfully.

Finally focused on her running, Ke marveled that she could outrun him in a race, but especially in long distance. So, he trained her regularly to run, flee, and not fight.

It wouldn't keep Peter from getting to her, but it might make the difference in her escape. She at least felt like she had a chance. It was important for her to remember that everything in Maisonville was temporary, just like in Hawaii, because the one thing she had to do was keep moving.

In fact, that very morning she'd gone over the reasons she couldn't stay in Maisonville or continue getting closer to the wonderful, welcoming group of people. But then she walked into the diner to Olivia and her relationship with Alexavier. That was better than most of the romance books she read.

Daisy bit her bottom lip to keep from smiling as she refilled a couple of water and tea glasses as she listened to Olivia. "My car is fine, and I will not take your fancy SUV." The blue-eyed brunette put her hands on her hips, which meant she was serious.

Sitting the pitchers down, Daisy leaned on the counter with her head resting on her hands as she watched the handsome Mayor of New Orleans charm the love of his life. "Olivia, baby, your car is an antique, and not in a good way. I'm just worried about you and Lucas when I'm not here. It would make me feel better to know when you drive across the lake that you will actually make it all the way across the twenty-four-mile bridge without your vehicle stalling or, worse, catching fire again."

Olivia rolled her eyes. "It was smoking, not in flames. You're being dramatic."

Miss Lynn giggled and walked over to stand next to Daisy. "I'll bet you a piece of pie that he wins this one."

"I can't bet, Miss Lynn. First of all, I ate donuts for dinner last night and I don't need to eat any more dessert. Second, I agree with you, he's going to win. Besides, I think he's right, too. Olivia should take the new car. She drove me home when it stormed last week and I wasn't sure we would make it the five blocks to the boarding house before the car filled with smoke. She told me it wasn't a big deal and to just roll down the windows. Lucas laughed and said it happens all the time. It was scary."

"He played the Lucas card, and that always works." Miss Lynn winked before patting Daisy's hand. "How are you doing today, honey?"

"Fine," Daisy said and then hurried to a far table to take an order.

Miss Lynn watched as Daisy scurried away before she had to answer any more questions. She was such a quiet little thing, and Miss Lynn wished she would open up to them. They already cared about Daisy and wanted to help her with whatever was troubling her, but she never said a thing about herself. Sure, she'd told them she moved to Maisonville from Hawaii, but she had a thick southern accent. According to one of their regular customers, Daisy had to have spent her formative years in the south, otherwise it wouldn't have stuck.

Daisy worked hard, volunteering for any and every shift they needed her. She never called anyone or received any calls or visitors. When Olivia asked about her family or friends, she said there wasn't anyone. There wasn't even an old boyfriend, according to her. But she definitely swooned over romance and smiled with Miss Lynn over Olivia and Alexavier.

The sweet girl spent a lot of time watching customers in love like Ryan and Sydney Gentry. Also, Reagan Gentry and her fiancé, Seth, whenever they came into the diner.

The longing on her face was unmistakable.

Yet Daisy didn't put herself out there to get close to anyone. She just carried that book bag stuffed with what looked like most of her belongings and a few tattered romance novels that she would read out back while on her break. It was enough to split Miss Lynn's heart, and she'd seen a lot in her years.

Olivia sauntered over and leaned up against the cash register. "Miss Lynn, do you think I'm wrong for not accepting Alexavier's car?"

Her headstrong girl, Olivia, was prideful. Olivia wasn't Miss Lynn's daughter, but she couldn't have loved her more. She cared about all the young women that worked for her. They were her family.

"I never think anything you do is wrong."

"Miss Lynn."

"I never think you are wrong, but perhaps you could accept it as a loaner until your car is repaired? That way, you and Lucas will be safe, and Alexavier will have peace of mind that you two are taken care of?"

Olivia weighed the idea in her head and then nodded before she walked back over to where she'd left Alexavier, eating dessert and drinking coffee. It looked like they talked it through and then hugged and kissed each other. All was right in Miss Lynn's world when her girls were happy.

Now to figure out how to make her new girl that way. But Daisy didn't give any hints about what she needed. She was quiet and kept focused on her work through lunch without stopping once.

Daisy rang up one of her customers and then went to wipe down the table they vacated. She was in her quiet little world and unaware that Olivia and Miss Lynn were talking about her.

"Did she even mention Reaper at all?" Olivia asked.

"Not a word," Miss Lynn said, shaking her head. "Maybe she didn't go out with him after all?"

"We practically put her in his truck, and he wants her like no other," Olivia said with a sparkle in her blue eyes.

Daisy looked up to see them staring at her. "What?" she asked before feeling her ponytail, the buttons on her shirt, and then apron.

"You know exactly what we want to know," Olivia said, squinting her eyes and making Daisy a little nervous.

"I'm afraid I don't know what you're talking about."

Miss Lynn shook her head. "Daisy Jones, did you or did you not go out with Reaper?"

"Oh, that?" Daisy avoided their stares as she grabbed several sets of silverware for the table she'd just cleaned.

It was quieting down at the diner and Daisy had worked to keep busy. She'd hoped Olivia would forget about her leaving with Michael last night, or at least leave a bit early before she had time for a big interrogation.

However, Olivia looked like she was settling in as she sat on a barstool and stared at Daisy. Just as soon as Olivia locked onto her, Reaper pulled his large truck into the parking lot.

"Well, that answers that," she said smugly and grabbed her

purse before she hugged Miss Lynn and gathered Lucas and his things to go home.

Lucas handed Daisy a picture of a hummingbird he'd drawn for her and then hugged her and Miss Lynn. "See ya later, kiddo," Daisy said after hugging the sweet little boy.

Miss Lynn smiled as Daisy waved goodbye to Lucas and then caught sight of Reaper through the front windows when he got out of his truck. The quiet young waitress was fanning herself as she admired the rugged man walking toward the diner door.

Suddenly, realizing what she was doing, she ran to get the broom to look busy.

Reaper sat at the counter and watched her without shame. The place was practically empty, and Miss Lynn was pleased to see Reaper making more effort to get Daisy's attention. The young waitress seemed so alone all the time, and he was willing to put in the necessary work to change that.

"Good evening, Reaper," Miss Lynn said, handing him a menu and offering him an iced tea, unsweetened the way he liked it.

"Ma'am," Reaper said, turning around to look at Miss Lynn. "Thank you," he added as he kept turning to watch Daisy, who wasn't paying him any attention.

"Everything alright?" Miss Lynn asked.

Reaper nodded. "Is she closing?"

"All alone," Miss Lynn said.

"Nah. I'll be here," he answered with a grin.

Miss Lynn winked at him and then, using a sing-songy voice, said, "Daisy. Customer at the counter."

As Daisy slowly walked over to the counter where Reaper was sitting, Miss Lynn gave her a quick hug before telling them both goodnight. She didn't waste a second grabbing her purse and heading out the door, leaving them alone inside the diner except for the two guys working in the kitchen.

"Are you ready to order?" Daisy didn't look at him, but instead focused on her notepad.

Reaper had hoped their time together the night before would have softened her up, but it was going to take more than coffee and donuts to make her comfortable around him.

"Good evening, Daisy."

She nodded as she tapped her pen on her paper hastily.

Reaper waited because her impeccable manners would kick in and she would finally look up at him.

The lengthy pause might have made a lesser man uncomfortable, but Reaper was more determined than most.

"H-Hi, Michael," she whispered.

His face lit up with his smile. "How's your day been?"

"Same as usual," she answered, looking up briefly and then back down at her notepad.

She was definitely shy, and it made him wonder even more what she was doing in Maisonville alone. He reached out to gently hold her hand, and that made her stop and look at him. "Do you have plans for Thanksgiving?"

Daisy shook her head. It surprised her when Miss Lynn gave her Thursday off. It was tradition for Lynn to work the holiday and she explained it was mostly people picking up holiday plates so they could go home and watch football.

"Could I interest you in a traditional family Thanksgiving meal at my folks' house?"

It had been a long time since she'd had a family holiday and the longing on her face must have given her away.

"I'll have to pick you up early because Thanksgiving is like my mother and sister's super-bowl. They start cooking the day before and then get up at dawn to put it all together. They don't want any help, but they expect me to show up and offer to help them so they can then push me out of the way."

Daisy laughed at his description of the events and then realized what she'd agreed to do. "Are you certain I won't be imposing? I mean, I'm sure Mrs. Bowers will include me in her lunch plans and it's not like I can't use the day off to get my laundry caught up or other chores."

Reaper let her ramble through a few more excuses before he stopped her. "I've already told them I was inviting you."

"You did?"

He grinned and leaned back on the stool, a little smugly. "I told them to make extra because you can really eat."

Daisy's mouth hung open in shock. "You didn't. That is not funny, Michael."

"I really did. I can't wait for them to meet you."

Shaking her head, Daisy tried to not laugh at him teasing her. Then she tried to think of an excuse to get out of going, but hearing him laugh and watching him smile did something to her heart.

She took his order and was relieved when the diner door opened, and she could excuse herself to go help others.

Reaper had watched her fidget as the realization of what she'd agreed to hit her. While he admired her work ethic, he understood she hid behind her duties so she wouldn't have to be social. There was no mistaking the look of relief on her face when she walked away to help the new customers.

Being overly nice and helpful was Daisy's nature, but Reaper watched as she nervously played with her apron ribbons that were tied around her middle and back around the front of her waist. She was jittery and had to repeat the new customer's order back to them twice. Putting the order in with the kitchen guys, she finally made it back over to him to refill his tea before she put on a fresh pot of coffee.

The cook rang the bell and Daisy hurried over to get Reaper's dinner. As she sat his hot food down, he reached out to touch her hand before she could take off again. “Daisy. Thanks for agreeing to go with me for Thanksgiving.”

She stared at his hand on hers. “Thanks for thinking of me,” she whispered, and he knew it was her deeply ingrained manners talking. But he could work with that.

The couple sitting at the other table finished up and, as they left, Daisy cleared their table and swept the diner floor for the second time that night. He watched her wipe down all the appliances and, after she'd finished cleaning everything, she could think of to avoid him—she brought him a piece of chocolate pie.

“How long were you in the military?” she asked, leaning against the counter.

Had she been thinking about him while she worked? "I was in the Navy for 10 years. I've been out for almost three."

She looked at him up and down. He still looked like a warrior. "Most of your adulthood?"

He nodded. "I'm 31, if that's what you were wondering."

Daisy shrugged. "I was going to guess early thirties."

"Is that a problem? You're what, twenty-six, twenty-seven?"

"Twenty-three. Is that a problem?"

He stared at her. Eight years younger than him? He would have never guessed that young. Sure, she looked young, but she was reserved and self-composed in a way younger women usually weren't. There was a story there, and he wanted her to tell it to him. "Not a problem for me."

She looked past him across the room, and he felt her nerves again, on edge. “Will it be a problem for your family?”

Before Reaper could answer her, she turned to tell the kitchen workers they could leave. She then went to turn the sign on the door around to say closed. Reaper stood up to meet her before she could go back behind the counter. He held her hands and pulled her close.

“My family are regular working-class folks. Don't worry.

Okay." He hugged her, and she leaned into him for only a second.

"Okay," she agreed, but she'd acted skittish from the moment she had agreed to go to Thanksgiving dinner with him.

He wanted to ease her mind, but she was a woman on a mission and that mission was to get out of the diner. Within four minutes, they were walking out the door, but instead of heading in the direction of the boarding house, Daisy walked the other way.

He stood there for a moment, wondering what she was doing. She looked overwhelmed as she made her way across the parking lot, but she must have felt his stare.

She turned around and spoke loud enough for him to hear her. "Sorry, I meant to say goodnight."

He tapped his foot, and she could see his jaw tense even across the parking lot when he crossed his arms in front of his chest as he looked at her expectantly.

She motioned in the direction she was heading and explained, "I-I need to run an errand after work."

When she said she needed to run an errand, he grimaced. She probably meant that literally because she didn't have a car. "I'll drive you."

Daisy suddenly reconsidered going to the post office, but she'd carried the letter around for several extra days already. It felt hot in her hands when she looked at it and she didn't know why, but she had to send it tonight. Forcing herself to let it go was a tremendous step and if she put it off again, then she'd just talk herself out of it for another week.

Reaper didn't like the turmoil he saw on her face. He walked over to her and gently squeezed her hand. "Angel, I'll drive you. Come on."

Daisy couldn't help the flutter in her heart every time he

called her angel. She nodded and then let him lead her to his truck.

All day she'd told herself that she had to keep her distance from everyone. They would not be long-time friends and the more she stopped hanging out with them outside of work, the better.

Yet, the moment he showed up and asked her to do something, she agreed. She would have to come up with some solid excuses so she could put some distance between them. She already liked him too much.

Sitting awkwardly in his truck, she looked up to see him watching her. Why did it always feel like he could read her mind?

I need—," she stopped talking and licked her lips.

Whatever you need, I can do, he thought as he waited for her to explain.

Chapter Eight

"I need to mail a letter. Could you take me to the post office?"

Reaper couldn't imagine what type of errand she needed to run that late in Maisonville, but the post office certainly wasn't it.

The more he thought about it, he realized the post office was on the other side of town and quite a way from the boarding house where she lived. He tried to hold in his anger at the thought of her walking there alone at night. "Of course," he said flatly.

Looking at his tense face, Daisy's stomach did flip-flops, but not for the usual reasons when around him. He was angry about something. She sat there awkwardly for several minutes, with the tension between them growing. Finally, she whispered, "Did I do something wrong?"

He shook his head but didn't look at her and he always looked at her. "It isn't safe for you to walk around this late at night by yourself."

"I had to close and didn't have enough time to go earlier." When he didn't respond, she added, "Besides, bad things happen all the time, not just at night."

That got his attention. Reaper stared at her and the serious look in his eyes was willing her to explain, but she didn't.

He shook his head and then watched the road as he drove her to the closed post office. Something seriously bad had happened to her or someone she cared about, and there was no hiding that fact. The air in the truck was thick with what she wasn't saying, and he knew it was futile to ask.

As he pulled into the parking lot, Daisy pointed toward the outside bins, and he pulled up next to the navy-colored postal box. She hesitantly handed a letter over to him. As he slipped it into the bin, he glanced at it and noted she hadn't put her name on the return address and that it was going to a restaurant in Lahaina, Hawaii.

He didn't know what was in the letter, but it clearly made her uneasy.

"Are we good?" he asked. She nodded, but the waves of doubt were rolling off her and he thought he saw her hand trembling when she'd released the envelope.

Reaper reached over and held her hand as he turned the truck around to head toward her place. Hopefully, she would relax now that the task was done.

She was quiet all the way to the boarding house, but as he parked his truck, she settled into the seat like she wanted to talk, just like the night before.

"Will I need to dress up for Thanksgiving? I don't really have anything fancy." She was still worried about agreeing to go with him.

He shook his head. "It'll be casual. Trust me, my father thinks wearing his good blue jeans and polishing his boots is fancy."

Daisy grinned, and the twinkle in her eye told him he'd amused her.

Something about Daisy told him that she'd lived an extravagant life and getting dressed up to her was a whole different lifestyle than his oilfield family from South Louisiana. But she didn't want to admit that to him yet, so he would let her keep pretending.

"Michael? Can I ask you something else?"

"Anything you want, angel."

Her cheeks were pink from his response, and it took a few seconds for her to pull it together. "Your parents were high school sweethearts and your sister and her husband were too? Did you date anyone seriously in high school?"

Reaper smirked, thinking about how he had to admit some truths about his past. His family surely would bring some of it up in front of her and he might as well get it out in the open sooner rather than later. "I guess it really was sort of a thing in my town, meeting someone in high school. But I was what my mother called a rabble-rouser when I was younger. I was bigger than most of the boys and played football from the time I was six. Hard-headed was another description."

Daisy grinned. "Well, that must have come in handy with football."

He laughed at her teasing him and noted that she hadn't done that before. "Yes, it did, but not with the girls so much. I dated half the girls in school, but no one seriously."

Daisy loved to hear him talk about his family and growing up. His family life fascinated her. She settled in for the longer conversation she hoped they would have.

"Are you cold?" he asked, watching her wrap her arms around her body.

"I'm okay. I'm sort of always cold."

Nodding his head, Reaper reached behind the seat for the blanket stowed back there and tucked it around her tightly.

He sat closer to her, and she watched him carefully. He could see she wanted to trust him. Trusting was her natural response, but something had spooked her. Would she ever tell him what had happened?

"So, how about you, Daisy? Any long-lost loves from high school?"

She laughed as she shook her head. "I wasn't popular in high school like you. I was a bit of a homebody."

"All the pretty girls were popular in my school. You would have caught all our attention," he said, reaching out to pull her feet into his lap.

She didn't say a word as she watched him untie her tennis shoes and then he rubbed her socked feet with his incredibly warm hands.

It was the single most thoughtful thing anyone had done for her in a long, long time and she fought to keep herself from moaning when he ran his thumb up the middle of her heel.

"Is this okay?"

She didn't trust her words, so she nodded instead.

Reaper could see how overwhelmed she was by the simple gesture, and it made him want to do it even more. But the only way she was going to sit still for him was if he kept talking.

"I told you how my mother ruled the neighborhood and was basically the leader of all the moms. I was the unofficial leader of all the boys. You name it, I tried it. Smoking cigarettes, drinking alcohol, sneaking out of the house, and cussing like a sailor before I was a sailor. But I got it out of my system quickly because no matter what I did, my mother always caught me or one of my friends. She whooped the stuffing out of us every time and then hauled us to church. None of us could get away with anything and to this day I still don't know how she did it, but she had eyes everywhere. I learned to enjoy fishing or hunting whenever my mother didn't have me working. I played football for the school, but my summers were free and the neighborhood kids all hung out together. A couple of my friends dated my sister, and I dated some of their sisters, but it never worked out. We usually ended up in a fight defending our sisters, which honestly wasn't worth it. Then Nina Calhoun moved to town. She was the youngest in her family, but her older sisters were already married. We all had a crush on her, and she was mean as a hellcat."

"A hellcat?" Daisy repeated, and then laughed.

Reaper laughed, too. "Another one of my mother's favorite descriptions."

"So, of course, you liked her?"

"I think I liked the challenge. But we were oil and water, or maybe more like water thrown on a grease fire."

"Combustible?"

"Something like that."

"So, what happened?"

"Probably not what you expect."

Daisy didn't guess. She just sat back against the door and waited for him to explain. He continued massaging her feet for a few more minutes, knowing he was going to tell her the whole story.

Nina was the same age as Reaper, and they'd met at age fourteen when her parents moved to town. Her father was a roughneck and gone most of the time. Her mother looked the other way when Nina did anything wrong. Nina bragged that her two older sisters wore their mom down and the woman no longer had the will to parent her.

If the boys smoked, so did Nina. If they drank, she did too. Anything the boys could do, she said she could do it better and even if she couldn't beat them—she tried it all.

"Nina had a great sense of humor and was full of adventure. She double-dog-dared everyone to do things they would've never otherwise tried. She liked to fish and walk in the woods when we were younger. Rode motorcycles as well as any of us boys. She was something else. As we got older, she was the life of the party.

We dated and broke up easily ten times in high school. Then she would date one of my friends.

"After we graduated, I planned to go into the military, and she cried because she didn't want me to leave. We spent almost every day together that summer. And I fell for her, hard."

Daisy watched as Michael told her the story, but he didn't show any emotion.

"We made some promises, and I left, thinking she was the girl for me. But two months later, when I went home on leave, she broke up with me.

"My mother was furious with her for doing it before I shipped out for six months." He shrugged, but Daisy could tell that it had been a difficult time for him.

"The next time I came home, Nina told me she'd made a huge mistake and begged me to take her back. She was a hard woman to say no to and so we spent the holidays together. Two weeks after I shipped out again, she broke up with me because she said she couldn't handle the long distance. We did that back-and-forth thing for seven years."

Daisy reached out to hold his hand, and he looked over at her and smiled. "What changed?"

"I guess she found the person she really wanted to be with because she moved away, and I haven't heard from her since."

"Her parents?"

"They moved back up north where her mother was from. Her dad was too old for manual labor, so he quit the oil rig and went to work somewhere up there."

"Do you miss her?"

Reaper looked over at Daisy when she asked that question. "Remember how I said my mother called me hardheaded?" He laughed like it was a private joke and Daisy could see the pain he'd endured.

"You really cared about her. They say the first cut is the deepest." She locked onto his eyes as she added, "I can only imagine it was difficult, especially since you couldn't be home and because I imagine your job was dangerous." Daisy reached her hand out to squeeze his in understanding, and he stared at her small delicate hand holding his. She didn't know she was the one that was special.

"I learned a lot about love, but also about human nature. Above all, I learned what I could endure and what was important. My mother and sister are brutally honest. I had mistakenly thought most women were like that. Nina would lie, even if the truth suited her better. What I thought was chemistry was more like competition and we both were at fault for that, trying to come out on top or make the other fall in love harder. I guess she won."

Daisy reached out with both of her hands this time and when he looked into her brown eyes, he saw understanding there.

"If you loved her and she left you, then she lost."

Reaper pulled Daisy close and kissed her hard on the lips. She wrapped her hands in the collar of his shirt as their mouths collided. It was raw and passionate, and they couldn't get close enough as they held on to each other. The windows of the truck fogged up before they stopped.

She avoided his stare as she moved away from him and righted her clothes. Everything Cage had warned him about Daisy was coming true. She'd kept him at arm's reach and then suddenly reeled him in with all that innocence and wonder. But he would bet his life that it was real, and she wasn't faking it like Nina. As she folded the blanket, he remained stunned for a minute. That kiss was going to be his undoing. The way she held onto him like he was important was everything he'd missed before and didn't know he needed.

Finally, he rubbed his hands over his face and reached out to her. "Daisy? What about you? If you didn't date in high school, then when did it happen to you?"

Daisy looked directly at him and smiled. "It's never happened to me. I-I've never been in love."

She leaned over and kissed his cheek before she slipped her shoes back on, opened her door, and hopped out.

Reaper almost tripped getting out of the truck. Daisy was stunning and, without a doubt, the most loveable woman he'd ever met. Every time he saw her on a break, she had a romance novel in her hand. How could she not have been swept up in a relationship at least once? That kiss was incredible, and he'd been kissed a lot.

He met her at the sidewalk and held out his hand for hers. She smiled, and he saw the moment she agreed to hold his hand because that beautiful face of hers couldn't hide what she was feeling or thinking.

They walked silently up to the boarding house and at the door, he explained he had to work for the next few days but would pick her up at nine on Thanksgiving morning.

He hugged her, and Daisy blushed when she said goodnight and went inside. Had he ever wanted to get to know another woman more than he wanted her? The incremental bits she gave him made him crave so much more and he felt himself becoming more protective as he spent time with her.

Reaper climbed into his truck, with her scent still surrounding him. It was soft like her, but warm like vanilla extract. Suddenly he thought about the doberge cake his mother would make for Thanksgiving and all the layers of chocolate custard in between the delicate layers of vanilla cake. It always amazed him as a kid to see those thin layers hold their own against the custard. It had always been his favorite, and he smiled, thinking of how fond he was of Daisy. She had been through something big and, even though she was small—she was strong.

Chapter Nine

Mrs. Bowers opened the front door and gave a curt smile to Reaper after she said he could come inside to wait. She used a cane, but he wondered if it was actually necessary for her to walk or whether it was a weapon as she wielded it in the air as she spoke.

"Daisy says you're taking her to your folks' house for a proper Thanksgiving meal?" She cut her eyes at him, and he understood his answers would be the difference between her coming along or letting Daisy go with him alone. Lord, help him with these over-protective southern women.

"Yes, ma'am. My sister, her husband, and kids will also be there."

Mrs. Bowers used her cane to point to the side table where a notebook and pen lay. "You can write the address down right there, young man."

He smiled and did as she asked. Then she pulled out her phone and snapped a picture of him. "I'm also going to need to see your driver's license."

Reaper looked at her for a moment and determined she was

not kidding. He pulled out his wallet and let her take a picture, too.

As Daisy walked down the staircase, Mrs. Bowers put her phone in her pocket and smiled sweetly at him. "Would you like a cup of coffee for the road, young man?" she asked, as if they were getting to know each other.

He politely declined and watched as the older woman hugged Daisy and told her how beautiful she looked.

Daisy was beautiful in her dark jeans and black sweater. She also wore short suede boots. He didn't miss the fact that she'd listened to him explain his father's dress uniform and used it as her own dress code.

She also had a gift bag with a bottle of wine and an enormous bouquet of fall flowers in her hands.

Mrs. Bowers followed them down the sidewalk and as he opened the truck door for her, Mrs. Bowers called Daisy back.

He watched as she whispered something into Daisy's ear and then finally agreeing, Daisy took the woman's phone and went to the back of his truck to take a picture of his license plate.

"Sorry," she whispered to Reaper as she walked over to give the phone back to Mrs. Bowers.

"Y'all have fun now," she said, but he didn't miss the way she pointed her cane at him again.

Reaper waited until they were out of her sight before he whistled. "Who knew an eighty-year-old woman could be so scary?"

Daisy laughed, shaking her head. "Don't let her hear you say she's eighty. She tells everyone she's only seventy-nine and will set you straight in a New York minute. But she means well. She's just looking out for me, is all."

Reaper laughed and agreed. "I'm pretty sure she was ready to hit me with that cane if she didn't like my answers."

Daisy looked at him and he told her about having to give

Mrs. Bowers his family's home address and let her take a picture of his driver's license.

She put her hand over her mouth to stifle the smile that filled her face. "Oh, my goodness. I sure hope your family is easier on me than Mrs. Bowers was on you."

He knew she was trying to kid around, but there was some seriousness in her voice.

"They will love you, angel." He pulled her hand to his mouth so he could kiss it and then threaded his fingers with hers. "The boots were a nice touch."

Daisy shook her head. "Miss Lynn called Sydney Gentry and the two of them, with Olivia's help, styled me." Her cheeks were rosy as she admitted, "I'm afraid none of these clothes are mine."

Reaper winked at her and told her it didn't matter because she looked great in everything she wore. He wanted her to explain where all of her things were, but he wouldn't push her today. He had given the information from the letter she mailed over to Cage, who was going to check it out. But today he was going to focus on spending time with her.

He turned on the radio and she nodded when he stopped scrolling on a country music station. Then she surprised him by singing. She seemed to know the words to all the new and old country songs and entertained him for most of the drive to his parents' house.

It wasn't until they pulled into the driveway that she reached over and held his hand tightly. She was nervous, and he leaned over and promised her they were a regular family and she had nothing to worry about.

"You didn't have to bring wine or flowers either, Daisy."

"It's impolite to show up empty-handed, and you said they wouldn't want me to cook." He could see her eyes were wide, and she was second guessing her choices again.

He pulled her into a hug and kissed the top of her head. "Come on. You'll see, they're harmless."

Before they got to the door, Mr. Thibodeaux opened it and stepped out to give his son a big hug. Then he grabbed Daisy in a big bear hug, too.

"You're a tiny thing, aren't you?" he said and laughed. "You can call me Mike. I used to be big Mike until this one here grew up." He slapped his hand on his son's back and laughed again.

"Come on in. The girls are in the kitchen." He led them into the house and Daisy smiled at all the New Orleans Saints Football memorabilia and the Louisiana State University items, including a large cardboard cutout of their mascot, Mike the tiger.

On their way to the kitchen, Reaper waved to his brother-in-law, Mac, who was outside throwing a football with two of his sons and the youngest daughter.

The kids yelled, "Uncle Mike is here!" and started running their way. He let go of Daisy's hand just in time to catch all the kids who surrounded him. He picked all three of them up at once and they squealed.

His sister and mother, along with the oldest daughter, came running their way too. All three of them had the same smile and beautiful teeth as Michael. "Put them down before someone gets hurt," his mother said, swatting him with a dish towel.

Michael put them all down and then picked his slightly round mother up and kissed her on the cheek. When he set her back on her feet, she swatted him again.

Abigail finally hugged him, and then they all turned to face Daisy expectantly. Reaper quickly rushed to her side and introduced the whole family to his new friend. He stressed friend and told them they could call her Daisy.

The way he said friend twice felt odd, she thought, but

everyone immediately started hugging her, so she didn't think about it too hard.

The kids all talked at the same time, telling her their names and their ages; Susie, Little Mac, Mark, and Dottie were 8, 7, 5, and 4. Daisy handed each kid a tootsie roll lollipop and then handed the wine and flowers over to Beth and Abigail.

His mother Beth winked at him behind Daisy's back, which was a good sign, but then she wrapped her arm around Daisy and guided her into the kitchen, telling him to stay out.

He wrestled with the kids for a few minutes, but he knew better than to leave Daisy alone for too long. His mother and sister were a tough crowd on a calm day, and he needed to be there to run interference when they began pummeling his girl with questions. Five minutes later, he headed into the kitchen for a drink and to stand by her side.

When he stepped into the room, his sister was explaining all about the trip she and Mac had taken to Hawaii a year ago and Daisy was stirring something. He'd never known his mother or sister to let anyone help do anything in the kitchen and marveled that she'd won them over so fast.

Daisy looked up and smiled at him, and he could see that she was absolutely in her element with the bossy women in his family.

He grabbed a bottle of water and sat at the kitchen counter to eat a cookie with his niece while his sister explained how much she loved Hawaii but flying not so much.

Daisy listened intently and then reached out to touch her hand. It was a simple gesture, but he could see how genuine it was for her to speak to his sister that way. "Here is my family secret remedy. And it seriously works. Take half a Dramamine tablet and an antacid together thirty minutes before your flight and do not drink anything with carbonation except for water. I swear it works every time."

Abigail made a dramatic expression and hugged Daisy tightly. "Where have you been all my life? Do you know how many times I've thrown up in those little barf bags they put in the back of the seat pockets?"

Everyone laughed and then Mama Thibodeaux said there would be zero talk about vomiting in her kitchen.

Abigail bumped her hip into Daisy's and winked at her like they were co-conspirators, which made Daisy smile even bigger.

"So Daisy, Michael said you recently moved from Hawaii but he didn't say where you're from originally? Where do your folks live?" Abigail asked.

Daisy's smile diminished, and Reaper stood up and moved around the kitchen island. She shrugged her shoulder like it was not a big deal and then looked at Abigail. "They died when I was seven."

The entire room went silent, and Reaper pulled her into his arms to hug her tightly. His mother, who was standing behind them, gave him an ugly look and he mouthed, "I didn't know," to her silently.

His niece, who was still icing cookies, asked, "So you're an orphan, like Annie?"

Beth Thibodeaux snapped her fingers at her granddaughter, and the little girl looked confused.

Daisy winked at her. "It's okay. It happened a long time ago and yes, I guess I was a bit like Little Orphan Annie. My aunt and uncle stepped in to raise me, but they've both passed away."

Reaper lifted her hand and kissed the back of it and Beth tried to ease the awkward moment by telling her son that he needed to get out of the way so she could get to the oven and check the cornbread dressing.

Daisy used that moment to excuse herself to go to the restroom and as soon as she left the room, Abigail swatted her brother hard in the arm. "Why the hell didn't you tell us before I opened my mouth and put my foot into it?"

He simply reached over her head and pulled her ponytail holder loose, making her swat him again. Then he left the room to find Daisy.

Inside the restroom, Daisy washed her hands and patted some cool water on her cheeks, trying not to ruin the little makeup that she wore. She was terrible at this. The moment she'd agreed to spend the day with Michael and his family, it felt wrong. What was she doing? Letting her guard down and telling them the truth about her past would only make things harder when she left. It was dangerous for them to meet her and, even worse, to spend time with her in their home. Michael didn't need more clues about her. She needed to be forgettable.

After several minutes of giving herself a pep talk on keeping quiet, she was ready to face them all again. She would smile and divert the conversation over to questions about the kids. People loved to talk about their families and it was the only sure way to get the attention off her.

Feeling more determined than before, she headed out of the restroom and right into none other than Michael Thibodeaux. He was standing there waiting as usual and she honestly should have realized he would be there at this point. He pulled her into his chest and hugged her closely. When he kissed the top of her head, she felt it in her stomach. Why did he have such an effect on her?

Lifting her chin so she would look at him, he leaned in and gently kissed her on the lips. Before she could say anything, he stepped back and handed her a grape tootsie roll pop, making her laugh.

"Did you take that from one of the kids?" she whisper-scolded him.

He denied it and then took the wrapper off of it for her. She didn't have her usual emergency stash on her, and it was necessary for her emotional health. Somehow, he knew that. Leaning into him once more, she thanked him.

"They have given me the duty of setting the table with you. Are you up for it?"

"You have no idea. I happen to be a master table setter."

He pulled her hand into his and led her to the dining room, where his mother had already set stacks of plates and glasses so they could get to work.

Over dessert, Mr. Thibodeaux brought up their high school football team, and that was when Daisy realized that Michael and Abigail's husband, Mac, were the same age and played high school football together. She wondered if Mac was one of Michael's friends that he had to beat up over his sister. If so, you would never know it today, as they laughed and joked about the past.

Two hours after lunch, Abigail packed up some leftovers for her brother and Daisy so they could head back home. The entire family hugged her and then gave Michael a hard time about not visiting enough. He promised to come back soon and after about twenty more minutes; they were finally on the highway back to Maisonville.

The weather had turned cloudy that afternoon and it drizzled on their way home. Reaper offered to turn the heat on inside the truck, but he'd already rolled his sleeves up and she knew he was warm because his hands were like heaters.

He reached behind the seat and grabbed the blanket for her, making her smile, and about ten minutes later, she was drifting off to sleep.

When he pulled onto her street, he patted her leg gently to wake her up. She'd curled up under that blanket and he'd never seen anyone look more comfortable.

"We're here, angel."

Daisy slowly blinked awake and then her eyes were huge. “I-I slept the whole way?”

He laughed. “There must be something to that tryptophan in the turkey.”

She grinned at him, teasing her, knowing she'd only eaten ham. Then she leaned over to hug him. “I'm sorry. I wasn't much company on the way home.”

“I wouldn't have it any other way,” he said honestly. The fact that she'd slept soundly and comfortably meant she trusted him. He felt like it was an enormous step for her—them.

She leaned forward and kissed him on the cheek before climbing out of his truck. He met her at her door and hugged her.

As usual, he held her hand and walked her to the door of the boarding house, never asking to come in or making her feel bad for not giving more than she was ready to give.

She walked into his arms one more time and kissed him on the lips before rushing inside and locking the door. Michael Thibodeaux was too good to be true. He always said the right thing and showed her more than told her how he felt.

His honesty was humbling, and she longed to be more open and honest with him. It was her nature, but she knew the stakes. She'd lived through the terror of what Peter Miller was capable of, and she would never willingly put anyone else in his path.

Chapter Ten

Black Friday may have been a retail extravaganza in most towns, but in Maisonville and the diner it was a quiet little day to get caught up on gossip and deep clean the coffee machine.

Daisy walked in at eleven to Miss Lynn and Olivia sitting at the lunch counter enjoying their third or maybe fourth cups of coffee and laughing.

"Look at you all bright and chipper this morning," Olivia teased. "Am I to assume that you did not have company to stay over?"

There was no point in telling Olivia that it was almost noon because Daisy blushed at the mention of Michael sleeping over. "I don't kiss and tell."

"I think a night with that hottie would make you sing like a bird, my friend. And I, for one, cannot wait for it to happen for you."

Daisy's mouth hung open in shock, partly because they were discussing sex but also because what Olivia was saying was most likely true.

Miss Lynn stood and gently lifted Daisy's chin to close her

mouth. Then she walked over to make Daisy a cup of freshly brewed coffee, explaining that they had to make at least two pots today, so it tasted good after sending vinegar through it twice.

Olivia pulled a barstool over for Daisy, and then they discussed how she and Lucas had their first Thanksgiving with Alexavier's enormous family. It had been their first time to spend a holiday with his giant Italian family and if she hadn't been paying attention, then she wouldn't have noticed how it had overwhelmed her always confident friend.

It seemed that Daisy was a little more like Olivia than she'd first thought. Perhaps that meant she also was more like her Aunt Sue, too?

Miss Lynn expressed how happy she was on Thanksgiving Day to see so many of the regulars picking up traditional dinners for their families and then how she took all the leftovers to the mission in New Orleans, which included ten of her best pies.

Daisy hugged Miss Lynn and told her if she'd had any idea what Lynn was doing, then she would have stayed to help.

"Which is precisely why I didn't tell you, sweet girl."

Daisy shook her head and then told them what a lovely time she had with Michael Thibodeaux and his family. Then she admitted to falling asleep on the way home and how it was the most restful sleep she'd had in a very long time.

"Funny. I knew his name, but I've never heard anyone address him as Michael," Miss Lynn said, and Olivia shook her head.

Daisy couldn't miss the way Olivia's blue eyes shimmered as she leaned forward and whispered, "I bet in the throes of passion that you call him Reaper."

Daisy choked on her coffee, making Olivia smirk. Miss Lynn giggled at them both.

Getting more serious, Daisy added, "He was sweet all day. You don't think he was upset about me sleeping on the way home and not talking to him or spending time with him, do you?"

Olivia crooked her eyebrow. "He's the kind of man that would shoot you straight. You know, tell you exactly what he thinks. But how did he act when he dropped you off?"

"Perfect. As usual. I-I just don't want to lead him on, you know." Daisy sat her coffee cup down and then headed toward the back room to stow her bag that she still had with her up front. She needed to stop talking about Michael with Olivia and Miss Lynn. The truth was that she thought about Michael all night long, but if he lost interest in her, that would be for the best.

Suddenly, she heard Olivia and Miss Lynn talking more animatedly and stepped back into the room with her bag still in her hands. Standing there in all his overwhelming masculinity was Michael.

He laughed at something Olivia said and then turned that lethal grin on Daisy. "Good morning, angel. Miss Lynn says you aren't that busy, and I was wondering if you might spend the day with me?"

Olivia walked over and hugged Daisy around the waist. "I guess that answers your question." Her grin was just enough good friend and bad girl to make Daisy's stomach knot.

"What question was that?" Reaper asked in his deep voice.

"Oh, our girl, Daisy, was worried she might have made you mad last night by sleeping the entire way home and then for not asking you to stay the night with her."

"Oh, my gosh," Daisy whispered.

Olivia looked shocked as she swatted Daisy on the bottom. "You tell the truth, Daze."

"I-I was worried about the falling asleep thing, but that was all. Honest."

Reaper locked onto Daisy's eyes as she stammered her explanation, and Olivia teased her. He was having fun watching the two women, but finally had to help Daisy out. "Come on, angel. Let's get going before Olivia gets you into more trouble."

Daisy nodded as she slung her bag over her shoulder. When she walked toward Michael, who was holding his hand out for her, Olivia whispered, "Don't do anything I wouldn't do."

Daisy stared at her friend and mouthed "Stop," which made Olivia laugh as she waved goodbye to them.

Reaper settled Daisy into her seat before walking around to his side of the truck. It had been remarkably easier to get her to go with him than he'd imagined. He would have to thank Olivia for it later, but for now, he needed to calm down the adorable woman inside his truck.

"I'm sorry, Michael. Olivia gets these things in her head sometimes, but she was just kidding around. I-I don't always explain myself well enough."

He leaned over and kissed her sweetly on the lips. "Don't apologize, angel. I'm good. You good?"

She stopped talking and just nodded her head in response.

"I got over here early to pick up a few more architectural items from Ryan Gentry and thought maybe I could show you around my neighborhood. Are you up for it?"

Daisy nodded again, and when he threaded their fingers together, she smiled.

He turned the radio to the country music station that she liked and she seemed to settle in for the ride across the lake. It was a spectacular day with zero clouds, a light breeze, mild temps, and low humidity. It was a rare experience to have days like that in New Orleans, and people didn't take it for granted.

As they neared the French Quarter, there were tons of tourists and locals walking around taking advantage of the beautiful day. The tourists were easy to spot because they usually wore Mardi Gras beads, even though it wasn't the season.

Daisy scooted a little closer to him and he saw her scanning the crowd. "I just live two streets over. Everything all right, Daisy?"

She nodded but didn't look his way as she continued looking out.

When Reaper pulled up to a solid iron gate, she finally looked at him. "This is it," he said and pulled forward to an obscure driveway.

Her shoulders lowered as the gate closed behind his truck, securing them inside and away from the world.

"We're good?" he asked, making sure she still wanted to be there.

When her eyes got bigger and she bit her bottom lip, it took all of his resolve not to pull her into his lap. They weren't even out of the truck yet.

He led her through his brick courtyard to his back porch and only let go of her hand long enough to unlock the giant, dark green wooden doors.

She was still silent as he punched the security code into his alarm system. "I've had no trouble here, but since I used to be deployed for long stretches, I got into the habit of using this. It's nice to know a service is watching out for her while I'm away."

"Her?"

"I guess the house is kind of like a ship to me. Calling her a female felt right."

Daisy smiled. "Well, does she have a name?"

Reaper deadpan stared at her. "That would be weird. I just call her old girl." He winked and then walked through the entryway and Daisy laughed at him as she followed closely behind.

Daisy sat her bag down on a chair as she looked around. She wasn't sure what his house would look like, but had expected more of a man cave. Instead, it belonged in a magazine. There were exposed brick and wooden beams that looked like they were hundreds of years old. He had some expensive-looking leather furniture but also comfy chairs. He apparently collected art, and the walls were adorned with beautiful paintings and framed prints. It reminded her a lot of France and she'd loved France.

"You did all of this yourself?"

His face brightened and looked even more gorgeous when he was happy. What she wouldn't give to have met him before she'd met Peter. Now it was too late. She was damaged goods, had a price on her head, and this thing with Michael couldn't really be an option for her.

"You alright?" he asked, reaching out to touch her arm.

She nodded but didn't speak. The sudden urge to spill all of her secrets to the beautiful man was right at the tip of her tongue and she couldn't do it. She couldn't pull him into her situation because he was the kind of person who would get involved. And she wouldn't be the reason he got hurt—or worse.

Instead, she focused on his beautiful home. "The work you've done is exquisite. It's a great mix of French Provincial and French Country."

"You've been to France?"

"I've been to a lot of places."

He knew she'd been well taken care of, spoiled in a good way, sheltered even. But she was also quiet and unassuming. “With your aunt and uncle?”

“Uncle Ed passed away when I was sixteen and my aunt loved to travel.” There she went again, telling him the truth. She needed to stop talking. He was the guy who figured these things out for a living. Wasn’t that what Miss Lynn said he did with Cage and Rex? Security and some detective work? “That was a long time ago. You know I am from Hawaii.”

"But raised in Texas?"

She stared at him but didn't answer.

"You can't hide that sweet accent any better than I can hide my New Orleans one."

She gave him a slight nod, and he wished he hadn't made her so uncomfortable. But if she was trying to hide away or from someone, she needed to know her story was full of holes. He would spend a little more time with her and then figure out a way to tell her.

"I need to unload a few things from the back of my truck. Look around and I'll be back in a few minutes, okay?"

She nodded, and he slipped out the back door.

Once he was gone, she pulled the rubber band out of her hair and ran her hands through it to smooth the strands out. She considered what type of security work Michael did and thought about how he didn't discuss work with her. If she kept spilling details about her past, would he be able to piece things together? She had to stop sharing and listen more.

Wandering past the kitchen, Daisy walked into a front room that looked like a small den and office. There was a wall of shelves that held tons of old and new books, old radios, and radio memorabilia and pictures of Michael with other military men. She recognized his friends, Cage and Rex, but they were all younger.

She smiled, thinking about their nicknames as she studied another picture on the wall. That was when he stepped up behind her, making her jump.

"Sorry, angel." He hadn't meant to scare her, but it was a skill he couldn't help, silently walking into a room or anywhere. Next time, he would have to make noise so he wouldn't frighten her.

"Would you like me to show you around the rest of the place?" He offered, and she nodded. The main house had four bedrooms, three and a half baths, an office, a den, and a butler's pantry, plus the open kitchen-living room area. Across the court-yard he had three one bedroom and one-bathroom units with kitchenettes that he planned to rent out one day and at the end was a large workshop.

"They've been ready for a while now, but I like my privacy. I sit out in the courtyard early in the mornings. Not sure I'm ready to give that up just yet. There isn't a lot of solitude in the military, and I guess I'm making up for lost time."

"I've always liked my privacy too," she whispered and then turned away as if she didn't mean to admit it.

Reaper stood closely behind her, and she loved the heat from his body when he was near. "I know there are a lot of people in the French Quarter today, but it would be nice to get lost in the crowd together. You up for it?"

Nodding, she silently agreed, but when she turned around, he didn't miss the caution in her eyes. Reaper warmly wrapped his hand around hers as he led her out the front door of his home and into the bustling French Quarter in New Orleans.

"I'm starved," Reaper said before taking her on a food tour of his town. They had small bowls of crawfish jambalaya and seafood gumbo. There were bites of alligator sausage and boudin balls served with a spicy dijonnaise sauce. He introduced her to char-grilled oysters with warm French bread and then they finished with some bread pudding topped with white chocolate rum sauce.

Daisy had the rest of her bread pudding in a to-go box. It impressed him with how she hung in there eating small bites of his food so she could "pace herself," her words, and try it all.

It was dark when they strolled up and down streets as he pointed out architectural features of old homes and talked about the haunted history of the city. He enjoyed how she grabbed onto his arm when they stepped into the voodoo shop. He promised to take her on a cemetery tour soon and she admitted how much it equally excited and scared her.

Conversation between them was easy, and he wasn't sure

when she'd let her guard down but somewhere along the lamp-lit streets of the city, she told him a little more about her Uncle Ed and Aunt Sue and how much she desperately missed them. Daisy admitted to not making friends easily because she was shy and a bit too serious as a kid. She'd always felt older than her years and had little in common with her peers. Admitting she wasn't a risk taker like most teens, she wasn't interested in sneaking out of the house or drinking underage, so the other kids didn't invite her to many parties. She figured tragedy at a young age could do that to a person and then stopped talking.

He held both her hands in his to warm them up and then kissed her forehead. "A shy, beautiful girl wouldn't have had to do anything for attention at my school," he said, wanting to make her understand how she was special. When he'd been in school, the girls from his neighborhood were outspoken and assertive. In fact, there were a few shy guys, but not one girl. They intimidated more than one of his friends and he figured it was due to all the moms ruling their world. He smiled, thinking how he would have had to fight off all the other boys for beautiful Daisy.

As they walked back into his house, she sat her to-go box on the table next to her bag as he made them each a cup of strong coffee. She added cream to hers and then he guided her to the couch so he could sit closely beside her.

"You traveled a lot as a kid too?" she asked.

He grinned before shaking his head. "No. But I've already told you that I did all the things you didn't do and more. My friends and I snuck out of the house and into every bar in town. I could drink more than anyone else since I was so much bigger. I didn't travel until I joined the Navy." He lifted her chin so she would look at him. "But I can promise you that if you had been in my high school, we would have been friends. Close friends."

She took a deep breath, and he leaned in to kiss her. It was sweet and warm as he pulled her closer to him. As their bodies touched, she held onto his shirt again, tighter, and the kiss became hotter and deeper. He wrapped one hand in her hair and the other on her hip, pulling her body against his. She leaned into him, and her quick breaths were going to be his undoing. His body vibrated as she pressed against him and then, as quickly as it started, she pushed away, stood up, and avoided looking at him.

She was trying to catch her breath and he could see the panic in her eyes, but there had been desperation in her kiss. Daisy was warring with her feelings as she stepped further away.

He stood up slowly and when she glanced his way—he thought he saw tears in her eyes. "Look, angel, there's no rush," he said as he motioned between them. Before he could say anything else, his doorbell rang.

Daisy looked frightened, and he figured it was adrenaline causing her fight-or-flight reaction. He smiled her way and held his hand out for her.

She didn't reach back to him, but looked at the door where a light knock came next. Reaper wasn't going to answer it until she was calm. He walked to her and pulled her into his arms, and that was when he felt her trembling.

What the hell had happened to her?

"Daisy? You don't have anything to be frightened of here. We're friends. Right? You can trust me, angel."

His words must have gotten through to her somehow. She was still shaking, but leaned into him as he hugged her.

He kissed the top of her head and he heard her breathe deeply in and out a few times. After a minute, he leaned back and looked into her eyes. She grinned, but it was just her way of making him feel better. She wasn't relaxed like she had been before their heated make-out session.

The doorbell rang two more times, and she looked at him

expectantly, which made him smile. “I’m not answering it unless you’re okay. I don’t give a damn who is out there.”

She smiled that time and it lit up her eyes. “You would just let them stand out there?”

“The only person I’m concerned about is standing in front of me,” he said and didn’t miss the way she gasped.

He lifted her chin and kissed her sweetly on the lips. When she stepped back that time, she seemed more sure of herself. “I’m going to the restroom. Go answer the door.”

He winked at her and watched her walk toward the hallway before he went to see who in the hell interrupted them.

Chapter Eleven

Daisy felt better as she washed her hands and dug the dark cherry tootsie roll pop out of her pocket. She slowly unwrapped it as she thought about how great Michael Thibodeaux felt when he pulled her close and how she was in way over her head.

She sat on the side of his bathtub as she ate the tootsie pop and admitted to herself that she wanted him like she'd wanted nothing else in her life. Sure that was saying something since she'd lost more than most and wished for loads of things in her twenty-three years.

But at that moment, it was the truth.

He was the most caring and attractive man she'd ever seen, and just being near him calmed her soul in a way that she couldn't explain. The way he read her mind, let her know he would read her body in the most delicious of ways.

Couldn't she stop over-thinking things with him? Spending one night together would be worth it, and then she could deal with the consequences in the morning. The thought of leaving town and never knowing what it would be like to be in his arms just once was inconceivable.

Standing back up and splashing cold water on her face, Daisy took a deep breath and tried to find the confidence that Olivia would have in this situation. Then she laughed because that would never happen.

But she could go out there and kiss him like she meant it again. She could show him how much she wanted him and he would certainly take over. Showing her how it should be done.

Waking up in his arms would be the respite she needed to bolster her next move. It was going to be impossible to leave her new friends and life in Maisonville. Even harder than Hawaii. But memories of her time with Michael would give her the will to live her life and take control.

Daisy rushed out of the restroom and stopped when Michael wasn't standing there waiting for her. It was silly, but that had never happened before.

She could hear his low, deep voice, but couldn't make out what he was saying. But he sounded angry. Cautiously heading to the table where she'd left her bag, Daisy crept quietly across the room. The door was hidden from view, so she couldn't see who he was talking to and they couldn't see her.

But as soon as she got to her bag, a woman stormed into the room past Michael. "Are you kidding me, Mike? Have you told her about us? Does she understand what you and I have?"

Michael moved to stand in front of Daisy. "You and I have nothing. I haven't heard from you in years."

The attractive brunette had fire in her eyes and a light sprinkling of freckles across her face. She was taller than Daisy, with an athletic build. There was something of a girl next door look to her, but she also had a cruel expression.

"It doesn't matter how long we're apart," she said, locked onto Daisy and not to Michael. "We are soul mates. We have known it since we were kids and I've tried to deny it."

Michael threw his arms up in the air. “Get out of my house, Nina.”

Daisy tried to bow out and offered to give them privacy, but before she could move, Nina stepped even closer.

“It’s okay,” Daisy said. “You two seem like you need to talk.”

Michael shook his head, but Nina grinned. He turned toward Daisy, effectively shutting Nina out behind him.

“I have nothing to say to her. I told you that she’s been gone for years.”

Daisy reached her hand up gently to touch his cheek. She’d wanted so much more tonight, but he needed her understanding. “It’s okay.”

The moment was lost when Nina loudly announced, “It has been years since we’ve seen each other, three years and nine months, give or take a couple of weeks.”

Michael turned around and glared at her.

Nina only had eyes for Daisy. “Because our son was two weeks premature.”

The air in the room seemed to disappear and Daisy felt like she couldn’t breathe. Nina lunged toward her as Michael put his arm up to stop her. But Daisy ducked past them both, grabbing her bag on the way out the front door and into the street. She could hear Michael, but there was no stopping her. She ran as fast as she could and didn’t stop until she found a crowded bar on Bourbon Street.

She waited in the restroom for fifteen minutes and inside the bar for another half hour. Drinking a diet coke, she tried to talk herself down from the reality of what had happened. Had Michael known that Nina was pregnant when they broke up? Was he the kind of man to abandon his child? It really did change things.

As she sat there worrying over the chaos brought in by Nina Calhoun, Daisy noticed a man across the room wearing a green ski jacket that kept looking her way. He looked nothing like Peter's security guards, but she knew better than to trust anyone.

Ke had taught her to always be alert, and that guy definitely was watching her. When she stood up, he looked nervous and then left the bar completely.

Smiling that she'd overreacted and was safe for the foreseeable moment, Daisy was ready to find a taxi to take her back to the boarding house. The bartender explained she wouldn't be able to hail a taxi nearby because the street was closed off to traffic on the weekends. She would have to make her way out to one of the main outer streets in order to get a car. It was getting late, and she no longer wanted to be there.

So, she slipped back out onto the street. It was colder than she'd remembered as the wind cut through her light jacket. It was also quieter as she walked away from the French Quarter toward the river, where she'd seen a large hotel earlier that day. She knew from experience that the concierge would call her a taxi and she focused on getting there.

However, her mind kept going back to Michael and the events of the night. Could he have been lying about Nina? He'd said she broke up with him and then disappeared. He'd said emphatically that he didn't have any children.

Her heart told her that he'd been sincere, but her head knew she'd been tricked before and this wouldn't be a stretch. She had to keep to her plan. She couldn't stay anywhere for too long and this was her sign that it was time to go. Michael's ex-girlfriend was back, and they had a child. A toddler. And that changed everything.

He had no business with Daisy, and she certainly couldn't stay around knowing that she could put him and his kid in danger.

The universe had a way of making changes in her life where

she might not be strong enough to handle if left to her own devices.

Swiping at her tears, Daisy could see the hotel sign up ahead—two blocks. She had to stay focused on getting there and less on her breaking heart. It was Keola Kahale's number one rule. *"Don't get emotional. Stay focused on your goal,"* he would tell her.

Scanning the area, she suddenly realized the man wearing the green ski jacket from the bar was keeping time with her across the street. Had he been following her all along?

Daisy had been walking pretty fast, and perhaps she'd caught up to him? Slowing down to see if he was watching her, she thought he was staggering like he was drunk.

Relieved that he was most likely out of it, she jogged the rest of the way. The front of the hotel was lit up so brightly, and she was close now.

As Daisy picked up her pace, suddenly he did too. She was just a block away from the hotel, but he would catch her before she reached it.

Her heart pounded, and that was when he pointed at her and grinned. She started running backward and turned around, but from out of the shadows, a large arm reached around her and picked her up.

The struggle was real, but as she swung her elbow around and felt it slam into someone's head, she heard Michael laugh. "I think I need to change your nickname to hellcat," he said, still holding her. She was so relieved that it was him, but still terrified of the green ski coat guy.

When Michael realized she'd been running from someone, he pushed her body behind his and stalked out into the street. "What did he look like? What was he wearing?"

But there was no one else around. The man had vanished.

Michael grabbed her hand and led her down an alley where

he'd conveniently parked his truck. He didn't speak to her until she was safely tucked away inside.

He took his jacket off and handed it to her as he started his truck. "You're safe, Daisy."

She nodded, but her fear was at the surface, and her voice trembled. "Please, can we go?"

Reaper nodded, and within minutes, they were on the highway. As he headed toward the bridge to take her home, he apologized. "Please, Daisy, you have to believe me. I didn't know. I haven't seen or heard from Nina in almost four years."

"But she said you have a son."

Michael looked crestfallen. He held out his hand and waited for Daisy to reach back and take it. She finally did, but he could feel her trembling.

"Damn," he cursed under his breath before changing over two lanes and pulling off on a service road meant for the bridge patrol officers and maintenance workers.

Daisy watched as he threw his truck into park and took off his seatbelt. "Come here," he said as he pulled her into his arms.

She'd put his jacket on after her seatbelt and was completely tangled up in them both, making him laugh. It took a second to right the buckle, and he pulled his jacket around her shoulders as he scooped her over to him.

They were a breath apart, and eye to eye, as he explained. "Angel, I was raised to not say derogatory things about women and I won't start now in front of you. But the one you met tonight would lie, cheat, or steal to get her way."

"She wants you back."

"If there is one thing I know for sure, it's that she doesn't want me. She just can't stand the idea that I would be happy with someone else. Chances are, word got around that I was seeing you after we went home for Thanksgiving."

Daisy shrugged. "She's done this before?"

Michael kissed her forehead, nose, and then lips. "I know this may be hard to understand, but have you ever known someone that was rotten to their core? Who wakes up every day with nothing but bad intentions and a purpose to hurt others as much as possible?"

Daisy stared into Michael's eyes. "I may know someone like that," she whispered, and he smiled, thinking there was no way someone as sweet as Daisy knew someone as evil as Nina.

"Seriously, Daisy. Nina wasn't the person she pretended to be, and I was the focus of all her ill will. My sister was the one who caught Nina fooling around with other guys. I was sending her money to help pay her bills while she supposedly went to beauty school. She never took a single class and had several other guys also giving her money. The difference was that she was spinning some lies about me mistreating her and had a slew of men ready to jump me the minute I got to town. Abigail uncovered the entire scheme and called the police. She threatened to tell me if Nina didn't do it and after it was all over with, Nina left town."

Michael Thibodeaux had been in the Navy, and here he admitted that his little sister stood up for him. "Abigail protected you from Nina?"

"I guess villains come in all shapes and sizes. I don't know if I've ever admitted that out loud before, but they say the line between love and hate can be thin. And that line for Nina was undetectable."

Daisy threw her arms around Michael and hugged him tightly. She knew better than anyone how hard admitting something like that was, and he was so open and honest with her. Something she couldn't be with him.

"I'm sorry that happened to you. Especially with someone you loved."

Michael held Daisy close as he admitted, "I cared for her. We had been friends since we were kids. But she killed anything I felt for her and now I'm not sure if it was love. Not after all the lies and deceit."

Daisy leaned back and he could see the concern on her face. "Don't worry. I'm fine now, Daisy. She doesn't have any power over me at all. I just regret she pulled that stunt tonight while you were there."

Nina barging into his house to confront Tenille had startled her and right after she'd talked herself into giving into her feelings for him. Running had seemed like her only option.

Michael reached over and held her face in his hands so he could look into her eyes. "Angel, please don't ever run away from me like that again."

Did he know she planned to leave them all soon?

Before either of them could speak again, bright blue lights lit up the dark behind the truck and a loud voice came over a police speaker, telling them to get out of the truck with their hands up.

Chapter Twelve

Michael rolled his eyes as he winked at Daisy. "We aren't supposed to park here," he said as he opened his door wide.

"Stay here. I'll be right back."

She heard the policeman over the loudspeaker again, "I said put your hands up, you criminal." Daisy immediately had her hands in the air when she thought she heard laughter coming from behind her. Slightly turning around, she could see Michael shaking his head at a man in uniform, who was laughing so hard he couldn't stand up straight.

The next minute, they were both walking over to the truck together. "You can put your hands down, Daisy. This is Cage's brother, Keith."

"How ya doing?" Keith asked, giving her a friendly smile. Then he turned toward Reaper and punched him in the chest. "Man, I didn't know you were dating someone. I guess that explains where you've been lately."

Daisy blushed, but Reaper didn't correct Keith. He just gave him a serious look, and Keith grinned slyly. "I couldn't resist when I saw your truck. I figured you were down here up to no good and frankly, I'm just glad you both had clothes on."

Michael shook his head in warning, and Keith turned around and apologized. "Sorry, ma'am. I didn't mean to be disrespectful. It's just that the only people we ever catch down here are either hiding from the police or naked."

Daisy laughed and Michael smiled at her and then at his friend. It was clear that Keith really liked Michael.

"Cage said you guys have been picking up some new security work for the mayor and you might need me to put in some overtime on a new covert operation? Bridge detail is pretty boring, so hit me up if you need me."

Michael didn't talk about work, and she instantly wondered if it was dangerous. *A covert operation?* What had he done in the Navy?

The two men talked a few minutes more and Daisy enjoyed the distraction. Watching the two funny men laugh about old times was amusing. Michael had served in the Navy with Cage and Rex, but Keith had been a police officer for years. All four were honest, and hardworking, but single. Daisy listened closely as Keith teased Michael, saying he always charmed the pretty girls. "All I'm saying is you could leave one or two for me, buddy. And Lord knows, Cage could use a date once in a while." Reaper laughed at his friend, who then said he could find women but couldn't catch a fish with dynamite. Then they made plans to go fishing together soon.

It surprised Daisy that none of those men were in relationships. They all seemed to work too much, but they cared about each other and their family. And when the word got out that those four bachelors were available, women would come in droves to meet them.

Ten minutes later, they said their goodbyes and Michael

pulled the truck back onto the bridge, a little more relaxed than before, as they headed to Maisonville.

Time and time again, Daisy was reminded that everyone liked Michael. Everyone. Of course, he'd said Nina didn't like him, but the woman was obsessed with Michael. It may be difficult for Daisy to trust her own radar with people, men specifically, but everyone couldn't be wrong about him.

He was a good man. Honest and true. He loved his family, and if he was your friend, then that meant something. He would treat his girlfriend like she meant the world to him and one day, Daisy hoped he would find someone that deserved him.

What she would give for things to be different. But it couldn't be her. No matter how much she wished they could be together. His ex-girlfriend had put him in an impossible situation. Hearing that his sister had to step in and call the police to keep Michael from getting hurt upset Daisy. But Peter would do more than fight him. It was difficult for her to think about Peter hurting Michael, and she regretted she couldn't come clean about everything in her past. Lying wasn't something that came easily for her, but that was all she'd done since she'd arrived in Maisonville, to everyone she'd met.

It was unforgivable, and she could hardly stand herself for it. Besides, Daisy heard Michael loud and clear when he talked about Nina. He had cared about her since they were kids, but whatever he'd felt was erased because of her lying.

Trust was important in relationships and especially for him because lies destroyed his first love. Daisy couldn't bear to hurt Michael, too. If he couldn't forgive Nina, then he certainly wouldn't be able to forgive Daisy. They'd just met. He thought she was something she wasn't. He called her an angel, and she certainly wasn't innocent. She was putting everyone in danger by being there and should never have gone to meet Michael's family.

She shivered, thinking about the man in the green ski coat

and how he smirked as he pointed at her. Whether or not that man was working for Peter, he had put her on alert. And she should have been more careful all along.

If only Maisonville and all of its residents hadn't distracted her.

The ride across the bridge was long and Michael could see Daisy deep in thought. He patted the seat next to him so she would scoot over closer. "Hey, angel. Everything all right?"

"Just tired," she lied again. It rolled off her tongue easier each time she did it and she liked the after-Peter version of herself less and less. Realizing she was wringing her hands, Daisy unbuckled her seatbelt and scooted over next to Michael. When she put her head on his shoulder, he patted her on the leg and then reached across her to hold her closer to him.

It didn't go unnoticed that she was silent most of the way to the boarding house.

Reaper turned on the music, but she didn't even hum along. He reached behind the seat and pulled the blanket out for her. She pulled it over her legs and seemed to snuggle in closer, but still, she had that worried look on her face.

He kept his arm around her as he pulled up in front of the boarding house and Daisy looked up nervously when he didn't let her go.

"Angel, I'm not going to be able to leave unless you tell me what happened to you out there tonight."

She shrugged but didn't say a word. He cut off the engine and then turned in his seat to face her. The silence was deafening, and she wasn't sure how long she could take it.

"I-I was a little overwhelmed with your ex and then when she mentioned your son, it just felt like I shouldn't be there."

He reached for her hand and held it warmly. "Nina is over the top on her best day. And I'm sorry you had to witness any of that. I hope you'll give me a chance to figure all of it out before you pass judgment."

"I'm not judging you."

Reaper leaned over and kissed her sweetly on the lips. "Thank you. Now, what happened after you left?"

Daisy weighed the truth in her head and decided she could finally be honest about something. "I went into a bar and sat in the restroom for a while, trying to figure out my next move. When I came out, there was this guy in a green ski coat watching me. He wasn't there very long, but I waited a while before heading out to find a taxi to drive me back to the boarding house. I didn't realize it would be so hard to get one on Bourbon Street, but remembered seeing them in front of the hotel. On my way to the Hilton, the guy showed back up. At first, I thought he wasn't paying attention to me. Then when I started jogging, he did too."

Reaper watched Daisy's body language as she spoke. He could tell she was trying to make it seem less of an ordeal, but her chin trembled as she spoke.

"Did you know him? Have you seen him before tonight? What else did he do?"

She shrugged again and gave him a watery smile. Daisy was scared of someone or something, and that was clear whether she admitted it or not. "I didn't know him. He just gave me a look, like he knew I was alone, and pointed at me before he started toward me."

Reaper pulled her all the way into his lap as he hugged her tightly. "It was my fault you were out there in the first place."

In actuality, Daisy knew she had put herself into that position and regretted agreeing to go with Michael to his home at all. She was the one that had lost all sense of what she was supposed to be doing and from whom she was running. Her carelessness would be the difference between living and dying, and she had to pull herself together.

The Kahale family had put themselves in danger helping her. Nalani's cousin had spent months trying to teach her how to protect herself or get away if she was caught. She was betraying them by not doing her best. The more time she spent in the quaint little town, the more she kept forgetting the stakes.

"It wasn't your fault. It just happened," she said, trying to make him feel better as well as herself. His arms around her made her feel safe, but she knew there was no such thing as long as Peter was out there. Michael was everything she could ever want and exactly what she could not have. Her life in Maisonville had an expiration date and seeing the green ski jacket guy had reminded her it was past the time for her to go.

But she wouldn't be able to say goodbye to Michael. It would hurt too much. Besides, according to Nina, Michael had a son to think about and she wouldn't put him in danger too.

She leaned up to kiss him on the cheek and to thank him for a lovely evening, even though they had been interrupted. When Reaper walked her to the front door of the boarding house, she surprised him with another goodnight kiss that had more emotion than he'd expected. She hugged him again, and held on a lot longer than ever before. When he got back into his truck, he saw her standing in the doorway, watching him for a beat too long before going inside.

By all accounts, that night, Daisy had been the most affectionate toward him and before Nina interrupted it had felt like they were on stronger footing. He wanted her in every way, but was also prepared to let her take as much time as she needed to be comfortable. She wasn't the type of girl who ran headlong into something. She was worth waiting for and he'd planned to tell her that when she came back from the restroom, but Nina had shown up and blown the night to hell.

Of course, Cage had warned him that Nina would show up one day. It wasn't in her nature to leave him alone or let things go. She had to have the last word and if he ever settled down with another woman, his friend was certain she'd try to interfere. Cage had a gift with people, specifically women, and could read them like an open book.

Cage had agreed with Reaper that Daisy was hiding from something, but he'd also warned that she most likely wasn't the angel that Reaper thought she was and all that goodness didn't make sense. "Have we ever met a woman that was truly that guiltless? Seriously, they find out our background and then pretend to be all helpless so we can beat our chests and save the day. Neither of us have ever met a woman that couldn't stand up for herself and that's okay. Life isn't a fairytale. It's gritty."

Cage's words rang out inside the cab of Reaper's truck. Life was gritty. But Reaper had always known Daisy was hiding something. While he believed omitting the truth was the same as lying, he could feel the difference between her situation and the deceit Nina had put him through. No, Daisy didn't share her troubles because she either didn't want to admit them or she was trying to protect those around her.

His friend understood women, but Reaper could read a situation better than most, and as he slowly pulled out of Daisy's neighborhood, he couldn't shake the negative feeling that everything between them had changed.

Chapter Thirteen

It wouldn't make sense to most people, but Reaper had lived through some of the most dangerous situations in his life by following his instincts. Before he made it to the bridge out of Maisonville, he made a U-turn and headed back to Mrs. Bower's boarding house.

He wasn't sure if it was Nina, the man in the green ski jacket, or maybe even his latent response when she ran out of his house that had pushed Daisy. The only thing he knew was that the night had been going wonderfully before it blew up in his face faster than he could blink and he should have reacted faster.

Opening the door to Nina was his first mistake. He had a camera and could have looked at his phone before opening the door. Letting her yell and push past him toward Daisy was his second. But the gravest error was not getting to Daisy before she took off running into the French Quarter.

He should've left Nina there, but he'd done that in the past and she'd destroyed his apartment, turning over tables and furniture, and pouring liquids from his refrigerator onto the carpets.

That had been in their early twenties and perhaps she'd changed since then, but he wouldn't put anything past her.

When Nina smirked like she'd won versus Daisy, he'd wanted to let her have it. And Nina looked like she was ready for him to explode. However, Reaper had changed in the years since he'd seen Nina and she no longer could wind him up. She had a way of making him angry like no one else on the planet and then she liked to have wild make-up sex.

He wasn't interested in anything with Nina anymore, and couldn't get the hurt look in Daisy's eyes out of his mind, or the wild way in which she looked around the street before she ran like a bat out of hell. His heart sunk when she disappeared into the crowd.

It had given him the wherewithal to walk over to Nina, pick her up and carry her out of his home. She screamed and kicked like a crazy person, but it didn't matter. He had to find Daisy, and he didn't have time to deal with whatever cockamamie agenda Nina had cooked up for them.

It took him less than three minutes to remove Nina and then lock up so she couldn't get back inside before he got into his truck and searched for Daisy. He'd ended up parking and searching the streets and bars of the French Quarter for a half hour with no sign of her.

Time had dragged on as he'd searched and when he'd realized how much time had passed, he'd wished he'd called Cage or Rex to come and help him.

He'd refused to give up and when he jogged toward the river where they'd walked earlier that evening, she was there.

He was so relieved to see her that he hadn't realized someone was chasing her. But the guilt he felt when he saw how frightened she was had taken a piece out of him. If he'd found a single soul on the street near her, then he would have ended them.

She'd been in his care and was his responsibility and he'd let her down.

Now pulling up to the boarding house again, he regretted letting her go inside alone at all. If he called her, would she come back outside? Would she invite him in?

He couldn't bring himself to face the truth that he knew, so he sat there and watched the house for hours. He saw a light turn on upstairs that looked like a bathroom window and, after a few minutes, it turned off. And then he saw the large windows in what must have been a corner bedroom, Daisy's room, turn off.

Hopefully, she was getting some rest and could put the evening's events into perspective tomorrow. But he felt like the daylight hours would bring more change and he couldn't shake the ominous feelings he had about what was to come.

At daybreak, he saw Mrs. Bowers walk out to her front porch with a large coffee mug in one hand and a thick quilt in the other. She didn't notice him sitting there in his truck across the street as she pulled out her bible and what looked like a highlighter to underline passages.

The neighborhood seemed to come to life slowly as several cars passed by and he felt calm enough to head home. He would grab a few hours of sleep, shower, and be back for Daisy's shift at the diner.

They needed to talk. He hoped to get answers.

A few hours later, banging on Reaper's front door jolted him awake. He jumped up, and that was when he saw his phone lighting up like a casino slot machine.

Cage had called, texted, and now was trying to faceTime him. What in the hell? He grabbed his gun from his nightstand as he answered his phone and headed to the door.

"Open the door, sleeping beauty!" Cage yelled and Reaper could hear him through the door and the phone.

Reaper unlocked it, but instead of greeting his friend, he

flipped him off as he headed to the kitchen to pour a cup of day-old coffee into his mug.

"They would've kicked you out of our old unit if you'd slept like that."

Reaper was silent as he put his cup in the microwave. What his friend was saying was true, but he didn't need to agree with him.

"I thought maybe you weren't alone, and that was why you weren't answering."

Reaper threw a paper towel roll at Cage's head, but he ducked. "And you're slow, too!" Cage laughed.

Cutting his eyes at his friend, Reaper drank half his black coffee while Cage waited impatiently.

"Okay, what the hell are you doing here so early?"

Cage shook his head. No need to tell Reaper it was almost noon. His friend looked like he'd been through hell the night before and he'd catch on soon enough. "I had some news and figured you would want it as soon as I got it."

Reaper finished his coffee and then sat the mug in the sink. Cage was supposed to be checking into the restaurant in Hawaii where Daisy's letter had been addressed.

"You won't like it, but here it is, That Fish House Restaurant burned to the ground a few weeks ago. Some old man had been trapped inside, but he got into the standup freezer so he didn't burn to death. The entire place is a loss, and apparently it was arson."

Reaper wiped his face, and his focus seemed to be streamlined onto Cage. "They have any idea who did it?"

"Yup, and it has something to do with your girl."

Reaper shook his head. "She was already here three weeks ago."

"I don't know what to tell you, but they described a woman with Daisy's build and said her crazy ass boyfriend sent a guy there to do it. Apparently, that guy is now dead and they've been searching for her."

"The arsonist is dead?"

Cage nodded. "That place was locally famous and had been there for fifty years. The Hawaiian Family who owned it, also worked there, and are devastated over the loss. They're loved by everyone and do a lot for the community, too. Real salt of the earth type folks, you know. Local law enforcement is in an uproar. They've called in the feds and seem to be pretty desperate to find blondie."

Reaper shook his head. If someone told him that about Nina, he would believe them. But Daisy was different. Sure, he knew she was hiding something, but she wasn't the type of girl to run around with the criminal type of crowd. She wasn't a thrill seeker or troublemaker.

Cage pulled out his tablet and showed Reaper all the pictures of the fire destruction. It had totally wiped out the restaurant. The man from the freezer was on a stretcher, but there were no signs of life. He doubted anyone could make it through a fire like that. There were also pictures of the family and workers as they cried and hugged each other. They were shattered, and it was hard to see that type of anguish on their faces.

Cage called the lead detective, Detective Ghee, in Hawaii, and Reaper heard firsthand what had happened. There had been an accelerant poured all over the property and it was lit from multiple points so that the fire and thus the restaurant would burn rapidly. "It was a professional job. Then local law enforcement identified the body we found the next day on the beach as Mr. Samuel Foret. The feds knew him for this kind of crime and, well, I guess it caught up to him. We believe the real mastermind hired him and that the young lady is with that man or waiting for him somewhere."

"Can you tell us why you think she is with this guy?" Cage

could see the rage on his friend's face and so he took over the conversation with the detective.

"We believe she had an on again, off again relationship with him. They'd had some kind of disagreement at the restaurant ten months ago and she walked out. He blamed the restaurant owner and we think she told the boyfriend that they had helped her. Like I said before, we are just piecing this together. The family isn't saying anything and we only have a little information from some eye witnesses that were there the night it happened and spoke to the police. The boyfriend went ballistic that night and they hauled him into the police station. They fined him and he had to pay restitution for some property damage back then. We've concluded he hired Foret to come back and mess it up real good for him. Then he got rid of the evidence."

"If she walked away, why do you think she's back with him?"

The detective laughed. "That's easy. She was used to the good life he provided for her. It didn't take long living here and working a menial job for her to decide it wasn't for her. We have evidence she flew out on a red-eye flight not too long ago. Probably to go back to him, but maybe to wait for him to meet her after this job was done. Regardless, she got out of dodge before it got too messy. It's too convenient, if you know what I mean."

"It's circumstantial at best," Reaper said to Cage.

"If it walks like a duck, then—" Detective Ghee didn't finish his sentence. He didn't need to because they all knew what he meant.

When they hung up the phone, Cage watched his friend war with his thoughts. Cage cleared his throat. "I'm not saying she's trouble, but dude, she's in some kind of predicament and it's coming for her. You either need to get prepared or cut your ties."

Reaper shook his head. He was already in too deep. He couldn't walk away now. *Could he?*

He slammed his hand down on the countertop. He knew she

was in trouble the night he met her, but hadn't imagined it was worse than what Nina had gotten herself into and out of, time and time again.

Reaper grabbed his keys and stormed to the door. Before leaving, he asked Cage to get all the intel possible.

Driving with purpose, he headed straight to Maisonville and the only person who could give him answers.

Chapter Fourteen

Waving goodbye to Michael was the hardest thing Daisy had done in well over a month. It was difficult to admit that her life was just a series of awful events, but she could mark all of her years by the losses it had dealt her. Still, those were out of her control and while she wasn't the one calling the shots, it felt a bit like she was to blame.

The Kahale family in Hawaii had been so good to her. Nalani's parents and siblings were amazing and their extended family, too. At least, most of them. No one suspected Ke's wife would betray Daisy or them for a few measly dollars.

Keola had continued working with Daisy on her self-defense lessons to keep her sharp, and they'd become great friends. He was so worried for Daisy and poured his heart out to his wife late one night, only to find out what she'd done.

His frantic knocking on the front door of the apartment that night woke Daisy. But her roommate, Nalani, answered the door before she could get there. They all understood that Daisy had to run.

She hadn't tried to use her fake identification yet, but there was no time to wait. Nalani drove her straight to the airport and Nalani's uncle, who worked security there, walked Daisy to the airline counter paying cash for her one-way ticket to California. One of Peter's men, the one with a crew cut, was at the airport, but he didn't recognize Daisy with black hair and baggy clothes. Thankfully, Nalani's uncle spotted the man first and hid Daisy in a janitor's closet until her flight boarded. He then walked her to her seat and stayed on board until they were ready to push away from the gate. That was the last time she'd talked to any of them. She booked her travel on-line before she got to California and then boarded a flight to New Orleans and tried not to look back.

She owed the Kahale family everything and couldn't even thank them or let them know she was doing okay. Now she had to run again. But leaving Maisonville was going to tear her apart and there were lots of reasons why.

Daisy rubbed her eyes as she tried to stop thinking about the friends she would leave behind this time. She needed to focus on packing her belongings. Keeping it light would mean she could get in and out of the bus station quickly.

As she packed only the necessities into her bag, she tried not to think about everything else she set aside for donation. Someone less fortunate could well use those clothes and shoes. She swiped at a few stray tears. At least she wouldn't sob anymore.

Her Aunt Sue and Uncle Ed had been so happy when they met in New Orleans. That reason alone made the place feel more like home, and she hadn't been able to return to her actual home in almost a year.

Miss Lynn and Olivia were so much like her aunt and quickly felt like family, if she had any family left. Of course, Mrs. Bowers looked after her too, and Daisy wished she could stay and watch over the elderly woman. Mrs. B had outlived her family, and she needed someone. Daisy wanted to be that person for her and was going to miss her terribly.

Michael Thibodeaux would be the hardest one to let go of, and she had to stop thinking about him. He would probably reconcile with mean Nina and then they could raise their son in Michael's beautiful New Orleans home.

She closed her eyes and willed her thoughts away from Michael. Then she began writing letters to the beautiful friends she'd made. Daisy had only been there a month and some change. They would all get on with their lives, and she could keep them safe by getting out of town.

No need for tearful goodbyes. *Right?*

If her aunt were still around, she'd be incredibly disappointed to know that Daisy planned to leave notes instead of thanking them in person. It was a disgraceful way to thank Miss Lynn for giving her a chance. It was also cowardly, but Daisy didn't think she would have the confidence to leave if she didn't do it secretively.

It was late afternoon when Daisy finished and gathered her last things before quietly leaving the boarding house. She left an envelope on the kitchen counter near the coffeepot for Mrs. Bowers to find, then headed to work. No one knew it would be her last time to work the closing shift at the diner. But strangely, Olivia followed Daisy into the back room the moment she saw her face. "What's wrong with you?"

Daisy shrugged and willed herself to give a believable answer. "I just didn't sleep well last night. That's all."

Miss Lynn came in behind them and pushed into the tiny closet of a room to put her hand on Daisy's forehead. "Are you sure you aren't sick, child? Fever?"

Daisy's eyes watered, but she grinned through the heartache. "No ma'am, just insomnia. A good night's work will help me knock right out."

"I can drop Lucas off at The Gentry's house and come back to close with her," Olivia offered.

It was Miss Lynn's night to go play cards with her girlfriends and they didn't want her to miss it. She was the rummy champion and had to defend her title.

Daisy gave them both a genuine smile. "You two are going to have to stop babying me. I am fine. I just need to spend a little energy taking care of customers and cleaning the diner tonight, so I'll drop when I get home."

Olivia nor Miss Lynn believed her completely and so they decided Alexavier could pick up Lucas, Miss Lynn would go to her card game, and Olivia would stay until seven or closing if Daisy needed her.

It was going to be a huge problem if Olivia stayed and so Daisy put all she had into her last shift. She hugged Miss Lynn goodbye and then went straight to work on helping customers. In-between taking or delivering orders of food, she cleaned the front windows and wiped down every flat surface in the diner.

When Reaper showed up at 6:30, she barely nodded his way because she was deep cleaning the ice machine.

Olivia rolled her eyes as she brought him an iced tea. "Don't take it personally. She's trying to prove a point and let me tell you, our little Daisy isn't anything if she's not hardheaded."

Reaper looked confused, and that was when Olivia explained to him about the insomnia claim. And how Daisy was trying to prove them all wrong that she didn't need any help at all.

"But now that you're here, I guess I'll leave her to it. I'm exhausted by just watching her." Olivia winked at him and then walked over to tell Daisy goodbye.

Reaper picked up his own dinner from the kitchen window pass through while Daisy rang up a group of elderly men who each had coffee and a slice of peach pie.

The men frequented the diner, and each one flirted a little

with Daisy, making her laugh. But her warm laugh didn't reach her brown eyes, and Reaper instantly understood what Olivia was talking about. Something serious was wrong. But he'd known that last night.

"Are you feeling alright?" he asked when Daisy walked past him.

"Fine. Just didn't sleep well," she answered.

Last night, things had gone completely off the rails and he'd felt how upset she was even after he'd dropped her off. Sitting outside the boarding house all night and keeping watch over her had him on edge, but the final blow was the news from Cage about that restaurant in Hawaii. Hearing the detective talk about her made him understand that someone understood what this girl was all about and he'd hoped like hell that it was him. Now she was aloof and damn if the hair on the back of his neck wasn't sticking up.

He was grinding his teeth, a bad habit, but he was angry as he watched her avoiding him. It was almost a half hour before she came back by, seeing if he needed anything else. Sure, there were several couples in the diner, but she was avoiding him.

"A few minutes of your time would be great."

"Sorry, I have a lot to do to close up tonight and then I'm busy."

"You're busy tonight after work?"

"Yes."

"You've made plans with someone else?"

She couldn't mistake the cold in his eyes when he asked her if she was going to see another. It took a piece out of her heart, but she had to do it. They hadn't known each other long, but their chemistry might just be what those romance books she read were all about. At least she felt that way. It had kept her up all night and she couldn't stop thinking about him all day. She knew what she had to do to protect him and those that she cared about.

It was the same reason she'd left Hawaii.

She couldn't let Peter find her or find out that she had anyone that was important to her. He would hurt them in order to hurt her. Michael wouldn't understand that it was dangerous to be with her.

"I told you I'm not the girl you think I am."

He stared at her as he sat his knife and fork down. He'd spent his entire day talking to every contact he had to find out more about Daisy Jones. But there wasn't anything out there about her. She'd just appeared out of nowhere a month ago when she flew out of Maui and into California, then New Orleans. No government records and no social media. She was a ghost. The lack of information told him exactly what he'd thought. She was hiding from someone or something.

"Then why don't you have a seat here with me and explain who you are?"

Her face dropped. *Did he know? He couldn't know.* She took a deep breath. "You know I can't sit down while I'm working. If you don't need anything else from the kitchen, I need to let the cook go."

"I need nothing else from the kitchen," he said flatly.

Daisy shivered, knowing that he expected answers and she couldn't give him any. It was for his own good. Determined to stay on course, she turned away from him and told the guys in the kitchen they could go. Then she grabbed a broom to sweep up behind the counter instead of giving him a chance to confront her.

He waited until she turned the lights off in the kitchen, and then he stared at her. She trembled, but then quickly covered it up with anger. "Please, stop looking at me like that, Michael."

She went into the back room and grabbed her heavy bag, taking enough time for him to finish his dessert. But when she returned, he wasn't eating at all.

"Going somewhere?"

She cleared his dishes anyway and then wiped the counter in front of him. "I don't know what you mean. I always carry my backpack."

"I think you do. I think you're in trouble."

She placed an envelope next to the coffeepot before she turned off the rest of the interior diner lights and pulled out her keys. She avoided looking directly at him as she adjusted her heavy bag. "That's silly. You don't know anything."

He followed her out the door and when she locked it and turned around—he was standing too close.

"I know your real name isn't Daisy Jones." He lowered his head, so they were face to face, but she avoided his eyes. "I also know that you're not from Hawaii."

"I lived in Hawaii before I moved here."

"Was that before your boyfriend burned down that restaurant?"

"What?" Her eyes filled with tears and then she couldn't catch her breath.

"The Island Fish Company. I saw the name on that letter."

"It burned? Burned down completely?" She was shaking uncontrollably and dropped her bag.

The lost look on her face confirmed what he needed to know.

He pulled her into his arms. "Yes, angel. It's gone."

She felt the dark parking lot closing in on her. "No. No-no-no. That can't be. Tell me it's not true."

"I'm sorry. It is true." He grabbed her bag and then picked her up so he could take her to his truck.

"I-I can't stay here, Michael."

He nodded his head. "I'll take you anywhere you want to go."

Michael drove them to his house. Daisy didn't say a word, but he watched as she wiped her face and rubbed her eyes several times, trying not to let the exhaustion take her under.

He wanted to help her, but she had to trust him with the truth, first. He didn't think Detective Ghee in Hawaii had the full story, but he knew he didn't either.

His gut told him she didn't have anything to do with the arson or any other crime. However, he'd been so very wrong before when Nina walked all over him. But he'd always known Nina was a whiskey fire. He just couldn't accept it back then.

Daisy wasn't Nina, but he needed the answers.

As he drove through downtown toward The French Quarter, the crowds of people made her nervous. He watched as she slid down in the seat until her head was barely visible from the window.

"Almost home," Reaper said as he pulled around to the side of his house. He'd chosen that property because he had off-street parking. He could see her relief as the solid iron gates opened and then slowly closed behind them.

It was a fortress.

Daisy held her overstuffed backpack as she climbed down out of his truck. He met her at her door and relieved her of the heavy bag. Without him initiating it, she sidled up super close to him. She hovered as he unlocked the door and even as he put his alarm code into the alarm system inside. He could feel her shaking, even though they weren't touching.

Reaper had to make her understand no one was going to get to her as long as he was breathing. The gate, the locks, and the alarms seemed to help, but as he settled her onto the couch, he pulled a quilt around her because she was still trembling. He kissed the top of her head and talked to her calmly. "You are safe here, Daisy. Do you understand?"

She gave him the slightest nod, and he knew she wasn't so sure. "I'll be in your sight-line the whole time, but I'm going to make us some coffee."

It took him just a few minutes, and then he was back beside her with two steaming mugs. Daisy held her cup with both hands but it didn't matter how hard she tried, he could still see her shaking.

He needed to know the truth about her, but before he could ask, he needed to do the same. It was time for him to admit what he was and who he'd been.

"I'm ready to tell you where my nickname came from, Daisy, if you're okay with listening to my story?" He saw when she had the faintest glimmer in her brown eyes.

"Drink your coffee, angel," he said, remembering back to when he joined the Navy.

"I'm not sure how much you know about the military." Reaper said, and she shrugged, realizing he was honestly going to talk about himself and not grill her, which she'd expected.

"I was pretty set on joining the Navy, but my mother kept pushing me to go on college visitation trips with my school counselors. I was great at science and even thought about being a doctor. Can you imagine?" He grinned, thinking back to how much he thought he knew back then. "Thankfully, the recruiter gave me some great options, and I went off to BASIC training, knowing I was where I was supposed to be at the time. I had a blast during BASIC, but I'd always been mentally and physically tougher than most of my friends growing up. When I finished at the top of my class, I figured I'd throw my energy into BUD/S training."

She was biting her lower lip as she listened. She'd never known anyone in the military. "I'm afraid that I know nothing about The Navy or the military. And I've never heard of BUD/S training, either."

He grinned at her because he could barely remember what it was like to not know all the things relevant to that lifestyle. He tried to dial in on the details. "BUD/S stands for Basic Underwater Demolition/SEAL training. It lasts for twenty-four weeks. I was nineteen when I volunteered, and one of the youngest in my class to make it through. We started with a hundred and seventy-five and finished with only sixty-eight men. Cage and I were in the same BUD/S class. It was his second time going through because he'd gotten injured the first time around. We became friends, almost like brothers, as we kept each other motivated through training. I came out of there feeling like superman but have seen a lot of my friends get hurt or worse. In my mid-twenties, Cage and I served together on SEAL Team three and met our friend Rex. The three of us have been in some serious situations." He couldn't give her details, but he wanted her to know the truth. "The point I'm trying to make without going into the gory details is that men don't come out of that kind of training or career without feeling pretty immortal. But I have lost friends, close friends, during missions and when I say I've served with heroes, I'm not just bragging. These men—SEALS do things you can never imagine surviving."

Felicity had wondered if his security job was dangerous, but hadn't really considered what he'd done in the military. She remembered watching a movie a long time ago with her uncle, after they had watered it down for television, about some elite group of men and she thought they were Navy SEALS. "Like, what kind of things?"

"Things that I'm not at liberty to discuss."

"Bad things?"

"Things to keep our country and its citizens safe."

Daisy nodded her head, but he could see the questioning in her eyes. He couldn't, wouldn't, tell her specifics, but wanted to be as honest as possible so she would know who and what he was.

"I was fresh out of BUD/S and went against a group—let's call them pirates. We were just supposed to be backup, you know, in case the first team ran into trouble. They did. We were under heavy gunfire. When no one else could, I jumped into the ocean and swam around to get behind the bad guys and stop them. I was dubbed the Grim Reaper and later it was shortened to Reaper."

"You had to kill them?" Her hand was over her mouth, and she looked upset, which wasn't what he'd planned.

"The point I need you to understand, Daisy, is that if there is a bad guy coming for you, then my friends and I are the ones that could stop him."

She avoided looking at Michael, and he had mixed emotions about telling her his story. Then she spoke, and he knew it wouldn't matter what he'd said. She didn't want him involved. "I would never ask you or your friends to put yourselves in danger for me, though. I can't let you or anyone else get hurt."

If Daisy would just tell him what had happened, he could

reassure her, but he watched her face as she tucked the details inside. Olivia was right. She was hardheaded. She drank a sip of her coffee and then asked, "Was anyone hurt at the restaurant?"

"A single man was inside."

She sat her coffee down. "I appreciate the coffee, but I really have to get out of here."

When she stood up, he stood with her and gently turned her toward him. "Is the person you're running from the reason that your bag is always packed?"

"You don't understand."

"Try me."

"I can't let anything happen to Miss Lynn or Olivia. Oh, God, or Lucas. What if I've put all of you in danger?"

"You were leaving town tonight without saying goodbye, weren't you?"

"I-I left a note for Mrs. Bowers at the boarding house and one for Miss Lynn and Olivia."

He knew that was a goodbye letter by the look on her face when she set it down at the diner.

"You don't have one of those letters for me, do you?" They were just getting to know each other, but it still rubbed him the wrong way that she would have left without a word to him.

"Michael, you could get hurt just because I'm here."

He stepped closer to her. "It better be a team of people if they plan to get to you or to me."

Her face was ashen when she whispered, "Just one. One really bad man."

Reaper smirked. "Angel, weren't you paying attention? It would take a lot more than one."

She closed her eyes and wiped her face with her hands. Her eyes were red from rubbing them so much and she was tired in her bones. But she needed to make him understand. "He's not like other men. He's diabolical."

Michael pulled her into his arms and held her close. He wanted to tell her that she didn't know how dangerous he was, but at the moment, she needed his comfort instead. He'd always been more about showing instead of telling, anyway.

He would protect her.

"It's late and you're exhausted. Take a minute to think it through, angel. Why don't you shower and change your clothes, so you'll be more comfortable?"

She needed to catch a bus, but it was the last thing she wanted to do at that moment. Leaving his arms to sleep on a bus to nowhere seemed cruel.

He picked up her bag and walked her to his large master bathroom. When he turned on the water in his over-sized shower, she sighed. She really should be on that bus, but she couldn't say no to a hot shower.

Michael Thibodeaux was a giant, intimidating looking man and completely wonderful. Why couldn't she have met him first? She stood on her tiptoes and kissed his cheek. "Thank you, Michael. I won't take too long."

"Take as long as you like. There's no rush." He pulled out a couple of towels and then left her to it.

She quickly undressed and stood under the hot water spray for several minutes. It was heavenly, but she couldn't stay, could she? Putting Michael in danger wasn't an option and no matter what he thought, Peter was formidable. But if Peter wasn't there already, then maybe, just maybe, one night of planning her next move would be okay. She'd flown to New Orleans on a whim and that was how she'd ended up in Maisonville by mistake.

Honestly, it had been the best mistake she'd made in a long list of mistakes. But if she was going to evade Peter, she needed to be smarter. It was cheaper to travel by bus than by plane. She needed to change her name again and find someone that could make her new ID cards. She didn't know where to even start with that and if it hadn't been for Nalani's cousins helping her before, then she wouldn't have made it out of Hawaii.

"God, please let them be okay," she whispered and washed the tears away under the water. This wasn't the time to fall apart, and she had to pull herself together. She'd been lucky so far and she prayed that Nalani and her family were, too. Turning up the hot water, Tenille sat on the floor of the shower to let it rain down on her.

Once Michael walked out of the bathroom, he could feel his anger consume him. Daisy was gentle and quiet. How could someone that good and unassuming get into trouble? Hell, no matter how hard she was trying, he knew the moment he met her that she was hiding something. She had no poker face and basically no game, so how could she be mixed up in something that had her running scared? And she was absolutely terrified of someone. Someone she thought was extremely dangerous made her run for her life. How could a man like that even get close to her?

No matter what had happened, Reaper would help her. He wasn't even sure how she'd made it that far without being discovered. While she showered, he called Cage, who'd been impatiently waiting to hear from him.

"I don't know what, who, or when, but I will by morning. We're at my house and I need eyes on us for the night. She says he's diabolical and if that's true, then I expect him to have reinforcements. She's innocent though."

Cage trusted Reaper with his life, but he wasn't so sure his friend looked after himself that well. He agreed to call his brother and their friend Rex to help cover the house in the French Quarter. It was going to be a rough night waiting to hear what they were up against, but it wouldn't be the first time, and certainly not the last.

Chapter Sixteen

How long ago had it been when Daisy had taken a shower and lost all sense of time? It was a luxury she couldn't afford and yet, she'd mindlessly taken way too long in the shower. Getting lost with five massaging shower-heads in front of her and a large rain shower-head up above. There was enough room in there for five people and it was beautifully designed with hand-painted tiles. No doubt, Michael did all the work himself. He took time and care with each little detail. Still another quality she wouldn't have expected from him. He just didn't look like someone that could care about all the little things.

Tenille finally turned off the water and towel dried her hair and body before putting on navy sweatpants and a long sleeve flannel shirt. She looked a mess with her wet hair, but the plain-clothes would help keep her from getting noticed and, as a bonus, would be comfortable to travel. She dug out a pair of socks and sneakers, then stuffed everything else back into her bag.

The shower helped to wake her up and decide on her next step. She had to leave. She wouldn't tell Michael another thing about her past or burden him with her troubles. The less he knew, the better for him. She took a deep breath and headed out of the bathroom to ask him if he would take her to the bus station. After all, he'd said he would take her anywhere.

Daisy felt a bit more confident as she swung open the door, but there, leaning against the wall, was Michael Thibodeaux. She felt ridiculous when he startled her. Would she ever get used to him waiting for her outside of restrooms?

"Hungry?" he asked, and again he distracted her from the bus station. Taking the heavy bag from her shoulder, he guided her back to the living room, where he'd made a plate of grilled cheese sandwiches and two glasses of milk.

"I also have beer or wine?"

"I like milk with grilled cheese. Thanks."

Reaper couldn't explain why he liked that so much, but he did. He liked everything about her.

Once they were finally settled on the sofa and she'd taken a bite of the sandwich, she looked over to see him watching her. She smiled and took another bite, trying to avoid the impossible.

"What's your real name, angel?"

She put the sandwich down and took a drink of her milk. "Daisies are my favorite flowers."

He nodded, and she sat the glass down. She hadn't said her real name in so long it felt forbidden.

"Jones?"

She shrugged. "The guys who made my ID created Daisy Jones and honestly, I was just so thankful to have the forgeries. They could have named me anything. I had to get out of there." She looked at the grilled cheese sandwich. She loved simple comfort food, but now her stomach was in knots.

He kept watching her and when she didn't look like she was going to tell him, he used that deep gravelly voice on her. "I showed you mine," he said.

Her throat felt hoarse and her mouth suddenly dry. "Tenille

Sims," she whispered and then closed her eyes. She shouldn't have told him her real name. She shouldn't tell him anything else. But the way he looked at her and all the tenderness he showed made her want to tell him everything.

Wrapping her arms around her middle, she seemed to shrink with the truth.

It hurt him to see her feeling vulnerable. He moved in closer and gently reached over to move her wet hair away from her face. "How did you meet him?"

She couldn't open her eyes and face Michael as she thought about the first time she'd met Peter. She had been so naïve, and he knew exactly what he was doing. "It was a week after my Aunt Sue passed away. We lived in Sugarland, Texas, and I had to drive to downtown Houston and meet with our attorney. His office wasn't really far from my house, but by the time the meeting was over, I stopped at a bookstore and then grocery store nearby instead of getting into all the evening traffic. He talked to me throughout those stores."

She paused for a long time and Michael was certain he'd lost her. "He asked you out?"

Shaking her head, she began again, "When I went to load my groceries into my car, there was a homeless man who wouldn't leave me alone and out of nowhere, Peter showed up to help."

Now that she thought back to that day, and how calculating Peter Miller was, she had to wonder if he'd planned the whole incident. She looked even more upset, and Michael reached over to hold her hand.

"What is it?"

"You don't think he staged that whole thing in the parking lot so he could get my number, do you?"

Reaper didn't doubt it at all. "I don't know, angel, but men do a lot of things to impress a beautiful woman."

"Peter is more monster than man." She glanced at Michael

and saw that sweet understanding in his eyes. Then she admitted, "I believed his entire act. The incident shook me up and afterward, I agreed to let him take me to dinner. He took me to one of the nicest restaurants in the city and without a reservation, they seated us immediately, acting like he was a big deal. Honestly, I never really dated anyone before him. I was going through a lot at the time and didn't know what he saw in me, but felt lucky to have met him. He'd lost his parents when he was young, too."

Michael didn't have the heart to tell her that most manipulative people used the shock and awe method on innocent victims.

"I slept with him after just a few days. I had never slept with anyone before, and after that, he became possessive. Things were kind of hazy because the detectives were investigating her sudden death. I didn't really know what to do or who to trust, but he was there for me. When I couldn't stay at my home, he offered for me to move in with him temporarily. Under normal circumstances, I would've never done any of that, but I was grieving and not thinking clearly."

She stopped short of telling him the worst of it, but Reaper could read her face. What she wasn't saying was bad, really bad. He would have to know the gritty truth in order to protect her. But for now, he would just listen.

"He told me he would never let me go."

Her chin quivered as she spoke, and Michael couldn't take it. He pulled her close and kissed the top of her head.

The care Michael was giving her didn't stop the shame she felt, and she was scared out of her mind. Admitting just a little of what had happened to her took her right back to those horrible moments.

"But you got away, angel. And you are safe."

She took a deep, shaky breath. "But that's just the thing. I barely made it out of there. And I'm not so sure the people who helped me are okay. I don't think he's ever going to stop looking for me, and if he found out the Kahale family helped me, then I know he had their restaurant destroyed."

"I'll find out more details about the restaurant fire." He lifted her chin so she would look at him. "And I meant what I said. You're. Safe. Here. With. Me."

There was no reason to drive the point home about his Navy training and experience. She may not understand about his abilities, but it would take an army to get through him to get to her and he had back up coming too.

When her body finally relaxed into his, he'd thought he'd made his point known until there was a loud knock at his front door.

Chapter Seventeen

Tenille jumped to her feet faster than he'd ever seen her move. The frightened look on her face almost did him in. "It's okay, angel. I called Cage while you were in the shower."

She shook her head. "You don't know that for sure. What if it's Peter? The guy in the green ski jacket could work for him and could have followed us? Maybe he followed you to your house, and he's going to burn your house or-or-or—something worse."

Reaper held his phone up so she could see the screen. There was a picture from his security cameras at the front door and Cage was standing there grinning into the lens.

"I'm going to open the door now. Okay?"

Daisy nodded, but she was still shaken. Michael stepped to her and kissed her forehead. "I promise you're protected, okay?"

She didn't look like she believed him, so he held her hand and kept her close as he unlocked the door for Cage.

"Good evening, folks," Cage said. "Rex is already outside the back gate and Keith will be here in fifteen to watch the front. I'll circle the perimeter before I find a perch to watch from above."

Reaper thanked him and then cleared his throat before introducing Cage to her. "Cage, I'd like you to meet Tenille Sims. She's from Sugarland, Texas."

Cage was still wary, and he couldn't help it. He was a suspicious bastard by nature and he'd been there when Nina had used his friend. The worst criminals on the planet spit out were afraid of Reaper, but Cage knew his best friend's weakness for a beautiful woman in need.

"Sugarland, Texas? Not Maui, Hawaii?" Cage asked, looking into her eyes.

"I lived in Hawaii before I moved here," she said as she tucked her damp hair behind her ears. She knew they had no reason to trust her and honestly, she wouldn't blame them if they sent her on her way.

"Her ex's name is Peter Miller. He's also from the Houston area," Reaper said, letting his friend know who they were watching out for without actually saying it.

Cage nodded and then had her describe Peter Miller so he could give a description to Rex and Keith. "Will he be traveling with a crew, or should we expect him alone?" still he directed his questions at her.

"He never had any security or anyone with him when we were in Texas. It wasn't until he drugged me and put me on the private plane to Hawaii that I saw security guards or a crew, as you call them."

Was she really going to do this? Tenille pulled her damp hair around to her shoulder and twisted the ends as she considered how far this conversation should go. These men weren't in direct danger, at least not yet. She could tell them this was all a big mistake and get out of there.

"So, party or honeymoon in Hawaii, sweetheart?" Cage asked without masking his annoyance.

"Enough, Cage," Reaper didn't hide his irritation either, but Tenille understood why Cage felt the way he did and she respected it. He wanted to protect his friend from the selfish woman that would put him in harm's way and, she had to admit, he was right. She was awful for bringing danger to their door and because of that guilt, she told them more.

"He had a big deal to close with some men from the Middle East and that's why we were there. He didn't leave me alone after we got to the island. If he had to go out, he would leave armed men to watch me at the villa where we were staying. He had at least two of them watching over me at all times, unless I was with him. I got the impression that the security guys were there in case something went wrong with the sale."

Cage didn't change his expression as she spoke. "What was he selling, Crypto currency or insurance?" He laughed, but he wasn't funny.

"Guns," she whispered.

"What?" he asked deadpan.

"He was selling weapons, guns, ammunition. I'm not sure what else. I heard him on the phone and he made sure I understood how serious of a deal it was for him."

Cage stepped back. She was terrified just telling them that information. He didn't have to ask how Peter made sure she understood the serious nature of his business in Hawaii. It was written all over her face. The man had hurt her. "Get some rest. I can promise you that no one will get past us tonight." He nodded at Reaper, and then he was gone.

Reaper watched her walk toward the living room to pick up their plates and cups. Without a word, she took everything into the kitchen and cleaned. As he got nearer, he saw the tears silently falling down her cheeks.

She held her arm out to keep him away. "I'm so sorry I involved any of you in this mess. I-I don't know what I was thinking. I told you that I need to get to the bus station. You and your friends may be ex-military, but Peter is a super villain.

Someone is going to get hurt or worse, and it'll be my fault. You don't have to get involved. I don't want any of you taking part in this, okay?" She was really crying now and as she backed up away from him, he watched her looking for a door or window to get out of there.

"Daisy, I mean Tenille, look at me," he coaxed.

"Pl-Please don't say my real name again." She hiccupped as she tried to stop her tears, using the sleeves of her flannel shirt to dry her face.

"Angel, look at me," Reaper slowly closed in on her, but she was still looking at the closest exit. When she backed up against the cabinets, she still wouldn't look into his eyes. He gently lifted her chin so she could see his face.

"Angel, I've tried to explain that we aren't just ex-military. When the worst of the worst needed to be dealt with in the world, we were the people they called."

He could tell she didn't know whether or not to believe him, but she finally leaned into him as she stopped crying.

"Your barely functioning on the two bites of grilled cheese you ate and the no sleep. Please let me put you to bed so you can get some rest."

"I can sleep on the bus."

"I won't be able to sleep on the bus and there is no way I can let you go out there on your own. I'm involved now. So are Cage, Rex, and Keith. Won't you let us watch over things tonight? We can work out more details in the morning."

She hesitated and then, after weighing his words in her head, she finally gave him the slightest nod. It was the biggest relief he'd felt all night. Grabbing her hand, he led her into his bedroom and pulled down the comforter so she could climb in.

Reaper tucked the blankets around her and then reached over to turn out the lamp. She reached up to grab his arm.

"Where are you going to be?" she asked and he couldn't miss how shaky her voice was when she spoke.

"Wherever you want me to be, angel."

"Would you stay in here with me?"

He leaned over her and kissed her forehead. Then he pulled the covers back again so she could scoot over. He lay down next to her and slowly she moved closer to him. Tucking her head into his shoulder, he felt her body slowly relax. He stroked her hair for a few minutes and that was all it took for her to succumb finally to the exhaustion.

Reaper had never been so thankful for such a small gift, but he'd been on edge for hours and he needed some time to process all she'd told him. He was certain his team outside were already gathering information from what they'd learned and would have called in all the usual suspects to help.

Peter Miller may have been hunting Tenille, but Reaper and his team were now going to show him how it was done.

He just needed to make sure Tenille was safe during the process. She told them the who and the where it started, but there were a lot of details in between those bookends.

There was also the restaurant that was burned down and the Kahale Family that had helped her, not to mention Detective Ghee, who wanted to speak with her and probably the feds.

The whole thing was going to blow up in the morning, but he welcomed the chaos because as soon as things started flying, he and his team would take care of business.

It had always been that way for Reaper. It was like he needed pandemonium so he could laser focus on the problem. He'd told her about his early mission and earning his nickname, but it was six months after that when he'd been put to the test. His team was called in to assist the real badasses, Rex' original team, that was made up entirely of walking, talking super heroes. Men who were already legends in their world.

It was the early hours of the morning, which seemed to always be their go time. Rex' team was already in an underground tunnel half filled with water. Reaper and Cage's team were a few clicks back, waiting in the eerie quiet for their signal.

They were there to capture two top Al Qaeda operatives and should've been in and out in minutes. No signal came, but all the hair on the back of Reaper's neck stood up. He told Cage, shit was about to go down, but before he could respond, Reaper was in the water. There was a flash of light and an explosion. Cage had gone in after Reaper, and then the rest of the team followed. When they pulled up out of the water, the tunnel had mostly collapsed from the explosives. Rex was alive, but unconscious. Only one other member of his team made it out of there with all of his body parts. Reaper saved Rex and his teammate, handing them off to Cage so he could go back in. He then gathered the other injured men so his team could try to save them. It was when Reaper gathered all the dead, along with their body parts, that he proved himself because no one else had made it inside before he'd had everyone cleared out of the haze.

Reaper was his handle, but from that point forward they said it with awe. He was faced with an impossible task, yet refused to stop or slow down until all the men were gathered, alive or dead.

He'd never be able to tell that story to Tenille, but he would show her that she was safer with him than anywhere else.

If she gave him the chance.

Chapter Eighteen

Tenille woke up to the smell of freshly brewed coffee. As she stirred, she felt Michael's body heat surrounding her.

It was by far the most comfortable place she'd ever slept next to him.

"Morning, angel," he said, and his deep morning voice made her heart flutter.

"Good morning," she replied, sounding breathy and desperate even to her.

The grin he gave her was sinful, and she wondered if she could ever be intimate with him. Sure, she trusted him, and if she was honest, the physical attraction had been there since the first night he walked into the diner. But would her body ever let her forget her past? If she tried and couldn't, would Michael be able to forgive her?

Before she thought too hard about it, she leaned up and kissed him. It was all the encouragement he needed as he pulled her into his hard body. His tongue explored hers and everywhere they touched, she felt his heat.

It was frenzied and when she kicked off her sweatpants; he

grinned and pulled her on top of his body. Her nerves were getting the better of her, but when he licked her lips, she was instantly rooted to that moment with him again. Then he rolled over with her in his arms until they were beside each other. "Tell me what you're thinking, angel?"

She was hot and bothered, but could she talk about sex with him?

He lifted her chin and kissed her sweetly on the lips. "Tell me."

"I've never been on top."

He grinned wickedly and then pulled her onto his lap so she could straddle him again. Before she could think twice, he sat up, leaning against the headboard so they were face to face. "I would love nothing more than to show you how this is done, but we have a house full and I don't want them to hear us."

Her entire face was red as she nodded in agreement. His laugh was even more sinful before his lips slammed into hers. He had both hands tangled in her hair. She suddenly couldn't think of anything but him and how warm his body felt against hers.

When he stood up with his hands under her bottom, holding her in place, she went completely breathless.

He took her into the bathroom and closed the door with his foot. When he sat her on top of the bathroom sink, the cold got her attention.

I'm going to need a shower before I can go out there. She could see the effect their make-out session had on him, but it only made her hotter.

"I would ask you to join me, but I don't think I could keep my hands off you."

She shook her head nervously because in that moment, the only thing she wanted was his hands all over her.

He leaned down and kissed her on the top of her head before

pulling her into his hard body again. "We'll have plenty of time after all of this is over. Okay?"

Hanging onto his words would be the only way she could get through the next twenty-four hours.

Michael helped her down and then patted her bottom before she headed back into the bedroom to lie down until he finished showering. Crawling under the covers that smelled like him and were still warm from his body heat may not have been the best idea. She was consumed with thoughts of making love with Michael and grinned that she never once thought about calling him Reaper.

She only hoped that she would get the chance to tell that to her friend Olivia one day. And as she heard the shower turn on, she closed her eyes and fell back to sleep with thoughts of him and his hard body on her mind.

"Come on, sleepyhead. You need to eat something and then to get dressed."

Tenille smiled, thinking she was still dreaming. When she opened her eyes and saw Michael standing there with a plate full of breakfast food and coffee, she quickly scooted up in the bed to look at him.

He was fully dressed and had made her breakfast. What did she ever do to deserve him? "If you want to give me a few minutes, I could get dressed and come eat in the kitchen?"

He shook his head. "No need. It's going to be a long day. I want you to eat while it's hot and then you can get dressed and come talk to the guys. Okay?"

"Okay." she agreed. But just thinking about what she would have to tell them was difficult. She wasn't sure how she could talk about it. Would Michael still want her after he heard everything?

He smiled as he placed a large pillow across her lap like a tray and then set the plate down on top. "Thank you," she said before picking up the fork and scooping up some of the scrambled eggs with hash browns as he sat on the edge of the bed next to her.

Michael watched her take a bite. "You're welcome. I wanted you to eat and have time to get dressed for the day before—" he stopped talking when she looked up at him anxiously.

"Before you meet with the guys. Don't worry. I'll be by your side the entire time, okay?"

She nodded, but honestly didn't feel like eating anymore. But Michael picked up her fork and scooped up some hash browns for her. She took the fork from him so she could feed herself. It was going to be a rough day, but she would show them she was stronger than she looked.

It was what she'd spent her entire life doing, proving to herself and the whole world that she was more than the sum of all the bad things that had happened to her.

A half hour later, Tenille came out of the room, dressed and ready to face the guys. Reaper reintroduced her to Rex and Cage's brother, Keith.

Cage had spent the better part of the day tracking down Tenille's life in Sugarland. He didn't like what he'd discovered, but didn't let on in front of the others.

Rex had spoken to the Lahaina police detective, and he had a lot of news to share, too.

Settling Tenille on the couch next to him, Reaper waited for the men to sit before they went through the details. Rex wanted to get his information out, so they started backward from what had happened most recently and then before that and before that. It wasn't ideal because it didn't show the magnitude of what she'd gone through.

Still, Rex began, "Three days after you left, in the early hours before daybreak, Samuel Foret soaked The Island Fish Company in gasoline before setting it on fire. Before he got there, Mr. Akamu Kahale was inside doing prep work for the day."

Rex was telling the events more than reading them, but he looked at his notes to verify the names of everyone as he told it. As soon as he mentioned Akamu Kahale, Tenille put her hand over her mouth. She didn't utter a sound, but she was visibly upset.

"Foret wasn't happy with how the building was burning, so he walked around and ignited the thatch roof, too. Mr. Kahale was trapped inside because the roof fire took off. He called the fire department and then his family before he stepped inside the interior of his standup freezer."

Keith shook his head. "That would buy him some time, but most of what those freezers are made of is flammable turning it into an incinerator. That is, if he didn't die from the CO2 poisoning first."

Rex nodded. "Luckily, his sons got there quickly, and the freezer was near an outside wall. Before Mr. Kahale passed out, he broke a metal leg off a shelf and started beating the back wall of the freezer enough to warp it. His sons fought the flames back so they could rip through the freezer wall on their side to carry him out. He stopped breathing a couple of times before he made it to the hospital, but I'm happy to report that after being in the intensive care unit for two weeks, he is finally doing better and they are hoping for a full recovery."

Tenille covered her face with her hands as she tried to calm down. Mr. Kahale had been her champion the day she escaped Peter at his restaurant. Talking to the police and covering her tracks so effortlessly. Then he and his family took her into their home to make sure Peter couldn't find her. Now they've lost their family restaurant, their livelihood, and probably regret helping her at all.

Rex cleared his throat. "Mr. Kahale is going to be fine. No one else was hurt. Well, except Samuel Foret, who was found dead the next morning on a beach nearby. They first suspected drowning but then determined he was stabbed before being thrown into the water."

"I'm sorry," Tenille said before running into the guest bathroom. As soon as she closed the door, she slid down to the floor and held her head in her hands. How was this her life? She'd never hurt a single soul, ever. Her aunt would laugh because, as a child, she would even save spiders by sliding a piece of paper underneath them and scooping them out a door or window.

But since her Aunt Sue passed away, Tenille's life had been in a tailspin and she wanted to get off this ride. She stood up and washed her face, but before she could dry off, she heard loud voices coming from the living room. Were the men arguing?

Her heart was in pieces, but hearing the friends in the other room angry at one another scared her. Would things ever be normal again?

Before she could open the bathroom door, someone knocked.

"Tenille? Are you okay?"

It was Michael.

"Yes," she said as she stepped out of the restroom.

She searched his face for answers about what was going on, but he pulled her into a hug. "The guys stepped out for a minute. Let's get some coffee going before they get back."

Nodding and following him into the kitchen, she had to ask him what happened.

He seemed task oriented and pulled out coffee beans and a grinder. Next, he filled his machine with water as she leaned against the counter and watched him. He really made great coffee.

"Michael? I heard you guys while I was in the bathroom. Is everything okay?"

He walked over and kissed her on the top of her head. "I'm

sorry you had to hear any of that, but sometimes Cage is an asshole."

"I-I couldn't hear the words, just that you sounded like you were arguing?"

"He gets things in his head sometimes and won't listen to reason. He's just suspicious by nature, angel, so don't take what he says to heart. Okay?"

Was he warning her about Cage? She didn't have time to process it before the front door opened and Cage, Keith, and Rex bounded in with pastries they'd bought at a nearby bakery.

She helped pour cups of coffee for everyone and grabbed a roll of paper towels as they set up everything on the living room coffee table.

As she moved back into her seat and settled in with her coffee, she looked up to see Cage staring at her with an unreadable grin.

Chapter Nineteen

Cage and Keith had grown up in what was best known as the boondocks. It was South Louisiana, but better known as the back of beyond with water.

Their house was raised on stilts and originally meant for seasonal use, but when their mother and father both cheated on each other, they went with their dad.

He was the most stable of the two parents, which was still mostly a coin toss. They learned at a young age they could only trust each other. Until Cage joined the Navy and learned to trust Reaper and then Rex.

He just had a knack for picking up on dishonesty and hadn't met too many people that didn't lie about something. Lying about your age or weight was one thing, but still he rarely trusted others and always said if you'll lie about the little things, then lying about the big things will come easier.

Knowing that Reaper had already decided he wanted Daisy—Tenille, whatever the hell her name was, made it even harder.

Then, when he heard her in action saying that her ex had drugged her and taken her against her will to Hawaii, he'd changed his mind. Clearly, she'd been through something and it haunted her.

While on watch all night, he investigated her story and came up with more doubt than before and it was going to kill him to hurt his friend. But no one was going to uncover her background more openly or thoroughly than Cage, because he wasn't moonstruck over a pretty girl.

After all, his mother was a beauty queen all the way down to her fake smile and wave. She'd tear up as if on cue and lie to your face even if the truth would set her free.

Reaper was his best friend, and he owed it to him to expose all of her secrets so Reaper could make an informed decision. But he, for one, wasn't convinced she was worth all this trouble.

Everyone looked at him as he spoke. "I think you know it surprised me to learn you grew up five hours from here in Sugarland, Texas. It seems there was a lot of suspicion surrounding your aunt's death, and then they went back and exhumed your uncle's body, too. Isn't that right, Tenille Sims?" Cage stared at her without an ounce of emotion.

Reaper sat forward on the couch and his expression was a warning to Cage, but he didn't look away from her.

Tenille's voice cracked when she answered, "Yes."

"So the lead on that case, a Detective Berry, has apparently retired for medical reasons, and his partner, Detective DeVries is still handling the case. He was quite shocked to hear from me and to learn you were living in a suburb of New Orleans under an alias."

Just hearing their names made Tenille's stomach churn. The days after her aunt passed away set into motion all the craziness she was now trying to wade through.

"According to Detective DeVries, they suspected you of causing your aunt's death. Correct?"

Tenille nodded. How could she so easily go back to that dark place with just a few questions?

"Then when they exhumed your uncle, they found that he'd been murdered the same way. Right?"

Again, Tenille nodded.

Rex, Keith, and Reaper were all three on alert. Cage hadn't told them everything that he'd found out, but had warned that she didn't look innocent anymore.

They all three understood Cage suspected everyone of wrongdoing, even when there wasn't a reason, but he made a compelling argument here.

"Ironically, your aunt and uncle's house, your home, burned before you left town. They suspected arson there too, right?"

"Yes," she said, but instead of shying away from his questions, she found her backbone and looked directly at him. "If you spoke with Detective DeVries, then he told you I had nothing to do with any of it. My uncle was a forensic accountant and had uncovered something at a company he was auditing. The FBI told the detectives they found evidence someone from that company paid to have my uncle killed. They said that I needed to be careful because they killed my aunt and could come after me, too."

Cage shook his head. "That makes little sense. Your uncle died when you were a teenager. Why would they come after you and your aunt five years later?"

"That's what I said, but they disagreed." Tenille stood up now when she spoke. "I had just turned sixteen when my uncle died, and I didn't know anything about his business. Not really."

Smirking at her, Cage leaned back in his chair as he made eye contact with the other men in the room. The dramatic pause was almost more than Tenille could take as she crossed her arms and tried to control her breathing.

"But you know the executives that were angry at your uncle

didn't hire someone to kill him, your aunt, or to set your house on fire. Don't you, Tenille?"

She didn't move a muscle and the only sound in the entire room was her breathing and a distant antique clock from Reaper's office, ticking off each second.

"DeVries told me they unfroze your bank accounts and gave you back your passport. That same night, you disappeared. Like off the planet, and they suspected you had something to do with it after all. Especially when the FBI closed their case because the owners of that company who hated your uncle couldn't go through with having him killed."

"No." The giant tears that filled her eyes held for a few seconds before slipping down her cheeks.

Cage stood up to accuse her directly. "You did it for the money, Tenille. Admit it. Peter Miller was an intern at your uncle's company and together you two plotted the entire thing. But what, you double crossed him? You wanted to keep all the money for yourself? He went a little crazy when you wanted to dump him? Now you're going to use us to take care of him, your last remaining problem?"

Tenille ran out of the room and locked herself in the bedroom.

"Get out," Reaper said to his closest friends. Keith and Rex headed straight for the front door, but Cage locked eyes with him.

"Detective DeVries wants a word with her. Detective Ghee is already on a plane. I imagine all hell will break loose here tonight."

Reaper didn't respond. He just watched as his closest friend turned and walked out his front door.

Walking straight to his kitchen, Reaper pulled down the thirty-year-old scotch he'd bought when he left the Navy. It was the only time he'd drank it. Of course, Cage had been with him and they decided it was too good to waste, so he put the bottle away until one of them got married.

It made little sense that his mind went straight to that bottle and drink in the middle of all the mayhem. A therapist would have a field day with him because if Tenille was guilty, then all he wanted was to drink that scotch. The entire bottle.

Three fingers of the dark amber were all he needed. Pushing the glass away, he stalked to his bedroom, ready to bust down the damn door.

But when he got there, the door was unlocked, and sitting on the floor with her single bag packed was Tenille.

She hugged it in her arms, but he recognized the look on her face. She looked defeated.

"Do you think Detective DeVries or Detective Ghee will arrest me when they get here?" She'd apparently heard what Cage said.

Reaper expected her to deny it all, but she just asked the one question.

"I guess that depends on the questions they ask and the answers you give them," he said as he sat on the floor across from her.

She nodded as she stared at the floor.

They sat in silence for what felt like forever.

Finally, she looked up to see him watching her. "I'm sorry, Michael. I shouldn't have gotten any of you involved."

He shook his head in disbelief. "After all those accusations, that's all you have to say?"

"I already told you the truth about how I met Peter. What would be the point of me explaining anything else? There isn't any way to prove it. To prove my innocence and that's what you all are asking for me to do. To prove I'm not guilty."

She was right. All the circumstantial evidence about her was damning, and he did second guess himself and his ability to weed out the liars and cheats of this world when they wore a skirt.

Still, he couldn't help but think back to the way they'd met and the times he'd followed her just to make sure she made it home safely. She'd been truly scared, and he'd bank his life on that.

He watched as she stood up and put her bag over one shoulder. "Michael, there isn't any need for you to be involved with this situation or me any longer. The detectives are on their way to New Orleans, but if I turn myself in at the police station, then they could just go there instead of your house, right?"

Meeting her at the bedroom door, he stretched to his full height. He towered over her. Yet, she didn't back down. "What exactly are you going to turn yourself in for, Tenille?"

She shrugged as she avoided his face. "All of it. I mean, if I say I did it, then they would put me in jail, right? Men and women are separated, so he can't get into the women's jail."

What kind of person turned themselves in? Had he ever hunted someone that simply gave up without a fight? Who agreed to go to jail in order to avoid someone?

He put his arm out to block her passage out of the room. "Try me."

"What?"

"Try me."

"Michael. I'm tired. I can't run anymore. Turning myself in will make this all end. Peter will find out that I'm in jail and leave all of you alone so, you can go on with your life and get out of the line of fire."

She wasn't going to confess to avoid Peter. She was going to do it to save all of them?

He stepped into her space and she backed up until he had her cornered against the wall. She had her hands on his chest and he grinned, remembering the first time he'd offered to drive her home.

"Angel, it's time for you to tell me the complete story."

"I-I can't prove any of it."

He lifted her chin and leaned down a breath away from her face as he said, "Just tell me the truth and we'll figure it out."

Chapter Twenty

Tenille felt exhausted in a way that words couldn't describe. How was she going to tell Michael everything when she couldn't believe it herself?

He grabbed her hand and led her back into the living room after he gently removed the bag from her shoulder. "Have a seat," he said as he grabbed a quilt for her to cover up with and a bottle of water.

"I don't even know where to start."

"Would it be safe to say that the crux of this began the day your aunt passed away?"

The instant tears in her eyes told him yes. He reached out and held her hand. "I know it's hard to discuss, so I'll fast forward through the parts that I already know. You stop me if there is a detail that I leave out that's important."

"Okay," she whispered, and the hope in her eyes made him want to kiss her. He pulled out a piece of paper and glanced at his notes.

When did he take those notes?

"Your aunt, Sue Langley, passed away the day after Christmas. Approximately a week later, you had to meet with her attorney, I'm guessing to read the will?"

Tenille nodded, still watching him.

"The attorney's office was in Houston, which is about thirty minutes from your home, give or take with traffic. After that meeting, you went to a couple of stores where you first encountered Peter Miller?"

"Yes," she reached out and touched his forearm. He'd remembered every single word she'd told him and some details that she hadn't. How would she ever be able to explain how much that meant to her? To be heard seemed so small, but to someone who had been invisible over the last year, it was everything.

"My aunt and uncle were well off. I guess I always knew that, but didn't really know that. It was just the way I'd grown up and after losing my parents, money didn't seem that important. When I got to my attorney's office, he and a couple of other lawyers met with me. First, they told me that my aunt and uncle had set up an incredible trust fund for me which I hadn't known about. Aunt Sue was my best friend and losing her so suddenly was overwhelming. I hadn't even thought about how I would make ends meet. But Mr. Arceneaux explained I would never have to worry about money. Then one of the other attorneys said that there was some suspicion surrounding the way my aunt died. Before I could comprehend what he was saying, two detectives walked in and questioned me. I'd never spoken to a police officer before, much less a detective. My aunt and uncle's generosity overwhelmed me and then to find out that she hadn't died from natural causes. I couldn't even consider it. I sat in my car and cried afterward."

Tenille pulled the covers up higher and he watched her try to hold back her emotions. "That feels like a lifetime ago instead of eleven months."

Reaper reached out to squeeze her hand to reassure her, and that was when his phone went off and his front doorbell rang.

Tenille stood up. Were the detectives there already? She looked at Michael, who was looking at his phone. "It's my sister."

He looked as upset to be interrupted as Tenille felt.

Why couldn't they have a moment at his home alone without interruptions? Michael thought as he opened the front door.

"You have a minute?" Abigail asked as she walked in without being asked and then stopped short when she saw Tenille standing there. "Oh, hey there, Daisy."

When she turned around to look at her brother, he could see Abigail was about to explode over something. "Spit it out, Abi."

She shook her head. "Can I talk to you in your office?" She formed the sentence like a question, but pulled on his arm insistently as she tried to move him in that direction.

"We'll be right back," he said to Tenille, praying this didn't take too long. The day had already been a shit show, and he didn't know how much more they could pile on.

Abigail shut the office door and then whisper-yelled at her brother. "You didn't think seeing Nina the other day was important enough to mention? How about the fact that she's sporting a shiny little three-year-old kid? Did you know she's going all over town telling everyone that he's yours? Do you have any idea what that is going to do to mom and dad? You know they aren't getting any younger and Dad has already had some heart issues."

"I've been a little busy, Abi."

She cut her eyes at her brother. "No kidding. What do you think that news will do to sweet little Daisy?"

He shook his head. There was a lot he needed to unpack with her, but this was not the time. "I love you. I wish I could take care of the Nina thing, but it will have to wait. And don't worry, she already knows."

"How the hell does she know?" Abi threw her arms up in the

air. Her brother was juggling too many women and too many secrets for her to keep up. But she liked Daisy. She liked her a lot and didn't want her brother to screw it up. She punched him in the arm, hard.

"We all like Daisy, so don't you mess it up. You hear me?"

Michael laughed. His little sister had no idea what the hell was going on, and he'd already taken time away from Tenille that he didn't have to spare. So he gave her the simple answers. "Look, Nina barged in here the other night and announced it all in front of Daisy. I haven't seen the kid and I've never trusted Nina enough to have sex without a cover, if you know what I mean. But right now, I am in the middle of something important."

"Ew. Don't tell me about your sex life with Nina. And don't you screw it up with Daisy."

He stared at his sister.

"Okay, I've got to go. You take care of Daisy. And I've already taken care of the other." She strutted toward his office door, and Michael grabbed her ponytail to stop her. Old habits died hard, and he loved to pull her ponytail because it aggravated her when they were kids. It didn't matter that they were both adults.

Slapping his hands away, she tightened her ponytail and pointed her finger at him.

"You heard me, big brother. I've got this."

"Stay away from Nina."

"Too late."

Abigail winked at him and then headed into the living room. "Sorry to interrupt," she said as she hugged Daisy and gave her that trademark Thibodeaux smile. "You can have him back now. But if he gives you any trouble, call me."

Blowing a kiss toward her brother, she didn't miss a beat as she opened and then slammed the front door behind her.

She always blew in like a hailstorm and left the same way.

"Everything okay?" Tenille was worrying her bottom lip and

Reaper shook his head. No matter what his ex or his family stirred up, it couldn't compare to the trouble she was in, but still she worried about others.

"She just found out Nina was in town and wanted to warn me."

When Tenille closed her eyes, he knew she felt bad. It was just so easy to know what she was thinking. She was caring and thoughtful, which was why he knew as soon as he'd blown his stack about Cage's story that it couldn't be true.

He leaned over and kissed her on the top of her head, but she reached up to hug him before he pulled away. "I'm so sorry, Michael. You don't deserve to be in the middle of all of this, and I swear I wouldn't blame you if you just wanted to walk away and wash your hands of it."

"What? And let you have all the excitement alone? Not a chance, angel."

She'd fallen hard for the handsome man in front of her and she might regret it later, but she was grateful that he was with her.

Michael sat next to her on the sofa and encouraged her to continue. "So you went to dinner with the guy and then—."

"Then, over the next week, the detectives seized my passport, froze my accounts, and then searched my home. I was pretty devastated, and my aunt's three closest girlfriends tried to help me." She paused like she was thinking about those events, and Michael reached over to hold her hand.

"And where was Peter Miller?"

"He always seemed to show up at the right time. He knew about the law and gave me advice. But more than anything, I think he manipulated me into trusting him and not trusting my aunt's friends." Tenille had never said that out loud and was forming a better picture of the man who'd stormed into her world and wreaked havoc.

"Angel, where were your friends?"

Tenille shook her head. "You may not have noticed, but I've always been pretty shy."

Michael's movie star grin made her stomach feel hollow. He leaned over and kissed her cheek before he whispered, "Trust me, angel, I've noticed."

She locked eyes with him for a moment and then looked away. "I wasn't like that before my parents passed away and I remember having play dates with neighborhood kids. My parents were both teachers and pretty social in our neighborhood. We had a simple but happy life. Then one summer night after we'd gone out to dinner, we had a car accident. I was thrown from the vehicle, but my parents were trapped inside when it hit a tree. My aunt and uncle were there at the hospital and had to tell me what happened. I didn't talk for a year. I guess it took me a while to process everything. My aunt tutored me at home and my uncle had a spare room turned into my very own library when I started reading books out loud for them."

He kissed the back of her hand and then said, "Tell me you're rich without telling me you're rich."

She smiled and then whispered, "I also had my own secret garden outside."

Michael whistled.

"I didn't go to regular school until high-school but by then my aunt and uncle were my whole world and I just felt different from kids my age."

She'd certainly had a different life from anyone he'd ever met. And a ton of tragedy. "You were sixteen when your uncle died?"

Tenille reached for the water bottle and drank several sips before she answered him. "He'd been at work, and we'd been told it was his heart back then. But after my aunt passed away, the detectives said he'd been poisoned. My uncle was always active and healthy. He'd never even had a bad checkup, and he went every year for a physical.

"Aunt Sue was heartbroken, but also stronger than anyone I've ever known. It was that year that we started traveling every time I had a break from school. After I graduated, I told her I wanted to take a gap-year instead of starting college and she agreed. We had so much fun and ended up traveling almost non-stop for three years."

Michael moved to sit on top of the coffee table so he could face her. "This is a hard question to ask, but do you think your Aunt Sue knew someone was after you?"

Tenille's eyes watered. "I would have said no before, but I guess anything is possible. If she did, she never told me or let on that anything was wrong. But I know she and my uncle would have done anything to protect me."

She couldn't bring herself to talk about her uncle's journals or how she'd read them and found out the gory details of her parents' wreck and her injuries. She wished she could forget it all.

Michael watched her war with her feelings before he sat back down on the couch next to her. "I expect one or both detectives to show up in the next hour. Can you tell me how you ended up in Hawaii?"

"I don't want to lie to you, Michael, but there are some details that will be too hard for me to talk about with you, but it's mostly personal stuff and won't help."

He reached up and held her face in his hands as he kissed her sweetly on the lips. "You tell me as much as you're comfortable with, and I'll sort out the rest."

Tenille did her best. "I'd told Peter that I couldn't go with him to Hawaii and the next thing I knew, I was on a private plane with him and these big men I'd never seen before."

"That's when he'd drugged you?"

"Yes. Looking back, I can see the warning signs I'd missed,

but honestly, I was distracted by everything that was going on and didn't know he was such a dangerous man."

She'd expected to get emotional as she started talking about the details of Peter and Hawaii, but she didn't. "I flipped out a bit on the plane and he, in no uncertain terms, told me what he expected of me and I knew he meant business." She avoided looking directly at Michael when she added, "I mean, until then he'd never threatened me or hurt me, but I realized—."

Michael moved to sit beside her on the sofa and kissed the back of her hand as he held it warmly. "You realized he was capable of it."

"Yeah, I guess so."

They sat there in silence, both knowing that when real evil showed up, it didn't need an introduction.

Michael wrapped an arm around her and pulled her closer. Resting her head lightly on his shoulder, she began again for what felt like the tenth time. "He hid nothing from that point forward. When he discussed his illegal weapon sales over the phone or on a video call, he did it right in front of me. Whenever we went out to eat or left the villa for any reason, I dressed the part with the skin tight dresses and super high heels. He was obsessed with the attention. I was his trophy."

She shuttered, and Michael kissed the top of her head. It was killing him to hear what she'd been through, but he'd learned that intel was the most important part of taking down a bad guy.

"He was extra talkative in Hawaii. He told me it was his mother that caused the accident the night my parents died."

"Wait. What?"

"Yes. His father died the night my parents did. Peter said that his mother was driving and after running our car off the road, she tried to drive home but totaled the car into a tree. She pulled his dad out of the car, but he was dead, so she left the scene. The police never put the two accidents together, and she had the car scrapped and shipped in pieces out of the country. My uncle had hired a private detective to figure out who hit my parents' car, but they never could solve the case."

"So, Peter grew up knowing that his mother had killed his father and your parents?"

"You would think that he would feel sorry for us both, but he was left with an uncaring alcoholic mother. According to him, he hated me because his family lost everything that night. Their big house and all their money. My parents weren't wealthy, and we lived in a modest little town home. He said that it wasn't fair that I grew up in Sugarland in a fairytale house. His mother died when he turned eighteen and he was all alone. I had two loving people raise me. So, he hated me and tried to take everything from me, starting with Uncle Ed. So, it actually started a long time ago. I just didn't know."

Pulling her into his lap, he wiped her tears and wrapped his arms around her. "I'm so sorry, angel."

"Peter drugged our Christmas dinner with ketamine. But it only knocked me out. Aunt Sue had a thyroid problem, so it was worse for her. Then somewhere along the way, he decided that instead of killing me, he would rather—" It was hard to say it, but there was no stopping the words now.

"He would rather own me. Before we left for his dinner meeting that night in Hawaii, he said we would get married. Then in the parking lot he slammed my head into the window because I'd put my hair up in a ponytail holder instead of leaving it down the way he liked it. Nalani saw it. She was our waitress and helped me escape.

"I stayed with her and her family while he looked everywhere for me. The Kahale family faked evidence that I'd flown home to Texas and he left the island to go try to find me there."

Tenille left off the details of how she could barely get up and brush her teeth every day. She'd stopped eating and hardly slept.

It was a path of self-destruction she wasn't proud of and she might have to talk it through with a professional one day.

"I was so afraid he or one of his men would find me, so I dyed my hair dark, wore baggy clothes and dark lipstick so no one would recognize me. And tried to just disappear. I worked in the kitchen at a couple of restaurants while another one of Nalani's cousins tried to train me in self-defense."

"You took self-defense lessons?" Michael teased. "I hope you got your money back."

Tenille grinned. "He told me that I was a terrible fighter and so he taught me how to escape instead. When I outran him in a footrace, he said that was probably what would save me."

Michael pulled her into his body tightly and held her close. "Angel, you couldn't outrun me and I'm not willing to take a chance on whether you could outrun him."

"I actually get freaked out if someone is chasing me and you haven't seen me really run. I wasn't scared of you."

Michael smirked at her comment, noting that she was trying to tease him a second time. He could get used to that.

"He came back to Maui twice, but I didn't look like myself and no one had seen the before Peter girl, so I felt safe until last month. Nalani and I had moved into our own apartment. We'd only been there six weeks, but it was really nice to have my own space and feel normal. I had to be at work early the next morning and had already gone to bed. Nalani's cousin, Keola, was beating on our front door. He apologized and told us that his wife went behind his back and somehow contacted Peter. She'd even sent a picture of me to him and my address. Keola taught me to always keep a bag ready, which I did. So, I left everything else and Nalani took me to the airport. I'd already gotten fake identification cards but had never used them. Thankfully, they worked. Nalani helped me put money on debit cards and on the red-eye flight, I booked the next plane to New Orleans and my room at the boarding house. I haven't spoken to any of them, and they don't know how to contact me. They thought it would be the safest way."

Michael hugged her and told her it was the safest plan, that and being with him which made her smile.

"I just don't know how to prove that I'm innocent to those detectives. Or that Peter is guilty."

Michael stood up and reached his hand out for her. "You don't have to do either, angel."

The detectives don't have anything, or they wouldn't be grasping at straws and flying all the way here to question you.

Our biggest issue is if the police know where you are, chances are so does your super villain.

Tenille stepped into his arms again, knowing that Peter would come for her and try to take down everyone in his way.

Chapter Twenty-One

The biggest lesson that Reaper had learned from being a Navy SEAL was to trust his partners and to always have each other's back. He knew they wouldn't be far and now that Tenille had told him more about Peter Miller, calling his friends, his team, was crucial.

"Angel, if those detectives are making their way here today, we need to be ready."

She wasn't sure what else she could do to plan for them and so she waited for him to explain.

He appreciated that trust. There was no way she was some mastermind behind a plot to hurt anyone at age sixteen or later. Life had truly thrown her into the ocean without a life preserver, but he'd been a frogman most of his adulthood and he could help. At least with the help of his friends.

It was getting late, and Reaper offered to make her something to eat while he called the guys. She smiled because he seemed to eat every couple of hours and she didn't have the heart to tell him she only ate once or twice a day.

"I need to give the guys the rest of the facts so we can figure out our next move."

"Michael, I'm not so sure they'll believe me. And I can't blame them. If someone told me this story, I wouldn't believe it either."

He held her hand and led her toward the kitchen. "We don't have to believe the story, angel. We believe you."

Tenille threw her arms around his neck and hugged him. How had she ended up here with this incredible man and his friends? She had to have some pretty powerful guardian angels looking out for her.

She excused herself for a few minutes while Reaper called Cage, who picked up on the first ring. "You still pissed at me?" Cage asked.

"Nope."

"Alright, well, that Detective Ghee checked in to his hotel and wants to see your girl."

"He'll need to wait long enough for us to talk and get something to eat."

Cage started making his way down from his perch above Reaper's house the moment he got the call. He motioned to Rex, who followed him and knocked on the front door of Reaper's house while he was still talking.

"Dude, you should have those cameras recording the street out front 24/7. You could set up a YouTube channel and make a fortune. People are crazy in this town. I saw four guys dressed like 9 foot fire ants walking down the street and it isn't even Mardi Gras."

Rex chuckled. "They had Santa hats on too."

Reaper grinned. His friends had stayed close, watching over the house while he talked to Tenille. He figured they would. It was what he would have done. But it still meant something to him.

"Sandwiches?"

Rex and Cage both nodded as they grabbed drinks out of the fridge.

"Keith had to go to work, but he'll be back tonight if we need him. I was thinking of calling Ryan Gentry?"

Reaper pulled out a loaf of bread and started making a stack of sandwiches. He could eat three and he knew they would do the same, not knowing where this night would go. They needed to fuel up.

He gave them all the details and understood that Cage was still doubtful. Unfortunately, Tenille walked in during the heat of their conversation.

"So you're going with the poor little rich girl story and not going to even consider the money as a motive?" Cage said roughly, and that was when they saw Tenille.

All three men watched her as she walked over to them with concern in her eyes. "I'm sorry that you're all involved. It wasn't my intention. But I can go to the police station alone and let the detectives meet me there. That way, your names stay out of it. Or I can answer any questions that you have?" she said.

Cage nodded as he looked at her. "So what about all the money that you inherited?"

Tenille shrugged. "I guess it's all still there. I mean, I couldn't call Mr. Arceneaux, but he was close friends with my Uncle Ed. He always took care of things for me and my aunt before. He's probably still doing the same until he hears from me or that something has happened to me."

"You didn't know Peter when he worked with your uncle?"

"Uncle Ed worked for a large company but traveled most of the time. I didn't go to his office, but once or twice in my entire life. I only remember meeting his secretary and a junior accountant that worked with him."

Before Cage could ask another question, his phone rang.

Reaper gave Tenille a sandwich, but as she sat at the table, Cage told them that Detective Ghee was a block away.

"If you need more time, then we can tell him to wait," Reaper said to her.

"No. It's fine," she said, but he noticed she only ate a couple of bites of her sandwich before the doorbell rang.

Detective Ghee was in his late forties and a short, slightly rounded man. Definitely Hawaiian, which set Tenille at ease since she'd loved The Kahale Family.

He was friendly as he greeted everyone and accepted a cup of coffee from Reaper.

A local NOPD officer accompanied him, which didn't go over as well. He wasn't friendly or talkative and watched Tenille intently.

They all sat around the table together, which wasn't preferable, but Detective Ghee didn't figure the men would leave Tenille alone as he questioned her.

"So, Miss Sims, you and Peter Miller arrived in Hawaii together, correct? And you were seen eating dinner at local places and walking on the beach before the night of the breakup? Can you tell me what happened that evening specifically to cause you to argue and then run away?"

Tenille swallowed hard as she searched for the words she needed. "I never agreed to go to Hawaii, Detective Ghee. There was still an active investigation going on regarding my aunt's death—and I was overwhelmed with the news Detective Berry and Detective DeVries had given me about my uncle and the FBI investigation. I'd told Peter that I couldn't go with him, but he'd already drugged me. I woke up on a private plane with Peter and some men I had never met before."

Detective Ghee grinned. "You and Peter Miller were staying at the most expensive villas on the island and went to the nicest restaurants. But you're claiming that you were there under duress taking midnight strolls with him?"

"I was scared out of my mind. The man I had just met drugged me and got me on a plane without anyone stopping him. He discussed how he imported and exported illegal weapons in front of me, so I understood who I was really dealing with. Then he threatened my life and locked me in that expensive villa with armed guards, so I couldn't get away."

Detective Ghee pulled pictures out of a folder of her and Peter. "These are photos of you and Miller in the lobby and around the property. Correct?"

The photographs he had of her were stunning. She was wearing designer silk dresses with sky-high heels. In each photo, Peter had his arm around her or was holding her hand. She wasn't smiling in any of them.

Her eyes watered, but she swallowed back the emotion. She hadn't seen Peter in months and hated the way the pictures made her feel.

Reaper asked to see them, and Rex snapped several pictures of the photos so they could study Peter.

"Forgive me, Miss Sims, but those pictures tell me a different story. They look like a couple on vacation. Are you certain something didn't happen the night you left him at the restaurant that you don't want to admit?"

"Did something happen? Detective Ghee, look closer at those photographs and tell me that I didn't look like a hooker. I certainly felt like one and he raped me every single day that we were there and I couldn't do anything about it." She swiped at her tears, but didn't stop. Every single man in the room froze as they listened to her. "Nalani Kahale saw him slam my head into the window because he got mad at me before we walked into the restaurant. I had put my hair up into a ponytail because of the heat and he didn't like it. She waited on our table and when the intimidating men from the Middle East walked in, she was terrified for me. When they were distracted, she met me in the ladies' room and took me through the kitchen to her cousins, who got me off the island.

"I hid in her family home. The Kahale family saved my life and falsified evidence that I'd left the island, so he would leave. I owe them everything. Now, can you tell me what happened at the restaurant and how Mr. Kahale is doing now?"

Reaper stood behind Tenille and put his hands on her shoulders for support. She'd just shown the most strength he'd ever witnessed, and he wanted to kick everyone out of his house so he could tell her that she was amazing.

Detective Ghee looked remorseful as he nodded his head. "I'm sorry for what happened to you, Miss Sims. I wish we could have helped you." He looked up briefly and then continued with the island news. "Mr. Kahale is doing wonderfully. It was touch and go for a while because he'd inhaled a lot of smoke, but he should be able to go home this week or next. The restaurant was a total loss."

"No," she said with her hands over her mouth.

He nodded. "But it's being rebuilt as we speak. Everyone is pitching in and some local contractors have donated supplies. They could have it ready in a few months."

Tenille was visibly upset as she sat waiting for more news. Detective Ghee seemed to hold back something and Rex, who'd been the quietest of Michael's friends, spoke up.

"What else, Detective Ghee?"

The detective closed his folder and looked directly at Rex as he answered, "Well, unfortunately, Mr. Kahale's only daughter has gone missing."

Tenille stood up. "Nalani? She's missing? When? How long? Why didn't you lead with that information?" She stepped away from Reaper, who was trying to console her. "Tell me," she insisted to Detective Ghee.

"Miss Sims. You understand that I wasn't sure if you were still in contact with Peter Miller. The FBI is working on it. I'm here on behalf of the family. They're worried sick."

Tenille thought about what he said. The Kahale family had to be going out of their minds, but still they hadn't told the detective or anyone about her? She had to do something.

Cage, who'd been silent but studying the photos of Peter and Tenille, leaned forward in his seat. "The man you found on the beach was the arsonist? Was there any evidence that Miller was there?"

"His plane had to file a flight plan with the airport," Detective Ghee said. "It said he was on the flight into and out of the island that same day. Of course, there is no record of Nalani being with him, but if what Miss Sims is saying is true, and I do believe her, then he has paid someone to falsify those records."

"That was three weeks ago?" Tenille sat back down and her voice sounded weak even to her.

Reaper wrapped his arms around her from behind as he said, "That doesn't mean she's not okay. She's his leverage."

"He's a sociopath and has no conscience. He would hurt her without a second thought," she said, barely above a whisper, but they'd all heard her.

When the doorbell rang and Reaper's phone went off to alert him, everyone looked toward the door.

"I think that is Detective DeVries," Reaper said, shaking his head. It was official, when all this was over, he and Tenille were going to lock themselves in the house and not let anyone else come over for a month.

Chapter Twenty-Two

Detective DeVries was surprised when he walked in and met Reaper, Cage, Rex, Detective Ghee, and the NOPD officer there with Tenille Sims.

It had been almost a year since she'd disappeared and the young woman he'd met a year ago was certainly gone. She'd been meek and looked younger than her twenty-two years. He'd suspected her of murder back then, but it had been difficult to imagine such a sheltered girl capable of the heinous crime.

The woman standing in the room before him now was road worthy by comparison and he doubted himself as he watched her stand next to the behemoth man he knew had been a decorated Navy Seal.

He had to give it to her. She'd aligned herself with some muscle. He shook hands with everyone except for her and then had a seat at the end of the full table.

"Miss Sims. I would say it's good to see you but I'm a bit surprised that you're alive and well."

She didn't speak. She just stared back at him. The girl she used to be would have been scared out of her wits.

"I would ask you where you've been, but I've heard that you were in Hawaii hiding out for quite some time, and then here in New Orleans."

Still, she remained silent.

"I guess you've heard about Detective Berry?"

Tenille shook her head.

"He was in a hit-and-run accident and had to retire."

"Is there a question in there, Detective DeVries?" Reaper asked. He was still reeling from the last interrogation and the revelation of what Tenille had endured.

"Nope. Just wanted to catch her up on the latest."

Reaper nodded and if DeVries had been a lesser man, then he would have been nervous to continue.

"Anyway, let's get to it." He also pulled out a folder, and Tenille wondered if that was a prerequisite in detective school. You had to bring some kind of surprise evidence in a folder when questioning someone.

"The last time I saw you, the FBI was closing in on a couple of suspects who had hired someone to do a contract killing."

"To kill my Uncle Ed," she said, wanting to make sure that he acknowledge that her uncle mattered and they weren't just discussing the weather.

Detective DeVries nodded at that. Still, he couldn't get over the fact that she had matured so much in eleven months.

"They concluded their case and the two executives pleaded guilty for trying to hire a contract killer. But in the end, they didn't have the nerve to go through with it. So, it knocked us back to square one until you disappeared."

Tenille leaned forward in her chair to speak to DeVries. "You were worried about me? I mean, the last time we spoke, you told me that I needed to be careful. Right?"

He looked uncomfortable as he nodded. Detective DeVries

hadn't been concerned about her wellbeing. He'd just jumped to the lazy conclusion that she was guilty.

She ignored the obvious as she continued. "Don't worry. I've solved the case for you. But I'm afraid I'm in more danger than I could've ever known back then."

Detective DeVries sat up straighter, seriously interested in knowing what the hell had happened in this unsolvable case.

"Peter Miller killed my uncle and then killed my aunt and tried to kill me with the same poison."

DeVries smirked, thinking she was being a wiseass. When she sat there stoically, he realized she was serious. "The man you were seeing at the time?"

It made her sick to her stomach that anyone thought of them together. "I'd only just met Peter Miller after my aunt passed away. But it turns out, he'd known about my family since he was a teenager. His mother was the hit-and-run driver in my parents' accident. His father died that same night, but his mother made it out alive and hid the evidence. She got away with it, but apparently, they lost everything. He was jealous and in his own words to me, I had the fairy tale life he was supposed to have had. He decided to take that away from me and has succeeded. Wouldn't you say Detective DeVries?"

The detective didn't know what to say and Tenille sat there watching him process all the information that he'd never, ever considered.

He looked at her and then around the room at all the men that seemed to believe her incredible story. *What the hell was going on?*

"Uh, can you prove any of that, Miss Sims?"

Deadpan, she said, "Not a word of it. But that's the thing, right? You couldn't solve the case either. Now, I've told you the who and the what, and you know when and where. It's up to you to be the detective and find the evidence."

Detective DeVries wanted to argue, but he saw the way all the large men were looking at him. He'd thought he would walk in there and intimidate her again. This time, he'd been ready to get a confession. He was sure of it. Suddenly, he wasn't sure of anything and wanted to get the hell out of there. "I guess if you don't have anything to add to the investigation—"

Tenille stood up. "Detective DeVries? I've been missing for eleven months without a trace. Did anyone even look for me?"

His worn cheeks turned red. "Archie Arceneaux and your aunt's friends filed a missing person report."

She shook her head. He'd written her off as guilty and hadn't bothered to do more than some paperwork. If she'd ever wondered whether she could go home and tell the police what had happened, she knew the truth now. No one there would have protected her.

Turning her back on DeVries, she walked over to Detective Ghee and thanked him for everything he'd done so far to try to locate Nalani.

Rex walked DeVries to the door while Reaper watched the exchange between Tenille and the friendly detective from Hawaii. "I guess if the Kahale Family didn't tell you anything about me, then they didn't admit that it was their cousin, Keola's wife, who sold me out to Peter?"

He regretfully shook his head. He respected Mr. Kahale and had even worked part time in the restaurant when he was a teenager to earn spending money. But the man was loyal to a fault.

Tenille looked like she felt sorry for Keola's wife. "Like most people, they were having a hard time making ends meet. She'd lost a baby and couldn't work more than part time. When she'd found out that Peter was offering a lot of money for information on me, she was desperate enough to contact him. When she told

Keola what she'd done, he raced to get to me, to warn me. I was minutes away from being caught and while it wouldn't have happened if she hadn't called Peter, I wouldn't have escaped if it wasn't for Keola."

She reached out her hand and squeezed the man's forearm. "I don't know what I'll do if anything happens to Nalani because of me."

Detective Ghee squeezed her hand gently and nodded. "Nalani is a sharp girl. She's gotten into a few scrapes before when she was away at college. If anyone could get through this, my money is on her."

"Is there anything else that I can do to help?" she asked, and the detective shook his head.

"I'm afraid I've run out of options. I'll turn over all the information you've given me and hopefully the FBI will have better luck."

Reaper walked the detective to the door and Tenille paced the floor in the living room. When he returned, he sat at the table with Cage and Rex.

"We can't wait for the bastard to come after her," Reaper said. "It makes sense to dig deep into his background. If he has a company, then he must run his illegal business through the legal entity. Perhaps digging will turn something up?"

"I can make that happen," Rex said and then added, "What if we set up a buy and flush him out? Make him think he's got the deal of the century and when he shows up, take him down."

"That would take too long and cost a fortune to pull off." Reaper was angry that none of the detectives had any information about Peter Miller.

All the while, Cage sat there quietly, watching Tenille. She was upset and pacing the living room. "When did you send that letter?" he asked.

It had been a week since the letter had gone to the restaurant, but clearly they weren't in business and most likely not able to pick up mail.

But Tenille knew exactly what he was referring to. Someone may have picked that letter up and figured out it was from her.

It had her address at the boarding house on it. What if Peter went there and hurt Mrs. Bowers or did something to her friends at the diner?

Reaper could see the worry consume her. He was there, standing next to her in seconds. "Angel. The chances of him getting that letter and piecing it together are infinitesimal."

"You don't know him, Michael. He's exactly the type of person who could figure it out. And none of them have any idea what's coming. I mean, I've never even hinted that I was in danger, much less that it was following me."

Reaper held her hands to warm them. "We can watch over them, but you have to leave town until this is over."

Hiding in Hawaii for almost a year, Tenille accepted the fact that she couldn't protect herself and that running and hiding had been her only options. It was all she'd thought about from the time she'd arrived in Maisonville. But now, with everything in her, all she wanted was to stay.

But she couldn't let anything happen to her friends that felt like family. She had to warn them. Tell them the truth about her past and then she could go somewhere else, safe, and hide from Peter.

Perhaps this time he would leave everyone alone and just come after her? And when he did, Michael, Cage, and Rex would be there to stop him.

It hadn't worked out for the Kahale Family, but they didn't have three former Navy Seals looking out for them. This time, it could be different. It had to work out better for the sweet little town and the friends that had been so dear to her. But as she saw the way those three men were watching her now, there was going to be a battle just to go back across the lake because the clock was ticking.

Chapter Twenty-Three

"Like hell you are, angel," Reaper stretched to his full height in front of her and looked like a wall of muscle.

She wasn't afraid of him.

Turning around to pick up her backpack and throw it over her shoulder, he cocked his head to the side and watched her.

Tenille had just found her moxie, and he loved watching her stand up for herself with that asshole detective from Texas. But she didn't argue. Instead of discussing the situation and allowing him to tell her why it wasn't safe to go back to Maisonville, she simply picked up her things and would show him.

He couldn't help but like her gutsy side. Truth be told, he liked everything about her. But he still wouldn't let her go.

"You can ignore me all you want. But I'm not above picking you up and carrying you out of here in order to protect you."

That got her attention. She stopped and looked at him to gauge how serious he was, and he was pretty darn serious.

"Michael," was all she said, and he shook his head. "You just told me that the chances of Peter getting his hands on that letter and then traveling here were small. But I've lied to my friends for over a month. I need to be the one to tell them what's going on."

He looked past her and she knew he was trying to hold strong. Reaching out to touch his arm, she tried again. "You have to understand how important this is to me. Mrs. Bowers, Miss Lynn, and Olivia have all treated me like family, and I've put them in danger."

He looked down at her when her voice cracked with emotion. He knew she didn't have any relatives, and those women had been the closest thing to family to her.

"Mrs. Bowers goes to bed in an hour and the diner closes in two. We could hustle over there, talk to them all, and then be gone before ten."

She'd thought she'd made a good point, and he seemed to soften a bit as she talked, but then Rex stood up. "Reaper is right. We can explain to them what is going on and you can tell them you're sorry later. But the fact of the matter is that you need to leave town immediately."

"I thought you three could protect me?"

"Nice try," Rex said, and winked at her.

Reaper even laughed at that comment. "You and I are going on a road trip, angel. Rex and Cage will follow us, and then we'll call Ryan Gentry so he can be on watch until we can send in reinforcements."

There was no mistaking the disappointment on her face as she sat down on the sofa and listened to their plan.

It was obvious they knew what they were doing and quite impressive compared to what the detectives in Houston had done or not done for her. She figured it was the difference between police training and elite military training. But more than that, she was the only case they were concerned with, and those police detectives had tons of crimes to solve.

Reaper watched as Tenille got lost in her thoughts. He was

thankful she trusted him because he would do whatever it took to keep her safe from Peter Miller.

He stepped into his office to get them more firepower. He had a secret panel that opened up to his gun arsenal. Rex grinned when he saw his options and gathered up two additional guns with ammunition.

Reaper packed a bag for himself and Cage, who'd gone to pull his car around to the front of Reaper's house. Cage had parked around the block so no one would see his car, and it only took him about ten minutes to get there and then back.

They would need to get gas soon, but he figured they would also need to stop for coffee and more food, too.

Cage came in the front door and looked around. "Where is she?"

Rex looked at Reaper, who shook his head, then he checked the restroom. Jogging back into the entryway where they stood, Reaper practically growled. "She took my truck."

He showed them the camera and how she struggled with the side gate while Cage was pulling in the front. Two seconds later and he would have caught her.

"Son of a—" Rex said. "I guess we're going to Maisonville?"

"Damn-straight," Reaper spit out as he slammed the front door on their way to Cage's SUV.

He should have known she agreed too easily. If he'd taken a second to analyze the situation, he would've known she would take off the first chance she got. She had little to say in most situations and he had to accept that she, too, was all about showing and not telling.

Rex called the Mayor of New Orleans, Alexavier Regalia, who hired them for security regularly. He wanted to give him a heads up on what was happening so he could decide whether he wanted to take his girlfriend Olivia and her son, Lucas, out of town for a few days.

Cage called Miss Lynn at the diner and she was sweet as usual, telling him that Olivia was already there and that they expected Daisy in about fifteen minutes.

Reaper cussed a blue streak when he heard Cage's side of the conversation and how Tenille had thrown her safety and any caution about her situation to the wind.

She had zero self-preservation skills. He was an expert, and she would have to listen to him if he was going to keep her safe. She'd admitted that Keola Kahale had tried to teach her how to protect herself for months, but finally gave up. In a last effort to help her, he'd settled on teaching her how to run and hide. What the hell was that going to do for her?

By the time they made it to The Main Street Diner in Maisonville, he was even angrier at the situation. The sign on the door said closed, but the inside was lit up as they headed to the front door and saw the three ladies sitting at the bar talking.

Miss Lynn held Tenille's hand as she wiped tears from her cheeks. Olivia stood as soon as she saw Reaper knocking on the door.

The worry on all their faces defused his anger for the time being. He was staring at Tenille, but Olivia was questioning him. "What's the plan? You're taking her out-of-town tonight, right? Have you called Ryan, yet?"

Stalking over to Tenille, he held out his hand, and she handed over his keys. That was when Miss Lynn realized that sweet little Daisy, or Tenille, had taken his truck without his permission.

She winked at the young girl when she realized she was stronger than any of them had given her credit.

Olivia had Ryan Gentry on the phone when Alexavier stormed into the diner. "I'm sorry to interrupt your evening, Ryan, but we need you for a situation at the diner," she explained as Alexavier pulled her toward the front door. Lucas was spending the night with Alexavier's parents with a few of his young nephews, and he wanted to get Olivia out of there.

She held up her hands as she hung up with Ryan. "Wait, Alex."

But Alexavier was pretty bossy when he needed to be. "Immediate threat?" he asked Rex, who nodded.

"We aren't sure where Peter Miller is right now so we're going with immediate threat," Rex answered.

"This entire restaurant is lit up like a beacon. From out in the dark parking lot, you can see in here as clear as day," Alexavier said, as he told Olivia they had to go.

Miss Lynn shook her head as she turned off the interior lights with only a dim kitchen light beaming through. She had a small handgun in her apron, and Cage reached out as he told her that he would feel more comfortable if she let him hold it.

It was chaotic, and everyone talked at the same time. Reaper put two fingers to his lips and whistled loud enough to get their attention. Everyone stopped.

He looked at Tenille. "Angel, my truck, now!"

"Someone needs to follow Miss Lynn home to make sure she is safe and I need to go see Mrs. Bowers, and then we can leave."

Cage had never seen his friend angrier than at that moment and stepped in before he exploded. "Rex and I will follow Miss Lynn and meet you at the boarding house."

Ready to go all caveman on her, Reaper didn't say a word as he held her hand and walked her to his truck.

Everyone piled out of the diner as Ryan Gentry zoomed into the parking lot. It was another five minutes of explaining what was going on to Ryan that had Reaper hotter than ever. Ryan agreed to cover Olivia and Alexavier while they went to her house to get a few things. Miss Lynn agreed to close the diner for a few days and go into New Orleans to stay with Olivia and Lucas. Cage and Rex would meet Reaper and Tenille at Mrs. Bower's boarding house as soon as Miss Lynn was in her car and headed toward the bridge to New Orleans.

It was still a disaster, but as soon as Reaper and Tenille were in the truck and driving to the boarding house, he felt his blood pressure finally going back down.

"I'm sorry, Michael," Tenille whispered, but he held his hand up like he didn't want to hear it.

She shrugged and looked out the window as they drove in silence the five blocks to the boarding house.

He'd always disliked how much Nina always wanted to argue, and their fighting was off the charts. But sitting in the truck with complete silence when he had so much he wanted to say was killing him.

He pulled up in front of Mrs. Bower's house, but before he put his truck into park, Tenille hopped out and headed to the front gate. That was the final straw. He was on her before she could unlatch the handle and the fear in her eyes slayed him. He hadn't meant to scare her, and he immediately hugged her to his chest.

"Angel, you are testing every fiber of my being. I only want to keep you from harm, and yet you keep defying every single thing I've said."

She looked up at him and didn't need to say a word. He could see how sorry she was, and he didn't want her apology. He only wanted to make her happy. "Let's go see Mrs. Bowers and then, from this point forward, you stay by my side unless I tell you differently."

He kissed the top of her head and held her hand. But as they neared the front porch, they saw a figure sitting there in the dark.

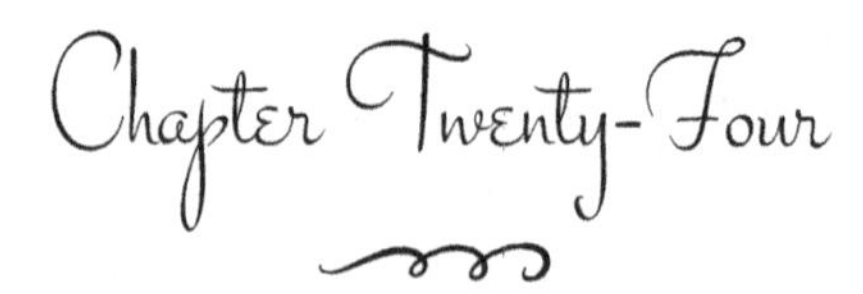

Chapter Twenty-Four

Tenille gasped as Reaper pushed her body behind his. The front porch light wasn't on, and it took a minute for their eyes to adjust. It was Mrs. Bowers slumped over in a chair. She was unconscious, and he dialed 911 as he checked her pulse.

Tenille spoke softly to the elderly woman, telling her she was there and everything would be alright.

Mrs. Bowers was sliding out of the chair and Reaper gently laid her on the porch with his jacket under her head.

Her pulse was weak, and she didn't stir as they waited for more help to arrive.

They heard the firetruck sirens fill the quiet neighborhood miles before it pulled onto the street. Then Tenille told them about the medications Mrs. Bowers took daily and how they'd found her outside like that in the dark.

"She sometimes sits out here with the lights off to rest her eyes, she says, but I think it's so she can spy on the neighbors when they walk their dogs. But she's never out here this late. I'm afraid she might have been here for an hour or more before we found her," Tenille said as tears filled her eyes.

One paramedic knew Mrs. Bowers and assured Tenille they would do everything they could for her. Then they put her on a stretcher and took her by ambulance to the hospital.

Reaper helped an emotional Tenille back into his truck. When he climbed into the driver's seat, she reached for his hand. "Do you think Peter could have gotten to her and poisoned her or something?"

"Angel, Mrs. Bower's is eighty years old and takes high blood pressure medicine. It could be her heart."

She nodded, but when they heard more firetruck sirens and Reaper's phone went off, they both feared something else was going on.

"We've got a situation," Cage said over the phone and then explained how Miss Lynn got an alert from the diner that showed there might be a fire. "She thinks she could have left something on the stove with so much going on tonight. We can't be sure until we get there. Rex called the fire department and they might beat us there."

Reaper cursed again. It was the day that kept on giving, and he was ready for it to stop. Olivia and Alexavier were driving across the lake already, and Ryan Gentry offered to take Miss Lynn there after they checked out the diner. So Reaper turned his truck around and they headed back to The Main Street Grocery, so that Cage and Rex could follow them out of town from there.

They pulled up at the same time as the guys with Miss Lynn. Ryan drove in behind them. There was definitely smoke coming from behind the diner and Miss Lynn rushed that direction.

"Hold on there, Miss Lynn," Ryan said. "What are you going to do? Throw dirt on it?"

She huffed at Ryan. "For your information, I have fire extinguishers in the back room."

Ryan pulled two out of his truck and headed to the back of

the building. Tenille held Miss Lynn's hand as they all followed behind him.

The back door was charred, but the only thing burning were the new wicker chairs and the wooden gazebo Miss Lynn had installed a month ago.

"What the hell?" Rex said, but Reaper had already drawn his gun when he realized the fire truck sirens had stopped.

He positioned his body in front of Tenille and Miss Lynn with Cage and Ryan flanking him. Rex stood behind the women as six large men dressed all in black stepped out from around the side of the diner with semi-automatic weapons focused on them.

Tenille was trembling when Michael reached a large arm back to pull her against his body. This was what he'd tried to protect her from, and she'd screwed it all up. It felt like an eternity before anyone said anything and she didn't know what to do except lean into Michael's body and pray no one started shooting.

When she heard Peter's voice, she knew things wouldn't be okay.

"Tsk, tsk, tsk," Peter said as he saw all four of the men surrounding Tenille pointing their weapons at his men.

"Tenille, you have a decision to make," Peter said to her, even though he couldn't see her behind the Neanderthal.

"Don't you speak to her," Reaper said in a voice she'd never heard him use. A really scary voice.

Peter smirked. "Nalani says, hello."

"Where is she, Peter?" Tenille said, and her voice sounded a lot stronger than she felt.

"She's safe. For now. But I can't guarantee it if you don't come with me."

"Not going to happen," Reaper spit out.

"Then a lot of people are going to get shot tonight, Tenille. Is that what you want?" Peter yelled a little louder.

Knowing what she had to do, Tenille dashed behind Miss

Lynn and toward Peter, stopping in the middle of all the guns. "If I go with you, promise they'll leave too. No one gets hurt. Please, Peter."

Tenille ignored the cursing behind her and Michael, who told her to step back to him.

Because in the middle of the back parking lot, with all the firepower pointed at her friends, she only had one choice.

"If that is what you truly want, my pet, then okay."

She turned and mouthed, "I'm sorry," to Michael as Peter pulled her back into his front and possessively wrapped an arm around her waist.

Tenille went pale and shivered when Peter touched her and it made Reaper want to kill him even more.

The coward, Peter, backed out of sight with Tenille's body shielding him. They climbed into the backseat of a black SUV with two of the hired guns getting into the front. The other four men stood stock still with their weapons pointed directly at Reaper, Cage, Rex, and Ryan Gentry.

As soon as the SUV zoomed out of the parking lot, Rex wrapped his arms around Miss Lynn and dragged her backward, pushing his body and her through the charred back door of the diner and out of the line of fire.

Ryan threw sand into the air and fell to the ground, rolling away from the scene, lighting the night up with gunfire.

Cage and Reaper both dove to the ground, also shooting at the men who would regret helping kidnap Tenille.

Two of the men got away and drove off, but they shot the other two. One was dead and the other crying out for his friends not to leave him.

A bullet grazed Reaper's arm, but everyone else was fine. He was the first one to grab the screaming man and punch him in the face. Cage took over, dragging him into the diner where they would get information out of him, one way or another.

Rex picked Miss Lynn up and apologized for being so rough. Ryan checked her out and then insisted on bandaging Reaper's bloody arm.

"I thought you were going to put a tracker on her," Rex said, frustrated that Peter had gotten the drop on them. There had been no signs that Peter was in the little town, and they'd all known better than to assume anything. They'd let Tenille lead them around, and that would cost them all dearly.

"I put it on her damn bag," Reaper said as he dug in his pocket for his phone.

Rex shook his head. "The bag that's in our SUV right now?"

Reaper nodded but was still looking for his phone as Ryan told him to be still as he taped him up.

"Wait. Fuck," he said as he stood. "Give me your phone," he barked at Rex. "Sorry, Miss Lynn," Reaper said, regarding his language. As soon as he logged into the phone, his fingers flew across the screen.

"Good girl," he said as he ran to the door. "She pocketed my cell phone. He hasn't figured it out yet and they're headed toward Interstate 12."

"Oh, the Saints will forgive you," Miss Lynn cried. "Go get our girl."

Rex and Reaper got into his truck as Cage pulled up behind them in his SUV. They tore out of the parking lot, kicking up rocks and dust in their wake.

Ryan secured the gunman and helped Miss Lynn sit down so he could call the police. He then called Alexavier to get blue lights in the air to assist The SEALS who didn't know what was waiting for them on the other side.

Nine miles ahead of Reaper was the SUV with Tenille, and only time would tell whether he caught up to them before Peter detected the phone. If he didn't, there would be no way to locate her.

Tenille had other things to worry about at the moment. She didn't know the man in the front passenger seat, but she recognized the driver with a short crew cut as one of the security guards over her in Hawaii. He'd known she was taken to Hawaii against her will and had made it clear that he wouldn't help her.

Peter gripped her wrist so tightly she was losing feeling in her fingers, but she didn't dare say a word since he was preoccupied with shouting orders to his men.

As they sped toward the interstate, Tenille suddenly realized she heard whimpering in the back of the SUV. It had to be Nalani, but there was no way for her to see in the dark.

Once they made it to the highway, Peter turned to give her all his attention. He wrapped his hand around her neck and lowered his face to hers. "Did you sleep with him?"

She acted like she didn't know who he was referring to, although there was no mistake about who was using his body as a shield to protect her when the guns came out.

He let go of her neck and slapped her hard enough to make her hit her head against the window. Peter had a thing about slapping her. "Did you f—" she cut off his crude question when she shook her head.

"No. No one since you," she whispered and tried not to shutter at the thought of what that would do for his ego. She had to play into him, but not so much that he thought she was lying.

He lowered his eyes at her. "Not even in Hawaii?" Peter wrapped his hand around her neck again and squeezed enough to cut off her breath. For a moment, she welcomed the dark. Anything to get her away from him. But he stopped short of her passing out.

She heard the whimpers from the back again. Louder. When she searched his soulless eyes, she knew it was Nalani.

"You have to let her go, Peter. There was a detective from

Hawaii looking for her. He said he was there for the family but that the FBI had the case and they are looking for you."

He squeezed her neck again, and she could feel the bruising. "I swear. No-No one was looking for me, but they won't stop looking for her because her family is politically connected."

He shrugged. Then, after a few minutes, he told them to pop open the trunk.

"It won't open, boss, while we're driving," crew cut said as he swerved quickly around a pickup truck that was probably going the speed limit.

"Slow down to sixty, put it in neutral, and then pop the trunk," Peter said as crew cut stared at him through the rear-view mirror.

She saw the man nod and felt the vehicle slow down. Surely it wouldn't work? Tenille cried out when she heard the trunk unlatching.

"No. You'll kill her, Peter." Tenille tried to hold on to him so he couldn't lean back and shove her friend out of the back of the moving vehicle.

It caught him off guard and crew cut was distracted enough to slow the vehicle down even more. Peter shook Tenille loose and busted her lip with his elbow as he climbed halfway over the seat. By the time he could shove Nalani's body wrapped and tied in a blanket out the back hatch, it felt like the fall might be survivable. At least Tenille prayed it was and that she would be okay. No doubt, Peter was going to shoot her as soon as they got to where they were going. Nalani at least had a chance now.

When the trunk hatch closed and they resumed their racing speed, Peter turned toward her and cocked his head. "You're different. Not as meek as you used to be." He leaned in close to her face. "You've gotten spirited." He handed her a napkin to wipe the blood off her face. "It'll be fun breaking you this time,"

Peter said, and didn't even look at her when he made that cruel remark.

If anything, their time apart had made him more vicious, and it emphasized how much less he valued her life. But he had a point to make and he would do whatever he wanted to her before he discarded her. She prayed Reaper was as good as he'd said he was and that he and his friends got to her first.

Chapter Twenty-Five

The Mayor of New Orleans walked a fine line of following the rules as a city official and taking care of his woman to the best of his ability. When Olivia heard Rex tell him that Peter Miller was on the run with Tenille, she flipped.

"You don't understand. She almost fainted because I gave her a pep talk about Reaper and how much he wanted her. She won't survive this."

"Baby, I'll take care of it," Alexavier said, and when he gave Olivia his word, he would do everything in his power to make that happen.

He called his Police Chief and good friend, Patrick Morales, who called the head of the local FBI office. Between the two men, they could get a helicopter in the air, albeit a half hour later than either of them hoped. Nevertheless, there would be air support coming soon.

Patrick Morales had been in the small town of Hammond at another officer's house for a cookout when he'd received the call about Tenille. His friend offered to help since they were halfway between Maisonville and Baton Rouge, where the kidnappers seemed to be heading.

When they rolled up on the scene of a woman's body wrapped in a comforter and secured with duct tape, He didn't know how he would call his friend and tell him they had been too late.

There was a pickup truck and driver first on the scene, and he told them she'd been shoved out of the moving vehicle and rolled across the highway into the semi-dry ditch.

The witness was an older man and not too steady on his feet, so he couldn't climb down the embankment to get her. Patrick was already heading down before the other officer got the entire story. He couldn't stand to think of her down there, even if she wasn't alive.

As soon as he ripped the tape off, the rest of the comforter fell apart. Her eyes were so swollen they were slits, but she still tried to open them. She tried to sit up, but it looked like her arm was broken. "Oh, sweetheart, you're okay. You're going to be okay. I'm here. I don't want to hurt you, but I'm going to carry you up the hill, alright?"

He had been in law enforcement for a long time and seen a lot of terrible injuries, but this was senseless and horrific. He gently slid his hands under her. "If it hurts too badly, nod your head, okay?"

The paramedics would scold him when they got there, he was sure of it, but she wouldn't lie there in the mud and muck with ants crawling nearby if he could help it. When he got to the top of the hill, the other officer tried to help, but Patrick held her firmly. "I've got her. Pull out a blanket and let's ease her into the back of that truck bed."

Everyone tried to help cushion the back of the metal truck so she would be as comfortable as possible. Then Patrick needed to call Alexavier back so he could let his friends know they had found her.

The helicopter still hadn't made it into the air by the time Patrick had made it to the scene, but he had the other police officer call the hospital to send one for her. Then they called the state police to help shut down the interstate so it could land nearby.

Minutes later, Reaper drove up on the scene. When he saw what looked like a body in the back of a pickup truck, his heart pounded in his chest. He threw his truck into park in the middle of the highway as he ran toward Patrick Morales. The phone tracker still showed them moving, but she could have dropped the phone in the car. At the same time, Rex received a call from Alexavier telling him they had dumped Tenille on the highway.

He got out of the truck and rushed to keep Reaper from seeing her that way. But when they got there, they both were relieved to see that it wasn't Tenille. This had to be her friend Nalani that had been missing for three weeks.

They told Patrick the details and gave him Detective Ghee's number so he could inform the family. Patrick's friend handed them a police light to put on top of their truck and then they took off to try to catch the bastards that had dumped a woman out onto the highway like road kill.

They had to get to Tenille before they did the same to her, or worse.

Eleven miles ahead of them, Crew Cut cursed the Baton Rouge traffic as Peter yelled at him to drive on the shoulder or switch lanes every few seconds before barking out another command.

Tenille could feel the tension rising between them and noticed all the debris on the shoulder. If crew cut listened to Peter, then they might get a flat tire and her chances of escape would get even better.

But as they crossed the bridge, traffic opened up and the flat tire possibility was probably gone. She'd figured they were going to the airport, but as they left the capital city behind, her mind whirled about his getaway plan.

He must have sensed her worry as he stared at her. "Wondering where we're going, aren't you?" Peter smirked. He always thought he was smarter than everyone in the room when, in actuality, he was just heartless.

Tenille shrugged like she didn't need to know, but it bothered him not getting to brag. "I figured those assholes would follow us and think we were going to fly out of here. The rest of the security team went to the Baton Rouge Airport. Our plane was there, but they took off about ten minutes ago. Get it? It was a diversion. While they are chasing the plane, we will get on a boat and head out to the Gulf of Mexico through the Atchafalaya River."

"The River of Trees," the other man in the front seat said and laughed. Tenille shivered as she listened to crew cut and that guy brag about their plan. It was a river swamp, and she'd heard about the animals that lived in the swamps. *Would frog men be able to navigate the Atchafalaya?*

She couldn't look to see if Reaper's phone was still working, but they'd been in the car for almost an hour and a half. What if the battery died? She sat there and focused on what the two men were saying as she bolstered herself for the midnight run through the woods or swim through the swamp river she would have to make as soon as they got to wherever they'd docked the boat.

Suddenly, Peter sat up and told crew cut to stop talking. "You hear that?"

"What?" Crew cut asked, crooking his head to the side like it would help him hear better. The other guy rolled down his window and looked out.

"Slow down. Take this exit," Peter said and pulled out his phone and map.

Tenille thought she heard a helicopter, but she wasn't certain. Crew cut made a wrong turn and Peter lost his mind. "I will shoot your ass right here if they catch us," he told his closest security guard and maybe only friend. Did sociopaths have friends? She guessed not since he just threatened to kill him and he wasn't joking.

Fifteen minutes later, they were driving under an overpass or bridge and the helicopter sounds were gone. They were no longer on a paved road and the other guy complained. "This is crazy, man. Slow down." He held on to the handle above the window and complained one more time, and that was when Peter held his gun up to the man's head and shot him.

Blood went everywhere, and Tenille screamed. Peter grabbed her face and squeezed her mouth tightly and she closed her eyes, trying to remember not to get emotional and to stay in control. As the car swerved around bushes and large dips in the dirt, she wondered if there was even a phone signal out there for Michael to follow.

As they slowly rolled through some thicket, she heard the tires make a whirring noise and realized they were stuck in the mud. Would it be too wet for her to run?

Peter gripped the top of her arm and dragged her across the seat toward him. He was bigger than she'd remembered, or maybe she was more frightened of him than before as he lifted her over the muddy tracks and onto the straw-like grass next to him.

It was dark out here. Swamp dark. But crew cut grabbed limbs and covered the top of the car as Peter looked on with approval. They had put some time into this plan and she wasn't so sure she'd make it out of this situation.

Michael's phone was inside her sock and as she stepped over

the thick brush, she felt it slide down further until it was stuck inside her sock and her shoe. She was thankful it hadn't fallen out, but it hindered the way she walked. Peter saw her having trouble and gripped her arm tighter, lifting her up and over the worst areas as he navigated it easily.

Finally, they came to a clearing next to the water, and she saw the boat he'd talked about. It was small and looked old. It was scary.

"We're going into the Gulf of Mexico in that thing?"

Crew cut laughed, but Peter glared at her. "Don't forget that we're out here because of you," he sneered, and shoved her ahead of him toward the rickety boat dock. She didn't have time to run, but she could swim, and she'd wait for her opportunity.

He pushed her to sit next to him at the back of the boat as crew cut started the motor. Peter was still angry at her and got in her face. "Just because we've been busy doesn't mean you aren't going to pay for what you've put me through. I have spent hundreds of thousands of dollars trying to find you and don't think things will go back to the comfortable way it was when we were in Hawaii."

Tenille stared at him. He'd assaulted her every day while they were in Hawaii, some days multiple times. If she died out on this river, it would be better than letting him take her anywhere else.

Crew cut jumped up to remove the rope from the dock, and Tenille surveyed the water. The only lights around them were the stars and some bridge lights in the distance. There was no way Michael and his friends were going to find her.

She looked up at the tiny sliver of a moon and remembered a song she once heard that said the ones you love are looking at the same bright moon.

It comforted her as she seemed to hyper focus on the quiet hum of the boat. It didn't sound very strong, and the loud frogs and crickets were almost drowning it out.

She thought about Nalani and prayed that she would be okay. And then about Michael and how mad he probably was at her for making them go to Maisonville and then for walking away with Peter to try to save them all.

Peter stood and walked to the bow, and she prayed Michael would forgive her one day as she leaned back to slip over the edge and let the water take her under.

Chapter Twenty-Six

Michael hadn't spoken for half an hour, but when he took the exit at 85 miles per hour, he asked Rex to turn off the police light. They'd gained on the black SUV and were only minutes behind them when they'd taken the exit, but he and his team had known that sometimes minutes were all you had.

He cut off the headlights but had to slow down in the mud. Cage had somehow kept up with him and he was thankful they were together, no matter what was about to go down.

According to the GPS, they were close to where the SUV stopped and it looked like Tenille wasn't moving fast. "They must be on foot now. We'll need to walk from here," he told Rex, who told Cage.

Rex covered his light hair with a black cap and then began smearing a camouflage stick in black under his eyes and around his face. He handed it to Cage and another one to Reaper so their faces wouldn't reflect any light when they ran up on Peter Miller and his security.

They saw the SUV partially covered and then blood all over the windows. Rex checked, but the man's face was blown off and he was definitely gone. It made them all feel even more desperate to get to Tenille.

The signal on the phone GPS was strong, but out there near the water, it wouldn't be as accurate. It actually showed where they were standing was part of the river, so Cage used his hometown tracking ability to lead them in the dark.

When they heard a boat motor start, they all began running. Arriving at the river bank just as the boat pulled away from shore, they watched as Peter walked to the front to look out and the only other man on board steered. No one was watching Tenille.

The night was only lit by a few stars and Reaper didn't know how he knew, but when he saw Tenille alone, he shook his head. "Don't do it, angel," he said. None of them had wet suits, but when Tenille slipped under the water, Reaper took off after her, with both of his friends close behind him.

Underneath the black silky water, Tenille tried not to think about the alligators she was certain were out there. Perhaps it was too cold for them or for snakes? As she swam up to the top to take a breath, she felt an arm wrap around her from behind. As a blood-curdling scream erupted from her chest, a warm hand slipped over her mouth. "Shhhh, angel, it's me."

She couldn't believe Michael was there in the water with her. How? She turned around and hugged him as he held them both up in the deep, black, freezing water. She hadn't even noticed how cold it was before.

He kissed her quickly and then swam with her under one arm faster than she'd ever managed before. They were on the bank and could hear Peter screaming her name and then heard him shoot crew cut in the head for not watching her. He had a flashlight looking over the edge of the boat into the black water as if he could find her that way.

From where they were crouching, they could just make out the silhouette of Rex and Cage as they each climbed onto the boat and grabbed Peter and pulled him overboard. Tenille held her breath as the water splashed around them and then she heard Peter scream and wild thrashing that didn't look human. Next they saw Cage rear back with his knife before he went under, too.

A few minutes later, Rex climbed on shore and then finally Cage swam up with a knife in his teeth and a grin on his face.

"Eight footer took him under. The gator's smaller brother tried to get me, but I was too quick."

"An alligator?" Tenille asked as her voice shook.

"Just a small one," Cage said as he winked at her.

Then they all four headed back to the vehicles without saying another word. It was over and Tenille didn't know what to say or do with herself. These three men had swooped in and ended her nightmare. How was that possible? What were they going to tell the police?

She was trembling as Michael picked her up and put her inside his truck. Reaper and Cage turned around as Reaper helped her remove most of her wet clothes and then wrapped her in the blanket he always kept behind the seat for her in his truck.

He turned up the heat and then peeled off most of his clothes too, as he talked to his friends. Rex and Cage volunteered to hang there until the authorities showed up and Reaper agreed to meet them back at his house when they finished.

Tenille finally found her voice when Michael climbed into his seat. "He pushed Nalani out of the moving SUV," she said, not making eye contact with any of them. Rex leaned forward and told her that Nalani was alive, but in serious condition. "She was taken by helicopter to the trauma center in NOLA, but I don't think we'll know anything until morning."

"I-I need to call her parents," she said as tears slowly fell down her cheeks.

Rex told her not to worry because Mayor Regalia called Detective Ghee so he could tell her parents.

Michael kissed her on top of her wet hair and pulled her in close beside him.

A few minutes later, they were barreling down the highway headed to New Orleans, and the safe haven she knew was his home. Snuggled up next to him, she wrapped the blanket across his body and marveled at how his body heat was hotter than the heat in his truck. Halfway through their hour and a half drive, she drifted off to sleep next to him.

They pulled into his driveway at two in the morning and when Reaper tried to carry her inside—she laughed and stood up holding the blanket snuggly around her.

As soon as they walked into his house, he got a good look at her busted swollen lip, the bruises around her neck and then the broken capillaries in her left eye that had turned all the white area blood red. He turned around as he cursed and tried to reel in his temper.

When he looked at her again, the concern in her eyes was all he could take, and he picked her up and carried her into the bathroom. Sitting her on the bathroom counter, he pulled out some alcohol and cleaned her bloody lip and chin. He leaned forward and kissed her neck, gently. "Maybe we should put some ice on it?" he asked, more to himself than to her.

"I'm freezing. No ice."

"Angel, I think we should go to the hospital?"

She leaned forward and told him she was fine. "He did this before and it'll go away," she said so matter of fact that he wished he could bring Peter back to life so he could kill him again, slower than the alligator.

He turned on the shower but before he left her to wash up; he reached over and pulled some straw and sticks out of her long beautiful hair.

"I'm going to shower in the other bathroom unless you need

me," he said, and she hugged and kissed him again. Would she ever get used to his kindness?

She shook her head as she blushed and he wanted to stay and shower with her, but she was still coming down from the attack. But he knew she was thinking about it, too.

By the time she finished washing her hair and body, and then got a good look at her mangled lip and scary looking eye, she heard him outside her bathroom door. She only had a towel to wrap up in, but when she opened the door, he was grinning at her and holding a grape tootsie pop. "I thought you could use this, and maybe some clothes?"

She grinned and walked straight into his arms. He was the most wonderful thing that had happened to her in her entire life, and she hoped one day she could tell him.

He insisted on making her a grilled cheese sandwich and ate two himself as he watched her finally finish an entire meal in front of him. It was exactly what she'd needed and while they sat up waiting to hear from Rex and Cage; he pulled her to his side as he tucked a quilt around her.

He stroked his fingers through her damp hair as he held her close. "I don't know what I would've done if anything had happened to you. Do you know that, angel?"

He was always so open and honest with her, and she longed to be the same way. It was going to take some time before she felt like her old self again. And just maybe, she could be a stronger version instead.

"I'm sorry if I made a mess of things tonight. I did what I thought I should do, so no one would get hurt. But it seems like a lot of people got hurt."

"Only the bad guys, and in my book, that's a perfect ending."

"The bad guys and Nalani," she whispered, and he offered to call the mayor and see if he could find out anything.

"But it's 2:30 in the morning."

"I think he's probably up." He didn't want to tell her how they were all worried sick about her and the events of that evening. But if anyone was asleep, they weren't resting comfortably, and he had no problem calling Alexavier to ease her mind.

Alexavier answered on the first ring and he heard Olivia in the background ask if he'd found Tenille. "Yes. She's resting right here next to me on the sofa. Look, she's worried sick about Nalani. Have you heard anything?"

The seriousness in Alexavier's voice did not go unnoticed, but he didn't tell that to Tenille. She had enough on her mind. "My police chief, Patrick Morales, rode in the helicopter with her. He insisted they take her to the trauma center in NOLA and thank goodness that he did. She has three broken ribs, a broken arm, a dislocated shoulder, and a fractured ankle. There were also head contusions and they are watching her for a concussion."

"I see," was all Michael said in response, so he wouldn't alarm Tenille. She needed at least one peaceful night.

"Two of her brothers are flying here and Patrick is going to watch over her until they arrive."

Michael thanked Alexavier for all of his help and promised Olivia she could see Tenille tomorrow. When he got off the phone, he saw Tenille studying his face.

"What, angel?"

She bit her bottom lip and then winced from the pain. It was swollen, and he wanted to kiss her until it no longer hurt.

"What else did he say about Nalani? I saw you look concerned and then smile." She shrugged, and he grinned because his girl was learning his tricks about watching people.

"Curiously, the chief of police is at the hospital with Nalani. Apparently, he rode in the helicopter with her and insisted they take her to the New Orleans trauma center so she would get the best care."

"Why is the chief of police there? Is something wrong?"

Michael reached out to hold her hand. "No, he seems to be protective of her."

Tenille looked thoughtful and then smiled at him. "That is very curious."

Michael added, "He is also going to stay with her until two of her brothers get there. They are on their way and should arrive by mid-morning."

"Good. She's really close to her family." Tenille looked sad as she mentioned Nalani's family.

He pulled her into his lap and asked her if she was ready to go to bed. "I thought we were waiting up for Rex and Cage?"

Michael shook his head. "Come on, angel. You need some rest and I'll close my eyes until they get here. It'll probably be hours before they're back."

Tenille's body felt heavy, and her mind raced, thinking of everything Peter had put her through. She wasn't sure she could stop thinking about all of it, but cuddling up next to Michael in his bed was exactly what she wanted. And if rest happened, then she was even luckier.

Chapter Twenty-Seven

It was mid-morning before Rex and Cage showed up at Reaper's house. Tenille had fallen asleep at dawn and he didn't want to wake her. So he made a pot of coffee and sat outside in his courtyard when his friends dragged in.

"You two look like hell. Getting old isn't for the weak," Reaper laughed before pouring two mugs of coffee for his friends.

They were only old in Navy SEAL years, but still Rex rubbed his face with his hands before he took the mug and drank half of it.

Cage flipped him off, but took the cup of coffee with a growl on his lips. He told Reaper that every type of law enforcement in the area showed up on the scene. "I don't know if it was because of the mayor or Police Chief Morales, but damn, I thought we would never get out of there."

Shaking his head as he finished his cup of Joe, Rex looked concerned. "A news chopper was flying overhead, but the feds kept wanting to chat it up with us. That's when Cage told them about wrestling with an alligator. They all laughed like it was a joke until an arm and then a foot came floating by the river bank. After that, they had no more questions for us. But I'm pretty sure our faces will make the news. Of course, they dragged the river, trying to find any sign of him or his weapon. A few miscellaneous body parts were all they could find of Peter Miller."

Cage sat forward in the metal chair. "They're going to want to question her. We told them she was injured, and that you rushed her out of there before she went into shock."

Reaper nodded.

"Mayor Regalia had already filled them in on most of the backstory. You know that man is a talker. So, it shouldn't be too difficult. They'd already been to the hospital and spoken to Nalani Kahale before they got to us and she corroborated that Peter Miller had kidnapped her and flew her across state lines." Rex was good with the details.

It was then that they heard the door to the house open and Tenille, wearing a long sleeve navy t-shirt and a gray pair of baggy sweatpants, walked outside.

She smiled at the guys and said, "Good Morning," to them all. But Cage and Rex were both fixated on the dark bruises around her neck, her busted lip that was more swollen than last night and her left eye that didn't have a spec of white left in it but was blood red.

Reaper stood and kissed her forehead as he pulled a chair over beside him for her to sit. She whispered, "Thank you," and he watched her cheeks flush. He was completely mad for her, and his friends knew it.

Cage watched as Reaper poured her a cup of coffee and added cream and sugar before handing it over to Tenille. It felt like an intimate moment and they should probably leave, but it was great to see the two of them together. It made him feel even worse about how he'd treated her.

Feeling Cage's eyes on her, Tenille looked up and gave him a shy grin. He felt even more like an asshole. "I'm sorry, Tenille, for not believing you in the beginning. You weren't a damsel in distress or faking like you were helpless. I was wrong."

She reached out and squeezed his hand. "I was a bit D.I.D. there," she said and winked at him.

He shook his head. "No, ma'am, you were and are a sweet lady who was being terrorized by a sociopath for most of your life. You didn't deserve any of it, but you definitely didn't deserve for me not to believe you when you finally had the courage to tell someone."

"It's okay—," she tried to say, but Reaper leaned in and stopped her.

"Let him apologize, angel. Trust me, he never does that," Reaper said, and she nodded.

"Thank you for saying that, Cage," she added before sipping from her mug.

They talked for twenty minutes more about the Coast Guard and the two fishing boats that also came by the scene at the Atchafalaya River before saying their goodbyes.

Tenille and Michael made breakfast together, and just as they finished their toast and eggs, the doorbell rang. He looked around for his phone before remembering he'd left it on the charger in the bedroom. Lucky for him, going for a swim with it in her sock hadn't harmed it. He'd joked with her in bed that finally his iPhone was made from the same material as those mysterious black boxes on airplanes, which made her laugh.

The doorbell rang again, and he honestly considered not answering the door, but Tenille told him it was okay.

When Miss Lynn, Olivia, Lucas, and Alex were standing there, Tenille's face lit up.

"Oh, my God," Olivia said as she rushed to hug Tenille.

Miss Lynn had tears in her eyes as she and Olivia checked out all of Tenille's injuries.

Lucas poked at his own eye when he finally asked, "Does that hurt?"

Tenille shook her head. "I honestly can't feel it at all." She pointed to her lip and admitted, "But this here is pretty sore."

Lucas nodded and then hugged her to make her feel better. All their concern touched Tenille and as they got Lucas set up at the kitchen table with his transformers, all the adults went to the living room to sit down and chat.

"Any word about the damage to the diner, Miss Lynn?" Tenille asked nervously.

"The cook and kitchen guys assessed the damage this morning and said it was mostly superficial, but the whole place smells like smoke. We might have to stay closed for a few days, a week tops," she said. "But don't you worry about that right now."

Olivia added, "It will give those two food truck girls a boost with their coffee and pastry business. Word on the street is that they borrowed money from some jerk and if they are late with a single payment, then the business reverts to him and they will be hourly employees."

Miss Lynn looked at her seriously. "My stars. Poor girls. We'll have to help them."

"I'm happy to come and help get the diner cleaned up. Honestly," Tenille said.

Olivia's eyes turned to slits, but the smirk on her face was playful. "Look, you little overachiever, we've got this. You need to heal up so you can get back over there and take care of Mrs. Bowers for a few days."

Putting her hand to her heart, Tenille felt terrible for not asking about Mrs. Bowers. Miss Lynn patted Tenille's leg as she told her, "She's going to be fine. It was a good thing you went by the house when you did because she'd accidentally taken her medication twice and it had turned toxic in her body. The doctor said, you saved her life."

"It wasn't Peter, after all?" Tenille's eyes watered at the realization that Mrs. Bower's falling ill had been a legitimate accident. She looked forward to finally being able to appreciate having loving people around her and not having to worry that Peter Miller would hurt them in order to hurt her.

"Word has it we're going to get to meet your Hawaiian friends soon?" Olivia purposely changed the subject to a more positive one.

Grinning at her, Tenille nodded. "I can't believe Nalani is here."

"And two of her hot brothers," Olivia added, which made Alexavier raise an eyebrow her way. She shrugged and added, "Not that I care. I'm just looking out for our single girl."

Reaper then gave Olivia a look, but she smugly gave him one right back. There was a challenge in her eyes, and he knew it. He needed to stake his claim, or Olivia was going to put Tenille in front of every eligible bachelor in a fifty-mile radius. But now that Tenille didn't have to run, would she want to stay in Maisonville or New Orleans? What about her past in Sugarland?

It was too soon to hit her with all of those questions and his girl was looking wiped out as she explained more about her past to the sweet women who'd been like a family to her.

After a few minutes, Miss Lynn also noticed how tired Tenille looked. She instantly stood up and motioned to the door. "We need to let you rest, honey. There will be plenty of time for us to chat after you feel better. I assume you will be back home in Maisonville in a few days and aren't considering moving back to that house in Texas. You're one of us now."

Tenille stood and hugged the sweet older woman. But Reaper didn't miss how she didn't confirm or deny any plans.

After they left, Tenille walked back into the living room but didn't have a seat. "Would you mind taking me to the hospital to see Nalani?"

He wrapped his arms around her. "You sure you're up for it?"

She nodded as she gave him a quick kiss on the chin. It didn't take long for her to change her clothes and they arrived at the hospital just as Patrick Morales was walking into Nalani's room with a chocolate smoothie.

Tenille looked at Michael and he winked at her before knocking on Nalani's hospital room door.

The moment Nalani saw Tenille, they both cried. "Girl, I thought I would never see you again," Nalani said, holding her good arm out for a hug.

Tenille gently hugged her friend and then carefully sat on the bed next to her. "I wasn't so sure I'd ever see you again, either."

They looked at each other and there was a lot left unsaid between them, but there would be time for that later. "So how are you?"

Nalani asked as she checked out Tenille's injuries.

"Me? I'm fine. But look at you. How are you, sweet friend?" Nalani had acted like an older sister to Tenille from the moment they'd met. But it was Tenille's turn to take care of Nalani.

"I'm tougher than I look," Nalani said, winking at her friend, and that was when Patrick Morales stood up.

"Uh, huh," drink your smoothie, Sunshine. They told you that if you want them to spring you, then you have to take those meds and you can't do that on an empty stomach.

Tenille motioned back to him, and Nalani shrugged. He'd appointed himself her keeper for the time being, and Nalani kind of liked the bossy guy.

"So your brothers are on their way?" Tenille asked, hoping they wouldn't whisk her back home too soon.

"Of course, Jensen and Noa should be here any minute."

Nalani rolled her eyes. She was the youngest in her family and the only girl. Jensen and Noa were the two youngest boys, three and four years older than Nalani, but they watched over her more closely than her dad. They were also loud and fun, and the hospital wasn't ready for the likes of the Kahale Brothers.

"Do you know how long you'll be in the hospital? You could come stay with me at the boarding house to recuperate, if you want?"

Nalani smiled at her sweet, younger friend. Tenille had been in so much trouble and scared out of her wits for most of the time they'd been together. Despite that, she always had those sweet southern manners and tried to put others first.

"I'm not sure. They said if my cognitive tests come back okay that they might let me go tomorrow."

Patrick added, "But she is going to need around the clock help and she won't be able to climb any stairs for a while. Isn't Mrs. Bower's Boarding House a two-story colonial?" She didn't miss how he stepped in again to look out for Nalani. Whew, her brothers wouldn't like that, not one bit.

Tenille swallowed hard, and Nalani knew she was trying to hold back her emotions. "H-How is your dad and the rest of your family?"

"I talked to him this morning, and he's home and doing great. He had to be on oxygen for a while, but he was a ball of energy, you know. Hard to contain. Everyone else is busy trying to rebuild the restaurant and worried sick about me and you."

Tears filled Tenille's eyes. "I'm so sorry to have put you and your family in danger. I should have left Hawaii as soon as I got out of that dinner."

Nalani rolled her eyes and then held her head. *Should rolling her eyes hurt that much?* She wondered. "We wouldn't have let you go while that maniac was still around. You know my family is pushy. And it isn't your fault."

From the moment Nalani met Tenille, she'd tried to teach her not to apologize all the time. Instead, she would say, "Live your life with intention and if you make a mistake, then say something like 'my bad' and move on." Tenille would laugh at her and shake her head, but there was good advice in there, too. She wasn't at fault for all the things that happened to her or around her.

As they talked, Patrick stood up and handed Nalani her smoothie to encourage her to drink more. His timing was impeccable as a mean older male nurse came in the room and checked to see if she'd finally eaten so she could take her next round of medicine.

He also gave Tenille the side-eye for sitting on the bed, but when he saw her injuries, he stopped and smiled at her. "Have you had those looked at?" he asked, but instead of waiting for her to answer, he left the room and came back with a small framed female doctor. Her name was Dr. Singh.

She asked Tenille permission to look at her, and Tenille agreed. Dr. Singh gently felt around the bruises on her neck, all around her head, her lip, and then used a light to fully examine both of her eyes.

The doctor was caring and sympathetic. Overall, her sweetness was genuine. "You took some serious blows, little lady," she said and Tenille grinned because they were probably the same size.

"I've never seen the patakia of the eye that damaged before without damage to the eye itself. You were strangled? Did you lose consciousness?"

Tenille looked down as she answered. "Yes ma'am. Not completely."

"Does it hurt at all?"

"No, ma'am. My neck is sore and my lip kind of throbs, but that's all."

The room was silent as everyone watched the exchange. "You are going to need some rest. Seriously, a week or more. And I would suggest a thorough follow-up exam."

Reaper stood up behind Tenille and placed a hand on her back. He heard the doctor loud and clear and he was going to make sure Tenille followed those instructions starting that day.

Once the doctor left and Nalani took her medicine, a tech came in to take her for her second MRI. They hugged each other and Tenille promised to visit again.

Reaper shook Police Chief Morales' hand and as they headed out to the parking lot, two big Hawaiian men came running toward Tenille. Reaper was in front of her before they got close and had his gun drawn.

"Whoa dude. Chill. We're the Kahale Brothers, bruh."

Tenille laughed and kissed Michael on the cheek before she stepped around him to hug Jensen and Noa.

Noa lifted her chin and shook his head. "Dang, girl. How does the other guy look?"

She looked him in the eye when she said, "Well, he's dead, so he doesn't look so good."

Both of the Hawaiian brothers erupted in laughter and grabbed her up in a bear hug. They had never heard Tenille speak so bluntly. Her southern manners always stopping her from saying anything off-color. It was refreshing and funny as hell. "That's some good news," Jensen said.

"At least we won't have to go to jail for killing him," Noa added.

Tenille playfully pushed the big guys away and then officially introduced them to her overprotective body guard, Michael. But instead of calling him Michael, she said his name was Reaper. Instantly, the two half-Hawaiian men showed Reaper respect. They all shook hands and when Reaper put his arm around Tenille possessively, they didn't miss it. Tenille told them to go easy on Nalani because she was seriously hurt and still having some tests done. She then smiled and said Nalani had made a friend and for them to please go easy on him, too. They both looked at her like she was speaking a foreign dialect. "Seriously, guys. She's got a lot of healing to do and she deserves a little pampering."

They promised to be on their best behavior and then both laughed before they said goodbye. Jensen and Noa didn't waste any time as they headed into the hospital to find their little sister and figure out how she'd made a friend.

Tenille watched them bound toward the hospital and felt a bit relieved that Nalani's family was there. When Michael helped her into his truck and noticed how much slower she was moving, he was worried. She might have made some huge strides in speaking her mind or acting self-assured but asking for what she needed or taking care of herself was still going to take some time.

They had time; he hoped.

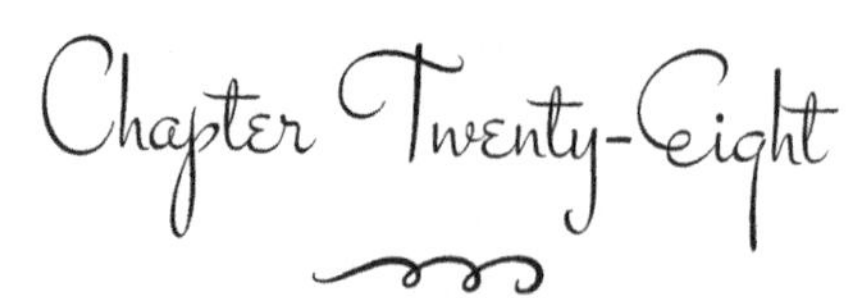

Chapter Twenty-Eight

Reaper relished the quiet of his home when he and Tenille returned. He offered to make her something to eat, but she declined. She seemed to have a lot on her mind. After making himself some spaghetti, he looked over at the sofa where she'd been sitting to find she'd fallen asleep.

He covered her up with a quilt and sat at the table to eat alone.

Cage sent a text that the FBI agents wanted to meet with Tenille that evening, but he explained what the doctor said and how she was asleep. Cage said he would put them off until the next day and, just as Reaper thought they would have a quiet evening, his doorbell rang.

Looking at his phone, he saw his father, mother, and sister standing there impatiently. Why would they all be there without calling first? He suddenly remembered Nina had shown back up in town. They were going to give him hell about her, and the mystery child she was saying was his.

Opening the door, he looked directly at his sister because

she'd moved to the bossiest spot in the family. "Tenille is asleep. Let's go to the courtyard to talk?"

They loudly followed him through the house, and he knew it was useless to tell them to be quiet. They just didn't have that in their DNA.

Outside on the patio, his father walked over to the woodpile and grabbed a few logs and sticks to build a fire in the metal fire pit.

His mother kissed him on both cheeks and settled into a chair, wrapping her fleece coat around her body tightly. She'd always told them she didn't get cold anymore since she turned fifty. Obviously, her sixties were a different story.

"Don't you have coffee in this place?" Abigail asked, shaking her head at her brother's lack of civility. He'd been raised better.

"I'm not sure why you're here, but I know you must have stopped somewhere along the way since you can't go thirty minutes without caffeine. And your house is two hours away, Abi. So, what's up?"

His father spoke first, and that had never happened. "Son, we're worried about you."

Reaper looked at his dad and then at his mother. "Me?" He knew they worried when he was in the Navy, but after countless missions where he came back healthy, they'd stopped questioning him. "Is this about Nina?"

Abigail made a big production of sighing and staring at him. "They didn't know about Nina, you idiot."

And that was when his mother lost her temper. "Michael Anthony Thibodeaux, do you mean to tell me that little Daisy is sleeping at your house, and you are still talking to Nina Calhoun? And just who is this Tenille person? How many women are you dating?"

He shook his head. "Of course not, mama. And I'm only seeing one woman."

Abigail intervened and told them the short version of what was going on with Nina. His mother looked angry, then sad, then angry again. "I have a three-year-old grandson that I've never met? And I'm just hearing about him?" Beth Thibodeaux said as she stood up with her hands on her hips, looking at Abigail to explain and then at her son.

"Wait a minute, if you didn't know about Nina, then why are you here and worried about me?"

Abigail stepped between her parents and brother, but pointedly looked at Michael. "They saw Rex and Cage on the news and insisted I drive them here."

He remembered Rex mentioning a helicopter from one of the news stations flying above them at the crime scene. He should have known his parents would see them and figure he was involved.

Before he could deny any of it, Tenille fumbled with the door as she balanced a tray with coffee and cookies for everyone while trying to walk outside.

As soon as his mother saw Tenille's face and the injuries, she gasped and ran over to her. "Michael Anthony, get over here and get this tray from her. My baby, are you okay?" Beth Thibodeaux gently pulled Tenille's chin left and then right to examine her.

"Yes, ma'am," she answered, but his family wasn't buying it.

"How did it happen?" Mike Thibodeaux asked his son, and everyone immediately looked at Reaper, too.

But instead of letting him take the heat, Tenille stepped in front of him. "It wasn't his fault. I'm sorry to have to say that I-I-I'm not exactly who I said I was when we met at Thanksgiving."

You could have heard a pin drop on the concrete when Tenille told them she wasn't who they thought she was. Reaper was certain he'd never heard his family that silent even when they were asleep.

"My real name is Tenille Sims, and I was born and mostly

raised in Texas. Michael didn't know the truth about me either when we met because I was too afraid to let anyone know my real identity." Tenille explained that the things she'd told them at Thanksgiving were true. She had lost her parents when she was young and was raised by her aunt and uncle in Sugarland, Texas. She gave them just the bare necessities of what had happened with Peter Miller and how Nalani Kahale and her family had helped her. Then explained that Michael, Cage, and Rex saved her life last night.

Beth Thibodeaux kept her hand over her mouth in shock the entire time. While his sister and father both listened, and drank coffee.

None of them questioned any of her behavior. Beth simply looked at Tenille's face again, examining her injuries. Her neck and eye specifically. "Child, have you seen a doctor?"

Tenille smiled shyly at the sweet Cajun woman coddling her. "Yes ma'am. Today. It amazed her that I didn't have more injuries or damage to my eye."

Beth Thibodeaux looked directly at her son. "I think she needs a second opinion. Bring her home to see Dr. Fontenot. You hear me?"

"Yes ma'am," he answered.

When Abigail tried to bring up Nina again, Beth shushed her. "Ma, it's okay, Tenille knows about her."

"Well, it seems like everyone knows what's going on around here except for us, Mike. And I, for one, do not like it."

Michael stood up and hugged his mother. "I'm sorry, mom. It wasn't intentional. It has just been a rough few days."

His mother acted like she wouldn't forgive him, and he kissed her on the cheek until she smiled. "Okay, you're forgiven. But you have to promise to bring Daisy, I mean Tenille, over more often." She had a tough outer layer, but his mother was mostly sweet on the inside.

Michael smiled. "Yes, ma'am."

"And what in heaven's name are you going to do about Nina?" she whisper-yelled.

Abigail threw her hands up and then made an exaggerated groan as she leaned back in her chair. Finally, everyone looked at her as she'd wanted. "I've been trying to tell you this since we got here."

"You have our full attention, Abi. Now get on with it," Michael said as he eased Tenille into a seat next to him.

"Well, you know I get my hair done with Sissy." Sissy's big brother Terrence had been close friends with Michael growing up. "Well, Sissy had an interesting story to tell me about her brother and Nina having a tryst about three and a half years ago. Of course she giggled and then asked if tryst was the right word for it."

Beth shook her head. "Did you say yes, if tryst means cheating with your best friend's girl?"

Abigail laughed. "You know I did."

Michael reached over to hold Tenille's hand. She was getting an up close and personal view of his family, not the cleaned-up and polished version from Thanksgiving. What he didn't know was that she loved every minute except the part where Nina had hurt him.

"Sissy then asked me if I'd seen Nina around town with a toddler and when I acted like that was the first I'd heard of it, she shook her head. Then she said she knew for a fact that it was Troy's little boy and that Nina was plotting to get her brother and Michael both to pay child support so she could quit working."

Abigail took a long swallow of coffee, no doubt for dramatic effect, before she continued. "Sissy isn't the brightest bulb in the pack, but she's sure got Nina's number because she talked her brother into getting the little boy to spit into a twenty-three & me test kit and mailed it off."

Reaper shook his head when his sister drank more coffee. His mother was about to explode, but it didn't make Abigail hurry to the punch line any faster.

His father didn't know what she was talking about. "What is twenty-three and me?"

"Dad, it's a DNA test you can take. You mail some spit in a tube or something and in two weeks you can find out all sorts of nifty things like your family lineage or whether you carry a genetic gene for cancer. But in this case, she found out that the sweet little boy was her bona fide nephew. And zero kin to us."

Beth Thibodeaux huffed loudly, because it was good news, but she would love all grandchildren brought into this world.

Michael sat back smugly that he'd been right all along. But also secretly thankful that Nina hadn't found a way back into his life.

Tenille was quiet as she watched the family drama play out before her. It truly was everything she'd ever hoped for, and more.

Did families realize when things went crazy how lucky they were simply to have each other?

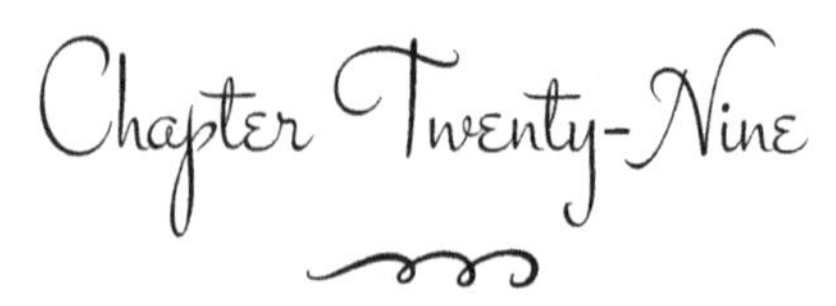

Chapter Twenty-Nine

The smell of vanilla and almonds woke Reaper up the next morning. It almost smelled like cake, he thought in his barely conscious mind, and that was when he felt the warm sweet kisses on his shoulder and then neck.

Instantly, he woke to find Tenille barely covered in a towel. Her hair was wet from a shower and her body with that sweet scent of cake.

That had to be her body wash because he was certain he had nothing like that in his house. He scooped her up into his arms and pulled her on top of his body.

"Good morning, angel," he said in that deep gravelly voice she loved.

"It is now that you're awake," she said, determined to drive him mad.

"Is there something I can do for you?" he asked teasingly.

She responded by sitting up on top of him and lowering the top of her towel. She used both arms to push her wet hair back out of her face, which made her breast rise to his attention. "I'm not sure. Is there something you can do for me?"

He sat up and pulled her into him tightly, leaving no doubt how much he wanted her. His tongue darted out and tasted her sweet lips, careful at first not to hurt her and then throwing caution to the wind when she pressed her mouth harder against his.

They explored and touched each other until he had to force himself to stop. It was going to kill him, but he had to make sure. "Angel. I think you know I'm on board for this or anything you want. But I heard what you said about what happened." He kissed her gently on her temple and then whispered, "I'll wait as long as you need me to. There's no hurry."

She kissed his bottom lip and then bit it softly between her teeth before looking into his eyes. "The thing is, when I think about sex, all I know is what he did and I hate thinking about him. But I noticed that when you touch me, I can't think about anything else but you. Make me think about you, Michael."

And he spent the rest of the morning giving her plenty to remember.

Wrapping her in his arms, afterward, Tenille fell back asleep for two hours. When she woke up, she smelled bacon and coffee wafting through the air. Had she ever been that hungry?

As she threw on his robe and headed out the bedroom door, Michael was coming her way with a plate of pancakes and bacon, along with one of the large coffee table books from the living room. She smiled at him curiously and thought she saw him blush.

"I don't have a tray and thought you could use this to eat breakfast in bed," he said.

Tenille stood on her tiptoes to kiss him on the cheek. He was truly the most wonderful man. "I'll eat with you, if that's okay?"

She was loveable, and he wanted to do whatever she wanted, but he would find a way to pamper her. "Come on, Ten, let's eat at the table."

The grin she gave him was like a wallop to his heart. Making love to her was even more wonderful than he'd imagined, and that was saying something. He'd never made pancakes for a woman before and one day he'd tell her that.

But this morning they had to wrap up things with the FBI, and possibly answer more questions with the Detectives from Hawaii and Texas.

His shy girl went straight to the difficult stuff. "How long do you think it will take with the FBI this morning?"

"Not sure, angel. I'd like to get all of that behind us, though."

"Me too. I'd like to call Mr. Arceneaux and my aunt's girlfriends, too. I want to be the one to tell them what happened and that I'm okay."

Reaper leaned over and kissed her. She was stronger than before. "Of course. If we can wrap things up early enough, I could drive you to Texas to see them?"

Tenille drank the rest of her milk and then shook her head. "I think I'd rather go see Nalani at the hospital and then Mrs. Bower's, if that's okay?"

He kissed the back of her hand and assured her that wherever she wanted to go, he would take her.

Then they spent the next three hours meeting or talking with law enforcement.

By the time they hung out with Nalani and her crazy brothers, they didn't roll into Maisonville until four in the afternoon.

Tenille stopped and picked up a couple of dozen flowers and put together the largest arrangement Reaper had ever seen. His girl was full of surprises.

But the look on Mrs. Bowers' face when they walked in to the hospital was priceless. She hugged and kissed Tenille while tearing up at the same time. She even hugged Reaper, but afterward asked a nurse where her cane was in case he got out of line.

"Sweet girl, after I read your letter, I didn't think we'd ever see you again."

"I'm sorry, Mrs. Bowers. I thought it was for the best," Tenille said before looking over at Michael. "But I know better now."

"So, you are staying put in Maisonville?" Mrs. Bowers asked shamelessly, like Miss Lynn. Reaper shook his head thinking about all the bossy Southern women that surrounded them.

"Well, I have a lot to take care of in Texas."

"And a place to stay in New Orleans, anytime," Reaper added and Mrs. Bowers asked for her cane again, making them laugh.

"But I'll be here whenever you need me, okay?" Tenille reached out and held the elderly woman's hand. It was the first time Mrs. Bowers remotely resembled an eighty-year-old woman.

Tenille fussed over her for another hour, making sure she had a proper dinner and then an after dinner hot tea as she liked to enjoy, normally on the front porch of her home.

Finally, they headed to Miss Lynn's Diner so Tenille could see the damage firsthand. It was almost dark when they arrived and Reaper told her it looked worse at night than in the daytime when she cried.

When they got back to his house in New Orleans, he could tell the trip across the lake wore her out. She barely ate any dinner and sat quietly on the couch as he surfed shows on television.

They went to bed before eleven and lying there in the dark, she asked him if he felt like going to Texas in the morning. "I could fly home, if it's too much trouble? I forget sometimes that I have money. You don't have to take care of me, you know."

How did he tell her he wanted to take care of her without sounding controlling? She'd been through so much and she was finally free. Did she want time alone?

He rolled over on his side to face her. "What do you need, angel?"

It had been so long since Tenille had a choice. She wasn't sure how to answer him. So she reached up to touch his masculine face. It was dark in the room and she couldn't completely make out his features except for when he smiled and his beautiful teeth reflected the negligible amount of light streaming in from the bathroom.

When she leaned up to kiss him, he met her halfway. Then he slowly made sweet love to her. It wasn't like that morning but instead, purposeful and everything she'd needed right then.

They didn't discuss going to Texas again, but in the morning, he was up and packed when she walked into the living room.

"Ready to go, angel?"

She smiled but stopped short of telling him how relieved she was that he was going to drive her. She was nervous about going home to Sugarland to face all the things she'd left behind.

Her home, the one her aunt and uncle raised her in and then left to her, had been damaged in a fire. Before that, the police had ransacked it while following a warrant to search for clues that she'd been involved in the murder.

She wished she could simply focus on the good things that her Aunt Sue and Uncle Ed had done with and for her. But those bad things that happened right before she kidnapped kept weighing on her mind.

Then there were Aunt Sue's friends that she hadn't spoken to in almost a year. Mel, Carol, and Amelia had been close to her for most of her life. The friends travelled with Tenille and her aunt to Europe every time they went. Contacting the friends while she hid in Hawaii would have put them in danger. Peter had killed her aunt and uncle. He would have surely gone after Mel, Carol, and Amelia if he thought they were helping her.

Still, she needed to explain it to them and had already tried to contact each one but had to leave messages. No one returned her call. Were they surprised to hear from her? Maybe angry to hear she'd been in hiding? Perhaps they believed Detective DeVries' accusations?

There were just so many questions, and Tenille worried over it all as Michael filled his truck up with gas and bought snacks for the drive. They listened to her favorite country music for hours, but after stopping in Lake Charles, Louisiana, to gas up his truck again, he climbed back inside with a serious look on his face. Then he presented her with a grape tootsie pop.

"You can only have this if you tell me when you started this habit?" He grinned as he handed it over and then popped another one into his own mouth.

"My earliest memory of my Aunt Sue was probably my third or fourth birthday. She was much older than my dad,her brother, but had such a fun personality. She and Uncle Ed never missed any birthday or holiday. Anyway, after my parents told her she couldn't buy me a pony, she rented one for the entire weekend for me to ride and feed. She stayed with me and the pony every minute and shared her tootsie-pops. When they came to pick up the pony, I was pretty sad and so she bought me an entire bag of these and told my parents they had to let me have them since they took my pony away. I've loved them ever since."

"Now that's a story," he laughed.

Tenille shook her head. "Years later, Aunt Sue admitted she knew they wouldn't let me have a pony. However, by letting them think she was going to give me one allowed her to use it as leverage to buy me anything else she wanted from that day forward." Tenille laughed. "Aunt Sue was something else. She bought me all the coolest toys and Uncle Ed always made sure I had a battery powered car, jeep, or go cart to match his car collection. They unabashedly spoiled me."

Her words and thoughts of her precious aunt and uncle hung in the air for the next couple of hours. When Reaper took the exit toward her house, she sat up in her seat and looked nervous.

Reaching over for her hand, he tugged until she unbuckled and moved over beside him. Once buckled back in, he kissed the back of her hand. "Just so you know, love should always be shameless."

Tenille couldn't stop smiling after he said that and although he hadn't said he loved her, it felt the same. As they pulled into her neighborhood, her nerves returned. But as they pulled into her driveway, Reaper whistled, making her smile.

"This is some house, Ten," he said as he got out of the truck and helped her climb out his door, too. He'd started using *angel* and *ten* interchangeably as nicknames for her and she couldn't help but fall even harder for him.

Strangely, the house looked, well, it looked perfect. She shook her head and walked toward the back. *When had everything been repaired?*

Walking back around to the front, Tenille shook her head. "I don't understand. The last time I saw this place, it had been set on fire and while there wasn't a lot of fire damage, there was a ton of smoke and water damage."

She unlocked the front door and when they walked inside, someone had put every single thing back in order. It looked exactly the way it had before her aunt passed away.

Tenille teared up and then went from room to room to find it was all put back together. When she went into the garage, her car, the car she'd wrecked before the house caught on fire, was parked in its proper place and had been repaired.

She'd prepared herself all this time for the worst, and yet, the house was much better than just repaired. It was perfect. "I don't understand," she said, and he hugged her, knowing that it was emotional just being there.

When the doorbell rang, she figured it was Mr. Arceneaux

since she'd told him what time she'd be in and he had some documents for her to sign.

But when she opened the door, there stood Mel, Carol, and Amelia. Before she could say a word, they swarmed her and all wrapped their arms around her at the same time. Had she been worried they wouldn't forgive her for not contacting them sooner? These women loved her as if she were one of their own. And it flooded her with emotion because that was how much they all had loved her Aunt Sue.

Aunt Sue had been the ringleader in the group and honestly, the women had been friends since college and more like sisters. They were relieved that Tenille was safe and sound.

The tears and joy were intense, and Reaper tried to stand back and give them space. After several minutes, Carol looked over and got a good look at Reaper. That was when they all stopped and stared at him.

"My goodness," Carol said. "I wouldn't have come home without that hunk either."

"Hmmmm-mmmm good," Amelia said.

Mel just laughed and giggled, but there was no mistake that she thought he was gorgeous.

Tenille laughed and walked over to stand next to Michael. "Sorry. They have zero filter and like to talk about handsome men as if they can't hear them when they speak."

He laughed, a little embarrassed by the older women checking him out so brazenly.

"This is my friend, um, boyfriend, Michael Thibodeaux," Tenille said and looked up at him to make sure that was okay to announce.

He leaned down to kiss her before stepping over and shaking hands with the three older women, who were swooning.

Finally, they calmed down, and that was when Mel asked, "So what do you think about the house?"

"Who? How? When?" Tenille replied.

They were all smiles as they admitted it was a team effort. "Archie was such a dear and filed all the paperwork with the insurance company in your stead," Mel said.

Since when was he Archie to her?

"That's right. He stepped in and made sure they covered everything and then hired a contractor to put it back in order. We pulled out all of our pictures and made sure they matched the paint samples. It took almost nine months," Amelia added.

"Yup, they just finished a few weeks ago," Carol said. "And it cost a mint. Thank goodness for insurance."

That was Carol, always talking inappropriately about money.

"So how is Archie?" Tenille asked suspiciously.

Mel held out her ring finger and showed off a beautiful yellow diamond. "Engaged," Mel said, and they all squealed like teenagers.

"What?" Tenille couldn't believe it. Mel was always the level-headed one and to think she was in love and engaged was wonderful.

"He is such a sweetheart," Carol said. "He was so worried that whenever you came back that you would have to deal with the house and mess, that he stepped in and took care of it. Mel spent a lot of time helping him and voile."

Amelia leaned forward, "The house is perfect and they are in love!"

It was hard to tell who was happiest about the engagement—Mel, Carol, or Amelia.

It was another half hour before Archie got there, and it gave Tenille time to tell them the basics of what had happened to her. There was no need to go through the gory details as the older women could fill in the blanks with their imaginations well enough. Tenille still had the battle scars from her last entanglement with Peter Miller, and none of them needed to ask how bad he really was because it showed.

Once Archie went over the business of her accounts with her and then gave her current credit and debit cards, it was late. She promised to keep in touch and Reaper hoped that meant she was going home with him.

As soon as they left, she asked if he was ready to go.

"Angel?"

She shrugged. "Does it seem weird that I don't want to stay here?"

He watched her carefully. Sure, she'd had a lot of tragedy in her young life, but this house had been her home. "Are you sure you don't want to stay? Not even the night?"

Chapter Thirty

Tenille felt at ease as soon as she saw her aunt and uncle's things put back in order. Knowing Mr. Arceneaux and Aunt Sue's closest friends could manage the beautiful home, the place they made for her, gave her peace.

But the truth of finding out that Peter Miller's mother had callously killed her parents had changed things. He'd spent the better part of his life vengefully taking away what was important to Tenille. This place where she'd been mostly happy held too many bad secrets. She no longer felt like it was her home. At least not anymore. She just needed to find the words so she could explain herself to Michael.

Michael could see Tenille fretting over what to do. She'd spent a year hiding who she was, and she no longer had to do that, especially with him. He pulled her into his body and held her close. "Why don't we go get something to eat?"

Climbing into Michael's truck, Tenille was extra quiet after she'd agreed to go to dinner. But he had a surprise for her because they weren't going to a restaurant. He'd noticed food trucks at a nearby park when they drove in and as he pulled up into the parking lot, he grinned that there was also a live band.

They ate street tacos and then he tried to show her how to dance the two-step. She couldn't remember laughing that hard ever before. Michael was tall and handsome, but also looked like a bad boy. Yet, he had some smooth dance moves and all the women there watched appreciatively as he danced with Tenille.

It was late when they got back into his truck, and he kissed her before buckling her in next to him. "Why don't we get a hotel room tonight? We can go by the cemetery tomorrow morning and then maybe run by the house and pack up whatever you want to bring back with you?"

Tenille nodded and then sat quietly next to him as he found them a place to stay for the night. Somehow he'd known what she needed, even though they hadn't talked about it. As they laid in bed, she told him the story of how her aunt and uncle met and fell in love in New Orleans. "They were so sweet together and had that type of love that lasted a lifetime." She stopped short of adding that it was special, even though they didn't live to be really old.

The next morning they ate breakfast at the hotel because Tenille told him that hotels with homemade waffle makers had the best breakfasts. Before going to the cemetery, Tenille again took large bunches of random flowers and made beautiful arrangements.

He held the flowers and her hand as they walked through the cemetery so she could introduce him to her parents first and then to her Aunt Sue and Uncle Ed.

She looked up at him and kissed him sweetly on the lips. "I know it probably seems strange for me to talk to them here like I do, but it feels like they hear me."

He kissed her on top of her head and told her he was sure they heard her whenever and wherever she talked to them.

When he drove up the driveway to her old house, he kissed the back of her hand before he turned in his seat to look at her. "This place is incredible, Ten, and I appreciate getting to see where you grew up. And we can stay for as little or as long as you need. But it's not your home anymore."

Tenille's face flushed, but she looked into his eyes. He was open and honest with her and she wondered if he had any idea how much it meant to her that he understood her so well?

The way he kissed her before they walked into the house suggested he knew exactly how she felt.

This time when they went inside, she was lighter and showed him all her uncle's collectible cars.

"I thought you meant model cars, Ten. You didn't explain that the man had actual drivable collectible cars."

She laughed at that and realized she really needed to learn more about money.

It took a couple of hours for her to pack the things she wanted, specifically some of her favorite clothes and all of her books.

Then Michael carried some of it out to his truck before she called Mr. Arceneaux to have the rest shipped to her, along with her car.

The drive back to New Orleans was easier than the drive to Texas, and she tried to understand why. Michael told her he thought the trip going home to New Orleans was easier because there was comfort in the familiar.

Tenille thought about that for a long time and smiled that being with him was feeling more and more familiar. But she wouldn't tell him that just yet.

But she and Michael talked for almost the entire trip, and when they pulled into his driveway, they were exhausted. He wouldn't admit he was tired, but once they carried all of her things inside, they ate cereal for dinner and lounged next to each other on the sofa watching reruns of the show friends.

"You know, I always wondered what it would be like to have a group of friends like that. Girlfriends to talk to and guys across the hall."

Michael growled and lowered his eyes at her. "There will be plenty of girlfriends but definitely no guys across the hall," he said playfully, and she laughed.

Later that night, when they crawled into bed, she told him he was right, that Texas wasn't her home anymore. Home was wherever he was, and he kissed her breathless.

Chapter Thirty-One

Tenille and Reaper sat on the floor in the living room of the French Quarter home, looking up at their beautiful Christmas tree. It was the first live tree Tenille had since her Uncle Ed passed away and she loved the fragrance and natural beauty along with the twinkling white lights.

Tenille had spent the week helping Mrs. Bowers get settled back at home. She prepared meals for her and hung up a few decorations. A friend of Olivia's from her hometown was visiting through the holidays and staying at the boarding house. Tenille made sure the linens were fresh, and the bathroom sparkled before their guest arrived.

Mrs. Goings lived next door to Olivia in St. Marksville for most of her life, but they'd only recently become close friends. Lucas was a huge fan of Mrs. Goings, and he couldn't wait to see her, too.

They joined her at the boarding house, along with Miss Lynn, to bake cookies and holiday treats. But Mrs. Goings came to town mostly to help Miss Lynn prepare a holiday meal for the needy.

Miss Lynn, Mrs. Goings, and Mrs. Bowers did all the prep work at the boarding house, since the diner was still under repair because Mrs. Bowers had the next largest space. They'd had a very busy time and Tenille, along with Olivia and Lucas, helped where they were needed.

Snuggling in next to Michael, Tenille laid her head on his shoulder. He couldn't remember ever feeling so settled. "Happy, angel?"

She nodded, and he kissed the top of her head. Her red sports car had been delivered, along with her things from Texas. While Tenille helped Mrs. Bowers, he'd cleared a space for her car in the garage and built bookshelves in the house exclusively for her use.

Together, they had secretly delivered gifts to Olivia and Lucas, then Miss Lynn and Mrs. Bowers. On Christmas Eve, Tenille's phone blew up with phone calls from all the ladies.

The first call was from Olivia. She was overwhelmed when she saw the new SUV in her driveway with a red bow on it, along with a velvet bag like Santa carried around. Inside, there were five Lego sets for Lucas.

"My neighbors described you, Tenille. I know it was you. I can't accept a car and those Lego kits cost a hundred dollars each. What gives?" Olivia said without taking a breath.

"I don't know what to tell you, Olivia. I stopped by and you weren't home. But I saw that the gift tags said from Santa."

Olivia didn't know what to say. But Tenille secretly had waited to pay Olivia back for all the times her friend had rendered her speechless over the past month, specifically around Michael.

"I-I don't know what to say, Tenille."

"How about Merry Christmas?" Tenille said and Reaper loved watching his girl smile so happily.

"Merry Christmas," Olivia said and as they got off the phone, Miss Lynn called.

"Hello, Miss Lynn."

"Would you happen to know anything about a gold envelope that was delivered to my house today with the full amount for the repairs for the diner in it?" Miss Lynn asked, a bit flustered.

"Sounds like Santa was at your house today, too." Tenille answered as she tried not to laugh.

"Insurance is going to cover the costs. I'm sure of it. It's just going to take a while for all the paperwork to be filed," Miss Lynn added.

"Well, Miss Lynn, I guess you will need to take it up with Santa."

Michael knew Tenille had wanted to help all of her friends, and honestly, loved how happy it had made her. She received calls from Mrs. Bowers and then Nalani, who was still staying with Patrick Morales.

Two days later, Mr. Kahale called her about the check sent to his contractors. Someone had mysteriously paid for all the repairs to his family restaurant and his medical bills.

Michael laughed at how easily she blamed Santa and his elves. His girl had been busy generously taking care of everyone that had helped care for her over the past year.

They spent all of Christmas Day at his parents' house and enjoyed the extra family time. But the week between Christmas and New Year's Eve, they stayed at home relaxing and loving each other. Tenille explained that week was like no-man's-land, since it was almost impossible to remember what day of the week it was and honestly, no one should even print those dates on a calendar.

Spending that time alone together was overdue, which was why they declined to celebrate New Year's Eve with their friends. As they sat together on the floor with only the lights from the Christmas Tree and the gas fireplace, they could hear a few of the contraband fireworks going off in the neighborhood. There were plenty of sanctioned fireworks crashing over the Mississippi

River, but still people felt the need to celebrate by doing it themselves.

As the clock ticked down the minutes to the new year, Michael handed Tenille her glass of champagne as he turned around to face her. "Angel, I've never met anyone like you and I need to warn you right now that it's already been difficult letting you go to Maisonville without me. If I could keep you here by my side all the time, I would. I think the only way I can accept it is if I know you are going to be by my side for the rest of our lives."

Tenille set down her glass and sat up on her knees in front of him. "What?"

Michael grinned, "I have it bad for you, Tenille Sims, and the only cure is going to be a lifetime of being together. Angel, will you marry me?"

He pulled out a black velvet box and held it out for her. But Tenille bypassed the box in his hand as she threw herself into his arms and wrapped herself around him. He laughed as their bodies collided.

She kissed him hard, and when she pulled back, he held out the box again. "You're supposed to open it, first, Ten."

She had tears in her eyes as she whispered, "My answer is yes, no matter what's in that box." She smiled and slowly opened it to reveal a beautiful classic solitaire diamond set in gold.

"I didn't get you anything for New Year's Eve," she said, pouting.

"You gave me a 1960s Jaguar for Christmas, Ten." He laughed. She had parked the classic car from her uncle's collection at Cage's house until Christmas Eve. Once they got home from delivering the surprise Santa gifts to her friends, Cage drove the car over. When Reaper realized what was going on, he couldn't believe it.

Pulling the ring loose from the box, Michael slipped it onto her finger. It fit perfectly, and she held out her hand, smiling at it.

He pulled her into another warm kiss and told her he loved that car, but seeing her wear his ring meant everything.

That was when they heard fireworks erupt and noticed it was midnight. Michael pulled Tenille in for a deeper kiss, and they didn't stop until all the noise outside quieted.

He watched her brown eyes dance, and then she slyly looked up at him. "You know, Cage told me the guys gave you your nickname before that mission. He said they called you Reaper because you slayed all the girls when y'all went out." She laughed and stared into his eyes. Was he blushing?

"Let's go to bed, angel," he said as he stood up and held a hand out to her. She reached out and let him pull her to her feet.

"You aren't going to tell me that story?" She teased him again. He loved her playful side.

Pulling her under the covers in bed with him, he leaned in close. "I don't remember anyone before you, Ten."

She was a breath away, but before she kissed him, she said, "He also told me you had him come to the diner to meet me that first day because you wanted his opinion. You already were interested but told him that could only mean one thing, that I was trouble."

Reaper laughed. He had big plans for them tonight. Tomorrow, they would pick out the day she wanted to get married. His family and her friends would be thrilled when they found out about their engagement, but for now, he had her all to himself.

"And I was right," he said. "You were and are the sweetest trouble." Then he showed her how much he truly loved trouble.

The Making of a Monster

BONUS STORY

It was said that the young woman's scream was heard throughout the entire gated community. Neighbors gathered, and friends talked while the police and the coroner showed up in front of the fairytale mansion in Sugarland.

A hard freeze was predicted in Texas, yet all the neighbors continued to gather outside as Tenille Sims stood on the grand front porch. She sobbed as they took the body of her Aunt Sue and last living relative away.

Tenille and her aunt had planned to go shopping. It was the day after Christmas, and they needed a few things before their trip out of the country for New Year's Eve. Half-past eight, Tenille dragged herself out of bed. She couldn't remember ever feeling that tired, and she headed straight to the kitchen and the coffee pot.

"Good morning," she said when she saw her aunt's silhouette sitting in the great room. Aunt Sue didn't respond, which made Tenille giggle because her aunt often would get up early, work on her embroidery, and fall back to sleep with her needlework still in her lap. But as Tenille walked into the room, she saw Sue Langley's pale form slumped in the chair, and she fell to her knees, spilling her coffee all over the floor.

Tenille didn't remember calling Mel, Carol, and Amelia, but they all showed up to help. They were Aunt Sue's oldest and dearest friends, and they quickly took over. They called the authorities, cleaned up the coffee, and fussed over Tenille.

As Sue's body was loaded into the coroner's van, Tenille broke down again. "This is so unfair. She's only 65," she cried. The crowd outside hugged each other, and several wept for her. However, the three older women standing on the porch with Tenille remained strong as they helped the younger woman back inside.

❧

IT WAS ONLY a week since she lost her aunt, and Tenille tried to put the lawyers off, but they insisted she needed to come into their office. Tenille wanted to use the excuse that she was preparing for her aunt's burial, but Sue prearranged her own funeral after unexpectedly losing Uncle Ed, Sue's husband, six years ago. The family attorneys knew it. They practically knew everything about her family and wouldn't be deterred. Those attorneys made Tenille nervous, plus she dreaded the Houston rush hour traffic.

As she pulled into the parking lot, Tenille thought about her aunt's friend, Carol. She'd stopped by the day before to help Tenille order flowers. Carol also suggested they needed a caterer to feed everyone that gathered at Tenille's home after the funeral to pay their respects.

"It's the way things are done around here," Carol said, and Tenille was thankful to have her help. She gave Carol a thousand dollars in cash to handle food and any rental items they might need, like chairs or tables. Carol tried to refuse the money, but

Aunt Sue always kept a stash of what she called "mad money," and Tenille felt like the situation warranted it more than anything before.

Carol lost her husband five years earlier, and that was when she and Aunt Sue rekindled their long-time friendship. Carol teared up as she reminisced about the olden days and how Uncle Ed almost went out with her instead of Aunt Sue. She swiped away her tears and tried to advise Tenille about the lawyers.

"It probably has to do with your inheritance. You'll surely be rich after this," Carol said.

As Tenille waited in the parking lot, she was bothered by Carol's comment. The young woman felt a lot of things, but rich wasn't one of them.

ONCE INSIDE, Tenille felt like the receptionists were whispering about her. She was told to have a seat and assured the attorneys would be ready in a few minutes.

Trying not to worry, Tenille half-heartedly read the novel she'd brought as she waited. The head attorney, Mr. Arceneaux, and her uncle were good friends, and he'd helped stealthily take care of their finances.

Uncle Ed was a forensic accountant and worked hard to give them a comfortable life. Tenille went to live with them when she was only seven years old and learned at that young age life was fleeting, and no one was guaranteed tomorrow.

Finally, she was led back to the conference room, where three attorneys sat at the end of a long table. One man ushered her to the side where a lone water bottle was placed. Two more spots directly across from her also had water, but no one was there. Would even more attorneys have to join them for this meeting? The only one she knew was the oldest in the room, Mr. Arceneaux. He began by explaining how much money Tenille had in a secret trust fund her aunt and uncle set up years ago, which didn't include their savings and some life insurance that she would also receive. It was overwhelming.

The attorneys all looked at each other when she didn't speak. Tenille admittedly had tuned them out as she tried to comprehend the enormous financial gift that her guardians had invested for her. She would never have to worry about money. How did she deserve them? They were always wonderful and generous to everyone but especially her. Now that they were both gone, it felt like they were still caring for her.

The youngest attorney in the room sat his portfolio down on the table loudly, and Tenille looked up. When he locked eyes with her, she knew there was more news. Bad news.

"A detective stopped by to ask questions about your aunt's will and your inheritance. There seem to be some discrepancies with the way Sue Langley passed away, and the coroner has to run more tests."

Suddenly, the rushing sound of Tenille's heart filled her ears. She wasn't sure if she would pass out or throw up. She pushed her chair back and put her head down on her knees.

Mr. Arceneaux hurried over and knelt beside her before opening her water bottle. "Miss Sims? Are you okay?"

Slowly, Tenille sat up and looked at Mr. Arceneaux. "Wh-what discrepancies?"

The third and final lawyer in the room took over. "They seem to think her death wasn't from natural causes."

"How can that be? I don't understand."

Mr. Arceneaux tried to calm her down as tears filled her eyes. "It's all going to be okay, Tenille. We'll be here with you the whole time," he said as he returned to his seat.

It hadn't registered what he was saying until two police detectives walked into the room and had a seat across from her.

Detective Berry introduced himself and his partner, Detective DeVries. He didn't waste time with pleasantries just got right to it. "How would you say you and your aunt got along?"

Tenille swallowed back her tears. This was absurd, and her aunt would have verbally mowed him down if she had heard him questioning their love for one another.

"She was my best friend."

"And you spent the holiday together?"

Tenille and Sue had spent every single day together for fifteen years. Once they took care of things at home, they planned to be off again on another adventure. "Yes. We spent Christmas Eve putting flowers out at the cemetery for my folks and Uncle Ed. We picked up our Christmas dinner, then went home and baked desserts to give to friends. On Christmas Day, we delivered the treats, had drinks with friends, and ate dinner late. It was perfect."

"Until she died the next day," Detective Berry callously said.

Tenille nodded. She was holding back her tears but just barely.

Detective DeVries added, "We know you have a plane ticket for Thailand this week, Miss Sims."

"Aunt Sue and I were going to Thailand together."

Detective Berry rolled his eyes. "Sure, you were, but perhaps having her around was cramping your style. A big fat inheritance would certainly make traveling the world more fun for a twenty-two-year-old."

Tenille couldn't stop the hot tears that fell after that accusation. "If anything, I was the one who cramped her style, but she always included me in everything she did. Ever since, ever since I was seven-years-old and lost my parents."

Mr. Arceneaux finally spoke up. "I think she's had enough today."

The detectives stood, and DeVries pointed at Tenille. "Don't go anywhere, Tenille. We'll have more questions for you later."

"Count on it, little lady. Your money won't protect you if we get the toxicology reports back and can pinpoint how your Aunt Sue was poisoned."

"Poisoned?" Tenille stood up and shook her head. "Please. Please tell me that isn't true. Who in the world would want to hurt her? This has to be a mistake."

"Yeah, right," Detective Berry added before both detectives left.

Tenille looked at Mr. Arceneaux and shook her head. "You should have told me before I got here what was going on. The rest of this could have waited, but I had a right to know that someone might have hurt my--." She didn't finish her sentence but instead grabbed her bag and left.

Too overwhelmed to move or do anything else, Tenille cried in her car. Finding her Aunt Sue like that in her chair was horrible. The detectives were wrong because she and Aunt Sue were together every minute of the holiday. Nothing made sense to her anymore. She and her aunt had plans. How would she navigate the world without her guide?

Suddenly there was a loud knock on her driver's side window. Tenille jumped. It was just Mr. Arceneaux. She wiped her face before rolling down the window.

"Are you okay, Miss Sims?"

Tenille nodded, but her tears continued.

"Let me reassure you that everything is fine for now. I'm not a criminal attorney, but I'll help you in any way I can. The detective's hypothesis is nothing more than that an educated guess. Try not to borrow trouble, okay?"

He patted her shoulder and told her he would be in contact as soon as he heard anything else.

Tenille thanked him, and as he turned toward his car, she

started hers and quickly left the parking lot. She hadn't borrowed trouble once in her entire life. But trouble seemed to follow her everywhere she went.

One block away, she saw a coffee shop, a bookstore, and a Whole Foods in the same shopping center. She imagined Aunt Sue whistling and saying that was the mothership calling them home, the trifecta of shopping heaven, or some other hilarious saying she came up with during random situations.

Tenille had an hour and a half to waste to avoid the evening rush hour traffic. She could find something distracting in one or all three of those stores.

She pulled into a parking spot just as a large black Mercedes pulled up next to her. A handsome man stepped out of the car and casually smiled her way.

He was tall, over six feet, and had short blond hair. He looked professional but also a bit intimidating. Tenille could tell he worked out under that suit jacket because of how the material moved around his body. How could a man be scary and handsome at the same time?

"Great car," he said and gave her a genuine smile.

"Thanks." Tenille grinned back at him. Uncle Ed had bought the cherry red Karmann Ghia new in 1968 and was the only owner before giving it to her. He had several collectible cars, but this was his favorite, and he said it made sense to give it to her on her sixteenth birthday because she was his favorite too.

She tucked her keys into her bag and followed behind the tall man into the bookstore. They continued to run into each other while browsing, and he grinned at her each time. When she finally made her selections, she saw him a little ahead of her in the checkout line. He had three books, and she smiled that he was a handsome reader.

Next, she perused Whole Foods and was surprised to see him again. They each were buying cheese and crackers. He had wine in his cart, and she'd bought some bread, but otherwise, they had similar items.

He covered the side of his mouth as if to speak to her privately, "We like the same things."

She nodded and didn't think much else of it as she checked out ahead of him that time. When she loaded her bag into the passenger seat of her small car and closed the door, a homeless man was waiting behind her. It startled her, and she immediately told him she didn't have any money.

As she walked around the front of her car to avoid him, the man dashed around the back and met her at her driver's side.

"You drive a hot little sports car but don't have any spare change for a man down on his shit luck?"

Tenille felt alone as she looked around the parking lot full of cars but without another person nearby.

The unkempt man reached out to grab her arm, but as he did, the handsome man who'd parked next to her grabbed the lowlife and threw him to the ground. He stood in front of Tenille, shielding her.

"The police are on their way. You'd better get out of here," he yelled.

Without another word, the man pulled himself off the pavement, flipped them both off, and hustled away from the parking lot.

Tenille was shaking when her rescuer turned around. His eyes surveyed her before he reached over and gently held her arm. "I'm sorry I didn't get here faster. He was in the store, and I was afraid he was following you, but I didn't see him leave."

"H-he was in the store too?" she managed to ask, but her stomach felt hollow, and she was lightheaded. She'd only fainted when she had to speak in front of a large group at school and while she got her ears pierced. But she'd been really stressed, and it had been a rough day. She prayed she wouldn't pass out in front of this guy.

"I think you may need to sit down," he insisted and opened her door and helped ease her to the seat. "I'll stay with you until the police arrive," he offered. Tenille leaned over to put her head on her knees for the second time that day.

It took twenty minutes for the police to get there and another forty-five before they finished questioning Tenille and the man who'd helped her.

His name was Peter Miller, and he had an office nearby. He waited until the last police car pulled out before speaking to Tenille again.

"You okay?" he asked.

She nodded, but he didn't look convinced. He looked ready to bolt, and she didn't want to hold him up any longer.

But he surprised her when he leaned against her car. "I don't know about you, but I sure don't feel like going home alone to eat now. Can I interest you in dinner?"

Tenille was surprised. She was sure this man wanted to get away from her. Perhaps he was just a nice guy?

"You don't have to do that." She wanted to give him a way out if he needed it.

"I think I do. You look like you could use some friendly company."

Tenille wanted to tell him that he had no idea how much she needed a friendly face, but instead, she agreed to follow him.

He pulled into a fancy restaurant that was just a half-mile away. The parking lot was full, and it took her a few minutes to find a spot. She saw him pull into a space on the other side, and she took a moment to freshen up her face and hair.

What was she doing having dinner with a stranger? She took a deep breath and tried to find her confidence. He was handsome, and he did stick around to make sure she was okay after the incident. The least she could do was buy him dinner for his trouble.

She looked back to the spot where he'd parked, but she didn't see him. Suddenly, her car door was opened, and she felt someone pulling her by her arm. It was Peter. Was he angry?

Tenille gripped her purse and stared back into Peter's eyes. He'd scared her, and she didn't know what to say.

His eyes warmed as he reached for her hand. "Sorry, I didn't mean to frighten you. But I'm pretty sure I saw that bum walking on the sidewalk a few hundred feet away from this lot."

Tenille gasped, and Peter didn't waste a moment hustling her into the restaurant where the hostess knew Peter by name. "Mr. Miller, we have your table ready," she said before leading them to a private area.

Tenille felt out of place. Sure, she had eaten at some of the finest restaurants in the world but never with a stranger whom she found so intimidating and attractive.

She avoided his gaze as she studied the menu. Don't borrow trouble was what Mr. Arceneaux had told her, and she was pretty sure she had landed right in the middle of it.

After a few minutes, Peter reached over and touched her wrist. "Are you okay? Changing your mind about having dinner with me?"

Tenille gave him a half-grin. How could he read her so easily? She studied his face briefly, and he seemed sincere and concerned. After losing Aunt Sue, she hadn't thought anyone would genuinely care again.

"I don't know what would have happened if you hadn't been there earlier. Thank you. And dinner is on me."

He gave her another serious look. She honestly couldn't read him at all.

"I'm just glad I was there. Why don't I order for us? And just so you know, whenever we're together, I will always pay for dinner."

His blue eyes were dark, which was fitting since she felt like she was at the deep end of the pool with him. She looked down at her place setting until the waiter came over with fresh bread and a bottle of wine. When did he order that?

Peter ordered four or five different items, and after the waiter poured the wine, he left them alone.

Tenille was happy to have something else to do other than talk to Peter. She drank wine as he buttered bread and put it on her bread plate.

"I work out early in the mornings, and if I eat late, I get hangry."

She glanced at his face but didn't talk to him.

He continued trying to ease things. "I work too much and haven't had a date in a long time. I eat here with clients or alone several times a week. They keep this table open for me and keep my favorite wines stocked. I hope you like it."

"Thank you," Tenille said. She was still second-guessing herself. She was sure the awkwardness was her fault but didn't know how to fix it, but she tried. "The wine is great. And I'm afraid I haven't eaten much today, and I'm probably hangry too."

He smiled at her and told her he had grown up in Houston but went to college out of state. "Are you from here?"

He refilled her wine glass as he waited for her to answer. The wine was what she'd needed after the awful afternoon, and she began to loosen up. "Yes. I live in Sugarland."

"That's a nice area. Is your family from there?"

Tenille picked up her wine and drank again. A glass and a half in was the only reason she talked so much, she figured out later when she thought back to that moment.

"Yes. But I lost my parents in a car accident when I was seven. My aunt and uncle became my guardians, and he passed away when I was sixteen. My aunt just passed away a few days ago. I'm all that's left."

"I'm sorry, Tenille."

She leaned back in her seat. "Honestly, I feel like the grim reaper is just following me around and taking everyone close to me," she shivered when she realized she'd said that aloud.

Peter seemed to relax for the first time all evening. "I lost my parents when I was young too. Drunk driver."

Tenille had never met anyone that had lost both their parents in a car accident too. She gave him a sympathetic look. "I'm sorry, Peter."

He locked onto her eyes. "I'm sorry for you too. Other people just don't get it."

She looked at him and felt like she was seeing him for the first time. "The reason I was in the city today was that I had to meet with my family's attorneys. Two detectives walked in and questioned me like I had done something wrong. I have never even spoken to a police officer before, and they acted like I was involved with my aunt's death."

Tenille drank the rest of her wine. Avoiding his face as she added, "If Aunt Sue were here, she would be able to tell me exactly how to handle this. She was strong and amazing and always knew what to do and when."

She looked up to see him staring like he was seeing her for the first time too. It was a little unnerving. Actually, it was tense, and she set her wine glass down and pushed it further away. She needed to stop drinking.

He put his glass down, too, and pushed it away. "I've been on my own for quite some time. It takes some adjustment, but you're going to be fine." He paused to stare into her eyes. "So, you're saying the police think your aunt was murdered?"

Tenille couldn't say that out loud herself, but that was what they were saying, wasn't it? She nodded as the waiter brought their food to the table.

They were relieved to change the subject. Peter rearranged items so he could line up the small plates between them. Once the waiter left, he grinned at her and explained each dish. "These are my favorite foods here, and I thought you might like them."

He wasn't flirting. He was kind, and at that moment, Tenille needed his kindness.

They ate and made small talk for the next thirty minutes and drank espressos before Peter paid the check. It felt like they were old friends, and she was surprised because she didn't have any old friends of her own. Tenille was introverted as a young child and a shy teenager. She would hang out with her aunt's friends and learned she liked older people and got along with them more easily. Peter was probably in his late twenties, about thirty-five to forty years younger than any of her current friends.

After dinner, he insisted on walking Tenille to her car. Instead of asking for her phone number, he gave her a business card with his number. Did he expect her to call him? Even in high school, she had never called a boy. According to her Aunt Sue, it was perfectly fine not to call them because boys usually did the chasing. The only problem with that was no one had chased her--Ever. As she looked at Peter, who'd handed her his card, it was evident that he didn't chase women either.

He said, "Goodbye," and closed her door. She planned to watch him walk to his car, but he pointed to her to start her car and go while he waited.

Was he still concerned about the homeless guy? His overprotective behavior moved her. She smiled, started her car, and waved before driving away.

She had never dumped personal information on a stranger like that and felt embarrassed to have over-shared with Peter Miller.

Tenille dug in her bag with one hand on the wheel and the other frantically feeling around for a tootsie pop. Her aunt always carried them for herself and Tenille, which started her life-long habit. But she did her best thinking while she had one, and she had a lot to consider.

It only took her twenty minutes to get home. As she pulled into her driveway, she saw a police cruiser pull in behind her.

❧

"ARE YOU TENILLE SIMS," the police officer asked when Tenille got out of her car. She pulled into the garage but left it open to speak with him, thinking it had something to do with the parking lot incident.

"Yes, can I help you?"

The police officer used his radio to tell someone that he had her, and she watched as an unmarked police car pulled into her driveway.

"Nice house," he said, staring at the large property.

Tenille wanted to go inside and lock the doors, but she saw Detective Berry getting out of the other car and realized this was worse than she'd thought.

"I have a court order for you to surrender your passport, Miss Sims."

"Wh-what?"

"You have means and motive, making you a flight risk. Give me your passport."

Tenille turned to go into her house with both men on her heels. When she got to the door, she told them to wait there. They were bullying her, and she knew it.

She was always quieter than most, but Aunt Sue always told her to stand up for herself. Perhaps it was Peter Miller's chivalry that night that helped her find her strength? But thankfully, she'd found the nerve to tell the officers they couldn't come into her home.

It only took her a few minutes to get her passport and return to the garage, where the two impatient men stood waiting.

When she handed her passport to Detective Berry, she looked him in the eyes. "I hope you're wrong about how my aunt passed away."

"I'm not, but you already know that don't you?"

She shook her head. He was a horrible, bitter man. "Get out," she said and pressed the button to close the garage."

The uniformed police officer walked away, but Detective Berry blocked the sensor on the wall so the door would retract and turned around to glare at her. "Just so you know, when I'm investigating a murder, I turn over every stone. If you're hiding something, I'll find it." He looked around the garage that held her car but also two of the five collectible cars her uncle had owned. "Must be nice having a rich uncle?" he sneered and walked away. Stopping on the other side of the garage door, he turned to stare at her again. Tenille glared back, pressed the button again, and watched the door close between them.

Tenille had never channeled her Aunt Sue harder than that moment, and she knew the woman would be super proud of her. She was always trying to get Tenille to toughen up.

Her mind raced as she went into the house. It was eerily empty, and it had never felt like that before, and what was she thinking, unloading all her personal information onto Peter? What must he think of her? She'd told him she was a suspect in her aunt's murder—a murder.

Peter Miller had saved her from an aggressive homeless man. She didn't see the man following her, and she was always taught to pay attention to her surroundings in the city. She was lucky Peter showed up when he did and was willing to help a woman in trouble. Not many people would do that anymore.

Showering and getting into bed, Tenille desperately wanted to talk to her aunt and get her advice. Aunt Sue would know what to do, but she wasn't there. She would never be there again.

Tenille plugged her phone into the charger as she stared at the clock. Before she could think better of it, she got out of bed to grab her purse and find Peter's card so she could send him a text.

"This isn't the same as a call, Ten," she said aloud to herself. Besides, they were just friends, and she could use someone closer to her age to talk to that understood about loss.

"Just wanted to let you know that I made it home okay. Thanks again for everything."

"Who is this?"

Does he have so many women in his life that he needs to verify who is messaging him? "Sorry, this is Tenille."

"I was kidding."

Tenille paused to think about that because she couldn't imagine him being funny. He was serious like her, and maybe that was why she was drawn to him.

"Tenille? Are you still there? Everything okay?"

The day was too much for Tenille. Couldn't she take a chance and trust someone? She quickly typed, "When I got home, a police officer was waiting for me, and the detective from earlier drove up."

"What? I thought they were investigating things. Did they figure something out?"

"No. The detective said he had a court order to confiscate my passport. He made several accusations and said I was lucky to have a rich uncle."

"That was completely out of line. Did you get a copy of the court order?"

Tenille felt sick. She never even thought to ask to see the court order. "No. Should he have given me one?"

"He isn't obligated unless you ask."

"I didn't realize." She didn't like admitting that she was so naive. He probably already had guessed it.

There was a long pause before Peter sent another message. "Tenille, I think you need to have your lawyers present if he wants to talk to you again."

"I just wasn't expecting it, you know? I told them they couldn't come into the house and told them to leave once I gave him my passport. He tried to scare me with his comments, so I shut the garage."

"Good. Don't let them push you around."

Tenille smiled because he seemed proud of her. "I was with my aunt just about every minute of every day, and I can't imagine anything nefarious happened."

"Nefarious, huh? Good word choice."

Tenille smiled. He was different than anyone she'd met before, at least anyone her age. He was intelligent and thought of things others usually didn't. She responded with, "Big vocabulary. I like big books."

"Me too."

She imagined he was amused with her. But he didn't give much away in person or over text, and she understood that on a deeper level.

"Hey, Tenille."

She was distracted thinking about him and how he'd come to her rescue that day. "Yeah?"

"If it happens again, call me. I'll come over and help."

Tenille smiled when she read that. Would he offer to help her if he didn't like her? Probably, but she enjoyed talking to him.

She smiled when he told her goodnight and laughed when he sent a smiley face emoji.

Peter Miller was a handsome considerate man. He also made her nervous, but maybe that was because he was nervous under the surface. Nevertheless, she needed a friend more now than ever, and it would be nice to have someone to talk things over with under the age of sixty.

❧

THE FOLLOWING day when the doorbell rang, Tenille immediately thought about ignoring it. But that was the old her, and she wanted something different. She wanted to be brave. Fearless.

Before she could talk herself out of it, she headed straight to the door and opened it. Her heart sunk when she saw the rude detective.

"Can I come in?" he asked but didn't wait for her to answer as he stepped inside the house.

"Would you like a bottle of water or something?" she asked and then scolded herself for being nice to him. But her upbringing was strong, and she couldn't help but have manners.

Detective Berry grinned, and Tenille tried to ignore the hair on the back of her neck standing up.

"No. Thank you," Detective Berry said and walked toward the great room, looking around the house as if he expected to find something or someone there.

Tenille followed him and watched as he sat down on the sofa. He looked expectantly at her as she sat in a chair and waited for him to speak first. This was a game she was good at, and he had no idea how comfortable she was with silence. After her parents had died, she didn't speak for a year.

Detective Berry said, "We've exhumed your uncle's body and are running tests."

Tenille blinked back tears.

"It will take some time, but we're sure it will show your uncle didn't have heart disease." He leaned in and whispered, "We have his medical records, and he was in impeccable health."

The detective's behavior was odd, and as Tenille watched him, she noted how he handled her more carefully than before.

"That's what my aunt and I told the coroner years ago. But he came back and told us that we were wrong."

Detective Berry leaned back on the couch, pretending to process what she'd just told him, but he had something else on his mind. "We'd like you to take a lie detector test."

Tenille gasped. She covered her mouth with her hands, shaking her head, no, before she could speak the words.

"I thought you might object. So, we've asked the judge to force you to do it. We should have an answer by this afternoon."

"I-I haven't done anything. And my uncle passed away when I was sixteen. At his office in front of a room full of people."

"Well, unless you had something to do with it, I don't understand why you wouldn't want the truth to come out. Take the test. Prove you're innocent."

"I am innocent."

"Well, from where I'm sitting, you are the number one suspect."

"Do you even have any other suspects?" Tenille asked. "This is ludicrous. They were my only family, and I adored them. I would give anything to have them back here with me now."

"It's my job to find justice for victims, and your tears and age won't deter me. I've had children that I suspected of murder."

Tenille rubbed her eyes. Hearing her aunt and uncle referred to as victims was devastating. "They were everything to me. I loved my uncle. If possible, I loved my Aunt Sue even more. What you're saying to me doesn't make any sense. Everyone loved them."

The detective stood, looking proud that he'd rattled her. "Miss Sims, I have never arrested a criminal that admitted he or she was guilty." He emphasized the words 'or she' to scare her more.

Tenille stared at him, and he sneered, "I have a warrant to search the premises that will be ready in a couple of hours."

Tenille stood and pointed to the front door. "I want you to leave my home now, Mr. Berry." She walked directly to the door and opened it, avoiding Detective Berry's face and harsh glare.

"I'll see you in a couple of hours, Miss Sims."

She shut the door before he could say anything else and began to tremble. This couldn't be happening. She paced the floor as she remembered her new plan to take control of her life. And the first thing she needed to do was call her aunt's attorney, rather, her attorney, Mr. Arceneaux. Then she would call Carol, Amelia, and Mel and catch them up on what was happening because she had a possible killer to catch, and if she needed a posse, they would have to be it.

The lawyer agreed to come, but it would take him some time, and the ladies beat him there. Tenille calmed down as they hugged her and promised to stay by her side. She may not know exactly how to handle the detective, but they reassured her that the older attorney would know what to do.

Amelia made them all hot tea after Tenille changed her clothes. Mel helped her pick out black pants and a black silk blouse that she said made Tenille look more self-confident. The pink joggers and t-shirt she'd slept in and wore when the detective had shown up made her look young, and she wouldn't look weak again the next time she saw him.

Mel reassured her that she could handle this, and Carol agreed. Amelia sat down with her laptop and googled what to expect from a search warrant.

Aunt Sue was always the ringleader of their circus, but they owed it to her to solve this case.

Mel's husband was a judge for years before he passed away, and she still knew a few people that could help.

They made lists of everything they already knew, but it was

tough for them to believe that Ed and Sue Langley were murdered.

"Your Uncle Ed kept journals, Ten. He had personal journals and work journals. Sue loved reading them after he passed. Perhaps something in those would give us a clue as to what is going on?" Amelia suggested.

Mel leaned in and whispered, "If they are in this house, those detectives will want them."

Carol looked at Tenille. "Do you know where they are?"

Sue and Tenille left everything in Uncle Ed's office the same way he'd left it. Even his favorite pen was still on the desk next to his leather journal he'd written in the morning that he'd died. The housekeepers were instructed to clean everything but not disturb the placement. Tenille loved to hear stories from her aunt when she read things he'd written about them. However, Tenille had never invaded his privacy by reading his journals. But she knew exactly where they were.

She quickly went into his office with all three ladies behind her. She dug into his desk drawer, pulling out five leather-bound books. Next, she went to the closet and pulled out three small plastic bins sealed airtight with dates written outside.

Each woman grabbed a bin while Tenille held the journals she'd found inside his desk drawer. "I can put these in my van," Mel told them, and they all agreed. But just as they headed out of the office, they heard a knock on the front door.

Could the detective have gotten the search warrant earlier than expected? Tenille didn't think Mr. Arceneaux could have made it that fast.

Amelia and Carol ran to the garage, with Mel stopping to grab the stack of journals from Tenille's arms. "You've got this, Ten," she said as she ran toward the garage.

Trying to calm down, Tenille looked out the side curtain.

Her nerves were getting the best of her that day, and she had to pull herself together.

"Fearless," she whispered.

She opened the door where she found Peter grinning at her.

"Hi," she said, staring at him wearing his perfectly tailored black suit and red tie. He looked powerful, and she couldn't help but feel relieved to see him.

"You look amazing. How are you?" He stood on the porch, waiting, unlike Detective Berry.

"Thank you. I-I'm okay."

He didn't look like he believed her, but she didn't want to discuss it with the door open. "Come in. Can I get you something to drink? Water? Coffee? Tea?"

He walked inside the door, but as soon as she closed it, he reached over to grab her hand. "I don't need a drink. Why don't you tell me what's wrong?"

Why did she constantly look like a damsel in distress in front of him? She didn't want him to think of her that way, but she didn't know how to change the narrative.

He heard noises coming from the garage and looked at her. "Hold on," she said and hurried to help her friends hide their evidence.

The ladies had gone out the garage side door and stuffed the journals into the van. It took them a few minutes. When Tenille returned with Carol, Amelia, and Mel, by her side, she was blushing. She introduced them and tried not to laugh as each woman approached Peter to check him out.

"Mmm, Mmm," Mel said, stepping to the side and still looking him up and down.

"Pleased to meet you," Carol whispered.

"Good job, Ten," Amelia said as if he couldn't hear her.

Tenille stepped around her older friends and led Peter by the arm out of the entryway. "I'm okay. Well, I will be okay.

I've got it under control," she said, answering his earlier question.

"Tenille, I've got some big shoulders, and I can help you carry some of the burdens," he insisted.

She stared at him. No one had ever spoken to her like that before, and she couldn't believe when she needed it most, she'd met someone like him.

She took a deep breath and told him what had happened with the detective that morning. Peter wasn't shocked or surprised. Instead, he remained calm as he listened to her. Afterward, he picked up his phone and called someone. "It's me. Cancel my appointments this afternoon. And call Mario and let him know I might need him in an hour or so with some legal issues. Yes. Just tell him to stand by."

When Peter finished, he smiled at her and her friends before asking for that bottle of water she'd offered.

Tenille hurried into the kitchen but could feel his eyes on her. Her stomach felt fluttery having him there. When she walked back toward him and handed over the water bottle, he motioned for her to sit on the sofa beside him.

The older ladies gathered around.

"Alright, let's discuss how this will go down," he said, and Tenille felt a bit more relieved. "First, no one can force you to take a lie detector test. Understand? No matter what he tells you, it isn't legal, and he can't make you do it. They are too subjective, and you shouldn't take it."

Tenille wondered who Peter Miller really was. How did he know these things? She wanted to kiss him right then and there in front of everyone. But she resisted the impulse and held his hand instead.

He winked at her and continued. "When the police arrive, they must tell you they have a warrant to search the premises. It will state where they can search. It could be your uncle's office.

It may say the entire house. But you can ask for a copy of the warrant so that we can verify. If it doesn't include your car or the outbuildings, they can't search them without your permission."

"Okay. Should I permit them? I mean, I haven't done anything wrong."

"I know you haven't, but this detective is an asshole, and he seems to be gunning for you. No need to give him more access than he's already taking."

Tenille took several deep breaths trying to keep calm. Why did it feel so good to have him there to take charge? How would she become that strong independent woman if the first time she was challenged, she leaned on him?

Peter stared for a moment, and she felt like he saw too much. She bit her bottom lip to distract her feelings. This thing between them was weird, but even if it was just friendship, she wanted him to respect her.

"Okay. I've got this," Tenille said, and Peter grinned approvingly.

"We've got this, Ten," Carol told her, and the other two women agreed. Tenille felt better because she wasn't alone.

Peter smiled at the ladies, too, as he drank half his water and stood to look around. "Nice house, Tenille."

"Thank you." Before she could ask him how he knew where she lived, the doorbell rang.

Peter pierced her with a look of determination. "Take a deep breath, Tenille," he instructed and did the same so she would follow. He motioned for her to stop as he whispered, "Slow and controlled. Don't let them see you sweat."

She nodded as she slowly went to the door to look outside. There stood her attorney, Mr. Arceneaux, but behind him were both detectives, Berry and DeVries, and six or seven additional police officers.

Tenille looked at Peter, who gave her another confident nod before she opened the door.

She introduced everyone to Mr. Arceneaux and took a few steps back as Detective Berry arrogantly walked inside to tell her he had a search warrant. She looked to Mr. Arceneaux, but before he could speak, Peter stepped in front of him. "Go ahead and ask the detective for the warrant, Tenille."

She stepped toward Detective Berry and asked to see the paperwork. He looked surprised that she had Peter and wouldn't just roll over again when he walked through the door.

Before Tenille could read the search warrant, Detective Berry instructed the group to spread out and go through the entire house. He looked at her and said, "I'm sending two officers to your shed and detached garage with all the fancy cars, okay?"

Tenille looked at Mr. Arceneaux, but again before he could say anything, Peter showed her those areas were not included in the warrant.

"Please only look in the areas allowed by the warrant, Mr. Berry," she said. Tenille remembered the first time she'd referred to him as mister instead of a detective. He was insulted. He wore that detective title like a badge of honor, and she didn't have any respect for him.

He glared at her but didn't say another word.

As they began to tear her home apart, Peter pulled out his phone and videoed everything. Tenille was so thankful that he was there, and later, she would tell him.

It took hours for the police to go through her five thousand square foot home. They gathered multiple computers, tablets, and two old phones, plus her new one to take with them.

After they left, Peter glared at her attorney, who hadn't said more than a few words the entire time the detectives were there.

"Exactly what is it that you do, Mr. Arceneaux?" Peter asked. Before the attorney could answer, Peter spoke again. "I know you're an attorney, but other than charging Miss Sims for your time to be here, you haven't done a single damn thing for her."

Mel looked proud of Peter, and the other two women glared at the attorney.

Mr. Arceneaux looked offended, but before Tenille could smooth things over, Peter opened the front door and motioned for the older gentleman to leave, which he did.

Tenille was too devastated over the condition of her home to defend Mr. Arceneaux. She was strong the entire time, but now that the officials were gone, the tears she'd held back were unstoppable.

She knelt on the floor in front of her library and stared at all her books strewn everywhere, and sobbed. Peter crouched beside her and hugged her.

There wasn't a single area untouched. Every mattress was stripped and flipped as well as every drawer. The home where she was raised was ransacked, and putting it back together would take weeks.

Peter gently pulled her face up to look at him and wiped her tears with his thumbs. "It's okay. I'll hire someone to come here and make this as good as new."

"Y-you don't have to do that. I can hire them," Tenille said weakly.

"I know I don't have to, but I will. Why don't we pack you a bag, and you can stay at my house until everything is back together?"

Tenille hesitated, and Mel stepped over to her. "You can stay with one of us, Ten," she said.

Carol's eyes widened as she stared at Amelia. Were they just being polite?

"I trust him," Tenille whispered to Mel, who looked skeptical at her.

"You're sure, Ten?"

Tenille nodded at the sweet older woman as Peter put his arm around her. She needed some time to clear her head, and perhaps a night or two away with Peter would help.

They dug through the rubble of her bedroom to gather a few things. Then twenty minutes later, Peter was driving her away from the nightmare of her day.

Just as they pulled up to a stark modern-looking house in Houston, Mr. Arceneaux called Tenille. Right when she thought she couldn't cry anymore, she was proven wrong.

"Miss Sims, I'm sorry to have to tell you this, but that Detective Berry got the court's permission to freeze your accounts temporarily. It will remain until you're removed from the suspect list."

Tenille couldn't stop shaking as she told Peter the news. He didn't miss a beat when he told her not to worry about anything because she could count on him for whatever she needed.

Overwhelmed, she thought about how she was right back where she'd started at age seven. That was the first time she was all alone and, of course, didn't have a penny to her name.

RED WINE WASN'T the answer to Tenille's problems, but it helped. She thanked Peter, who opened two bottles, one to drink immediately and the other to aerate for later.

His house was a harsh contrast to Tenille's home. It was all clean lines and soaring ceilings. His fireplace was black marble that scaled an entire wall, and his furniture looked custom-built for his height and the size of each room. Not a single thing was out of place, like the man himself.

He turned on the gas fireplace as he stood beside her and drank his wine. She wasn't sure she belonged there. But he was really helpful with the police. How would she have made it through the invasive home search without him?

Lost in thought, Tenille was startled when Peter spoke. "I know this is sudden. The way we met was unusual, and all the trouble that has followed is, well, strange too."

Cringing over what he must think, Tenille didn't know what to say. She'd never had anything like the last few days happen to her or anyone she'd ever known. "I'm sorry," was all she could say.

"Don't be. I like you. I want you to stay here."

She looked into his stormy blue eyes. He was challenging to figure out, but he was good to her.

"But if this is all too soon for you, I'll take you anywhere you want to go." For the first time since she'd met him, he seemed vulnerable, at least vulnerable for him.

She sat her glass down and walked straight into his arms. When she leaned up to kiss him, she'd caught him off guard. But the kiss quickly deepened, and an hour later, they were lying naked in his bed.

Tenille had never slept with anyone, and once he realized it, something changed in him. He was gentler, and his caring was her undoing. Afterward, he didn't say a word as he held her close. But when his phone rang several times, he apologized and said he had to take the call.

Peter stepped out of the room, and fifteen minutes later, he returned completely dressed to tell her he had to go into the office for a while.

"Make yourself at home. Grab something to eat, okay?" He kissed her forehead and then was gone.

Tenille waited until she heard the door shut before she got dressed, made his bed, and straightened things around the room that seemed out of order.

What was she doing? She was the thing that was out of order.

She wasn't saving herself for marriage, but she hardly knew Peter. Was she really going to stay at his house?

She went to his kitchen, poured herself a glass of water, washed it, and put it away. This was absurd. She wouldn't plunder through Peter's fridge or pantry because she could see that his perfect kitchen was never used. It was like something out of an Architectural Digest Magazine.

Tenille gathered her things and headed for the door but remembered she didn't have her car. Immediately, she searched for her phone, and that was when she remembered they had taken it too.

She couldn't even pay for a taxi because freezing her accounts meant she had no money or credit cards. She didn't even have "mad money" because she'd given it all to Carol for the after-funeral catering that wasn't going to happen.

There was nothing she could do. Even if she could contact Mel, Carol, or Amelia, what would she say? She'd practically insisted on going with him. How could she explain that she'd slept with him but thought she might have made a mistake? She felt foolish and wrapped her arms around her body. The cold was seeping into her bones. Tenille searched for the thermostat, but it looked like a computer, and there was a code to adjust the temperature.

Instead, she turned on the gas fireplace and curled up on the sofa, using her coat as a blanket. Hours later, when she woke up, it was almost midnight.

Peter was sitting across the room from her and watching her sleep. He had a strange look on his face, and she didn't know what that meant. But she sat straight up on the couch and tried to adjust the pillows around her.

"I guess you've decided to leave," he said, motioning to her suitcase by the door.

Had she hurt his feelings?

"I'm sorry. When you went to work, I worried that I might have overstayed my welcome."

"You sure it doesn't have anything to do with us having sex?"

Tenille blushed immediately and avoided his stare. "No," she said, but it didn't sound believable to her either. Of course, it had to do with them having sex. She obviously wasn't thinking clearly or acting rationally. She probably hadn't made a single decent decision in over a week.

Peter stood up. "I understand things have been difficult for you these past few days. And that detective has gone above and beyond trying to scare you, which I don't like. I want you to stay with me, Tenille. I can watch over you easier that way. But if you want me to take you back home or anywhere else, I will. Tell me what you need."

Tenille felt better just hearing him say that he wanted her there again. She didn't want to go home alone while everything was strewn all over from the detectives' search. And having someone watch over her for a night would be nice. She stood up and walked over to hug him. "Thank you. I don't know what I did to deserve you, but I appreciate everything you've done, Peter."

He kissed the top of her head, and she relaxed in his arms for a moment longer. "This is what I needed. This hug and maybe a slice of pizza?"

Peter laughed at the pizza comment, and it made her laugh too. He was a reserved man, but his dark blue eyes lit up when he smiled. "Do you like pepperoni?"

"Love it," she said, and he pulled out his phone to order them dinner.

A COUPLE OF WEEKS LATER, Mr. Arceneaux called Tenille and told her there were no updates from the detectives. She was still unable to access her accounts and utterly dependent on Peter for her basic needs.

"Please, Mr. Arceneaux, there has to be something you can do. How am I supposed to take care of the house and everything if I don't have access to my bank accounts?"

Archie Arceneaux felt terrible about the situation Tenille was in and wanted to tell her he was out of his depth with the criminal investigation. After all, he was a trust attorney and hadn't dealt with anything remotely similar to her case. But Archie owed it to her uncle, his friend, to look after her to the best of his ability. So he promised her he would take care of the house. "I will talk with the detectives again and get back to you soon."

Peter told her he didn't have much confidence in Mr. Arceneaux or his firm, and she, unfortunately, had to agree with him.

The truth was that Peter had taken care of her for the past two weeks. He'd driven her back to her house so she could pick up a few more things along with her car. Peter had filled her car with gas and bought food for them every night. He'd even bought her another phone. When he offered to hire a cleaning crew to put everything back for her, she'd politely refused. He was generous and considerate, but his responsibility wasn't to put her life back together.

In fact, it was going to cost a fortune to have the house restored to the way it was before, and Tenille wasn't comfortable accepting that much money from Peter. Their relationship had to be built on mutual respect, and if they didn't start on equal ground, she wasn't sure how long it would last.

Instead, while he was at work, she spent her days at her house. Sometimes she cleaned things up, but most of the time, she was combing through her uncle's journals.

Mel had brought them over that first day so she could talk to

Tenille in private. She asked if she could pull her van into the garage so no one would know she was there, and it had Tenille concerned.

They moved the table and chairs back into place so they could sit and talk. Over coffee, Mel was quiet until Tenille reached over and held her hand. "It's okay. Whatever you need to say will stay between us."

"I feel like I'm talking out of turn here," Mel finally said. "But I also don't want this to come out and you not know about it from one of us."

The room felt smaller, and Tenille moved closer to Mel. "Tell me."

"You know how Carol and your aunt lost touch for all those years, and after Carol's husband, Sam, died, they became friends again?"

Tenille nodded.

"Well, the truth was that Carol, Sam, and your aunt and uncle were all very close for years until Sam lost his job. Ed tried to help him out by loaning him some money. Instead of using it to pay for their house note or car payments, he gambled with it. Sam lost every penny. Afterward, he borrowed money from a loan shark. Carol returned to your aunt and uncle for help again, but that time to save Sam and herself from serious harm. Sue and Ed gave them more money but told Carol and Sam that was the last time because they had you to consider."

"Oh my," Tenille said. She knew her aunt was fantastic but to forgive Carol after all those years was a testament to how remarkable.

"I like Carol and all, but when her husband died, he left her with almost nothing. She's still hung up on money, and if it weren't for your aunt paying Carol's way to come with us on trips or to go out to dinner, she couldn't have joined us."

Tenille suddenly thought about the thousand dollars she'd

given to Carol. Did she even hire a caterer? Now that there wouldn't be a funeral for a while, shouldn't Carol offer to give Tenille the money back?

Why hadn't Aunt Sue ever told her that story? Tenille remembered Carol's inappropriate comments about her inheritance and how she would be rich. It was a lot for Tenille to think about, but she thanked Mel for telling her the truth.

Mel looked as if a weight had been lifted off her. She stayed for a couple more hours to help Tenille straighten the living room. After she left, Tenille sat at the table and read some of her Uncle Ed's notes.

She was instantly hit with emotion when she opened the soft leather-bound book. Uncle Ed had the most beautiful cursive handwriting.

Scanning through the journals, Tenille tried to find dates that corresponded with the story Mel had told her. Instead, she found notes where Uncle Ed had discovered Mel's husband, the judge, cheating on Mel. The judge had threatened Uncle Ed and told him he would kill him if he ever told her. The judge added that in his line of work, he knew people who knew people that could get it done.

Uncle Ed wrote everything in his journal and in big letters printed that if anything ever happened to him, look at the judge. He also wrote notes of when he told Aunt Sue and when Aunt Sue sat Mel down and told her the truth.

Mel didn't speak to Aunt Sue or Uncle Ed for over six months. Uncle Ed wrote that it was a classic case of Shoot the Messenger.

Tenille was stunned by the information. That night when she returned to Peter's house, he'd picked up dinner, but instead of eating, she sat quietly next to him. She couldn't bring herself to tell him anything she'd found out, but he knew something was wrong.

The following weeks went similarly. Every day, Tenille went back to her house, half-heartedly spent an hour cleaning, then read journal after journal. Sometimes, there were pages about how much he loved Aunt Sue or how much he loved Tenille. He recorded every book Tenille read as a child and had lists of books he wanted to get for her. She cried because she missed him and laughed out loud at some of his comments about her Aunt Sue's antics.

Still, every night she would go back to Peter's house. He encouraged her to settle in more and picked her up after lunch one day to take her shopping for a new formal dress and shoes. He had a charity event coming up and wanted her to go with him but he insisted on picking out her clothes.

He sat in the dressing room with her and helped with buttons, zippers, and clasps. It was intimate, and she felt so different from the person she was just a few weeks ago. When she narrowed it down to two dresses, he bought them both and insisted she would have another event to use the additional dress.

He told her about his work and how he imported and exported items for companies. Whatever they needed to be shipped and wherever was his specialty. His father had started the business, and it meant a lot to him to make it profitable.

It was the first time he'd shared anything more about himself. Of course, it was about work, but it made Tenille feel closer to him.

Tenille eventually found the journal entry about Carol and her husband. It was sad to read. Uncle Ed had really cared about Carol and Sam, and he was ready to blow a gasket when Sam had gambled the money away and sent Carol to ask for more. It was heartbreaking to read and confusing that Aunt Sue had found it in her heart to forgive Carol so easily.

Next, she found notes about Amelia and had to reread the passage. Amelia had worked for a big company. She was a single mom with three boys. Her boss hired Uncle Ed because he thought money was missing and didn't want people from the head office to come down and figure it out first. Through Uncle Ed's audits, he found how Amelia was skimming money from several accounts. It wasn't much from each one, but over time it had added up to a considerable amount.

Uncle Ed broke the news to her boss, William, and then agreed to sit in the room with the man as he confronted her. William had feelings for Amelia and didn't want to fire her or have her go to jail. She had children, after all. Boys he'd grown fond of too.

It was a difficult situation made worse by Amelia denying her involvement. She'd said some awful things to Ed before swearing she'd only done it to feed her kids and help pay her mortgage. That was all William needed to hear, and he promised her she didn't need to worry because he would repay the money. Eventually, they were married. Uncle Ed noted later that Amelia never liked him after that incident. He was always cordial to her but said people usually held a grudge when you caught them doing something wrong. He figured it was because they couldn't hide their dark side from you anymore, and almost everyone had one.

Tenille closed the journal and held it to her chest. Was anyone who she thought they were? Was Uncle Ed, right? Did everyone have a dark side? And how could Aunt Sue trust them all again?

Were any of those incidents motives for murder?

Tenille was overwrought with worry. She was a suspect in a crime she didn't even know existed, and now she was hiding evidence that could point the detectives in the right direction. All three ladies had offered to help her solve the crime and promptly helped her hide the journals. Had they used her vulnerability to conceal the truth?

None of them had visited or even called to see if they could help. Peter reminded her they were really her aunt's friends, and Tenille could see that he was right.

She dug in the pantry to find the bag of tootsie-pops that she was sure Aunt Sue had stashed in the back. It was a huge relief when she saw a giant-sized unopened bag.

Unwrapping a grape-flavored tootsie-pop made her smile, and she teared up as she thought about her aunt. They would play rock, paper, scissors whenever they were down to the last grape lollipop in the bag. It was their favorite flavor.

Sniffling back her tears, she sat down again with the journals, determined to find whatever clues she may have overlooked before. And that was when she found Uncle Ed's meticulous notes about her family's car accident.

Of course, she was so young then and could only remember the highlights. But Uncle Ed had the time, date, and the police officers' names at the scene.

Reading his details brought her back to that hot July night and how everything changed in the blink of an eye. Her parents, Zeke and Shelby Sims, took her to dinner and afterward stopped for ice cream to celebrate Tenille finishing her summer reading assignment early.

It began to rain on their way home, and everyone settled in for the thirty-minute drive as the windshield wipers rhythmically scraped across the glass.

When her mother took a curve a little too fast, Tenille's new book, The Little Princess, slid across the seat to the other side. She looked at her parents, who were distracted in their conversation before she quietly slipped out of her seatbelt.

Just as she picked up her book and sat back in her seat, a bright light blinded her, and that was where her memories ended.

Tenille was told that she was taken by helicopter to the trauma center and that she was asleep for three days when she woke up to see her aunt and uncle. She knew she'd almost died but reading the details in her uncle's handwriting made the memory feel worse.

She'd had head injuries and internal bruising over a lot of her body. The doctor's prognoses had given her only a twenty-five percent chance of coming out of it okay. She was lucky.

Next, Tenille read the details of the wreck she hadn't known. Her parents' car went over an embankment, not because of the rain but because it was hit from behind. The vehicle somersaulted down the hill before it caught fire against a tree. Her parents burned to death because they couldn't get out of the car.

The police found pieces of a bumper, some paint chips, and a headlight from the car that hit her parents. But neither the vehicle nor its owner was ever found. And her uncle had hired two separate private eyes to search for the hit-and-run driver.

Tenille sat stunned over the revelation that her parents' accident wasn't an accident. Someone had hit their car and left the scene. She'd made the off-color remark that the grim reaper was following her, but now she felt as if there was a bit of truth in her statement.

She couldn't read the journals anymore. Her uncle and aunt had hidden the truth from her about important things. Her parents' death and how close she came to dying or living a life with a brain injury. Everyone she knew had kept secrets from her. She couldn't stop the audible gasp that escaped her mouth. She looked around the home she'd grown up in and didn't recognize it. Sure, it was a mess but also, the memories she had there felt dishonest.

Tenille packed every single journal back into the plastic bins before surveying the disaster that was her house. She started picking up the debris and straightening everything with a determination she hadn't felt before, and she didn't stop for hours. Afterward, she was completely worn down. She couldn't think about the lies that had made up her life anymore, so she grabbed her things to head back to Peter's house. She was more desperate for Peter than ever before. He seemed to be the only person she could trust.

She swiped tears from her face and was distracted. It didn't register to her that the traffic light was red. She barely remembered looking up at the stoplight when she was hit by oncoming traffic. The little red Karmann Ghia spun like a top until it landed on a curb. Tenille wasn't hurt, but she was devastated that the car would need to be towed. The front-end damage was too much for her to drive it. Peter came to her rescue, yet again.

He barely looked at her when he got there but immediately took charge. He spoke to the police and the tow truck driver.

It wasn't until they got back into the car that he reached over and held her hand. "Do you want to tell me what happened?"

Tenille looked down at their intertwined hands. It grounded her in a way she couldn't explain. He always seemed to know what to do and how to handle the world at large. Something she hadn't navigated on her own before, and she felt lost.

"I-I didn't see the red light," she said. It was all she could admit, and he seemed okay with it.

When they returned home, he poured himself a scotch and quietly sat in front of the fireplace. Did he have a bad day too? She didn't know because her life was like a wildfire, and she was so busy trying to put out the flames that she never asked him about him.

She sat on the floor before him and stared at his face. "Is everything okay, Peter? Would you like to talk about your day?"

He stared at her, and she wasn't sure if he would ever speak. He just kept sipping the hard liquor and looking into her eyes. It wasn't uncomfortable, but she wished she knew him better and knew what he had going on inside that big brain.

"I want you to move in with me, Tenille," he said as he continued to look at her.

"I practically have been living here. But, Peter, I'm not sure about living together."

He didn't change his expression. He seemed to know exactly what she was thinking or feeling all the time.

"This is fast, but I do know you, Tenille. And I can help you. I know how to handle the police and get you untangled from that mess. I have an attorney that can take over your estate so that you can fire that incompetent old man lawyer."

Was that what he was thinking? That he wanted them to become more serious? It was the last thing she'd expected. But she wasn't ready for things between them to become more intense and certainly not permanent, at least not yet. She had to sort out what had happened to her aunt and uncle, and she wasn't good for him or anyone else until that was resolved.

"Peter, you are so good to me."

"Don't say no."

"I-I'm not saying no. Just not yet." Tenille's phone was on the counter and started ringing, but she ignored it.

He was still looking at her expectantly for an answer. Peter was the type of person that could answer any question the moment it was asked. But Tenille needed time.

"I don't think I can answer that question right now. I have a lot of work to do with the house and--," before she could finish, he interrupted.

"You can't tell me no because of the responsibility you feel for your aunt and uncle's house."

"That's not what I'm saying, Peter. Not exactly." She didn't want to disappoint him, but she couldn't tell him something he wanted to hear just to make him feel better. Tenille was dealing with so many lies or at least hidden truths from her past, and she wouldn't do the same to him. She hadn't discussed what she'd discovered, and she wasn't ready to examine their relationship.

Her phone rang again, and Peter shook his head. "Just go answer it."

She didn't want to answer her phone, but she didn't want to have to explain her feelings to Peter either. She jumped up and ran over to see who was calling.

It was Amelia, who she hadn't heard from in weeks.

"Hello."

"Oh, thank goodness, Tenille. Where are you?"

"I'm at Peter's house. What's wrong?"

"Honey, I don't know how to tell you this, but your house is on fire. I think you need to come here quickly."

Tenille wasn't sure if she even said "Goodbye," to Amelia. She grabbed her purse before she and Peter ran to his car so he could drive her home.

All she could think about was what else could go wrong?

When they pulled onto her street, she saw two firetrucks, several police cars, and a small crowd of neighbors outside. The house fire was out, but the smoke was still in the air.

Peter and Tenille walked toward the house, and that was when Detectives Berry and DeVries stopped them.

❧

"What now? You think I would try to burn down my own home?" Tenille's anger was unmistakable as she frowned at the two detectives. How could they possibly think she had anything to do with this or any other crime?

For the first time, both detectives looked apologetic. But Tenille didn't care about them and refused to say anything else.

She looked at Peter, who immediately spoke up to focus their attention on him. "She's upset, and you need to leave her alone," he said.

Tenille walked toward the group gathered in front of her

house when she noticed Mel, Carol, and Amelia standing toward the front with tears in their eyes. They were holding hands and watching the smoke still bellow from the roof.

When they saw her, they held their arms out, and she ran to them and hugged them tightly. The neighbors murmured, and she understood everyone was distraught over what had happened.

"Oh, Tenille, I heard that detective saying it looked like arson," Amelia said.

Nothing would surprise Tenille anymore. Every day there seemed to be another revelation in the mystery of her life. Yet everything in her world from the age of seven appeared to be an illusion.

As soon as Tenille graduated high school and told her aunt that she wanted to take a gap year off from college, Aunt Sue turned it into three wonderful years of traveling the world. Aunt Sue had turned sixty-two that same year, and for her birthday, they went skydiving.

"Ten, baby, you have an old soul," Aunt Sue would tell her. "And it's my duty to help you find your youthful spirit."

Sue Langley was daring, and after skydiving, she was also unstoppable.

Tenille wiped her eyes as she thought about those precious three years with her aunt. They'd had an incredible time together. They swam with sharks in the Bahamas and went surfing in Portugal. Aunt Sue's girlfriends, Mel, Carol, and Amelia, whom she'd known since college in the seventies, joined them to go snow skiing and snowmobile riding in Canada. The lists of countries and provinces she'd seen were endless.

They hadn't returned home to Texas for more than a day until that Christmas, and the day after, Aunt Sue was gone. Had Sue Langley used the travel to hide with Tenille or escape someone?

It took another hour before the firefighters left, and the crowd dissipated. The detectives quietly sat back and allowed Tenille to cry with her friends. Once Mel, Carol, and Amelia left, Detective Berry walked through the house with Tenille and Peter.

It wasn't as bad as she'd thought from the outside. Most of the damage was from smoke and the water used to put out the flames. Peter reassured her that there were companies that could come in and restore things like new. "It's not a total loss," he said.

Tenille couldn't speak as she saw her aunt and uncle's beloved things on the brink of ruin.

Detective Berry walked over and told her he was sorry for her loss and that he would find out who caused the fire. "I will have to tape the house off until the investigation is over, but afterward, you can have crews come in and fix it all, Miss Sims."

When she gathered more clothes and shoes from her room, Detective Berry helped Peter carry the items to his car. Tenille took one last look around, and then she saw the journals.

The fire didn't damage the kitchen, and the water that penetrated the room hadn't hurt the airtight bins that held the books. What if the arsonist did it to destroy the evidence?

Defeated and worn down, Tenille showed Detective Berry her uncle's journals. "There is a lot of information in there that you might be able to use. But, if possible, I would really like to have them back in good condition?" Tenille said meekly, and the detective promised her he would take great care of them.

It was one in the morning when Tenille and Peter returned to his house. He poured himself another scotch and offered her one, but she declined. When they climbed into bed, Peter kissed her and pulled her body into his.

"I'm sorry, Peter. I just don't feel like it."

"What does that mean?" he asked, and she looked into his face, which was void of any compassion.

"I just watched my home destroyed in a fire, and I'm upset.

Can't you understand that?" she was saying the words but couldn't believe she needed to explain herself.

But Peter had drunk more than she realized, and he wasn't happy about the situation. " I have done everything humanly possible to help you from the moment we met. I don't ask anything of you, Tenille, but if I need you sexually, it's the least you can do for me."

Tenille pushed away from him and ran into the bathroom. She'd never seen that side of Peter, and she didn't like it or him very much at that moment. She didn't cry, her tears seemed to have dried up after the fire, but she was shaken by his behavior and a little afraid of him.

She stayed in the restroom for over thirty minutes, and when she unlocked the door, she quickly exited the bedroom.

He didn't stop her or come after her, and she felt silly being afraid. She was overreacting. After all, he'd protected her from the homeless man, her hapless lawyer, and the detectives. She lay on the sofa and tried to go to sleep and forget about the fire.

At three in the morning, she had drifted off but awoke to Peter in the living room with her. He was quietly sitting across the room and watching her sleep again. He was drinking more scotch and looked upset.

She sat up and decided not to speak to him until he apologized.

He didn't.

But he did start talking.

"I don't think I've explained how stressful my job is. I had a tough week. After our charity auction dinner tomorrow, I need to go out of town to meet with some new clients. It's a big damn deal, and I need you with me. I realize how difficult things have been for you, but that detective appears to have moved on to other suspects."

Tenille had noticed that Detective Berry hadn't harassed her at the fire.

"That detective doesn't seem like the brightest bulb in the pack, and I don't have a lot of faith in his ability to figure this whole thing out. But he should leave you alone. I'll have a crew at your house as soon as the good detective returns the property to you. Okay?" Peter drank the rest of the alcohol in his tumbler glass.

So, they weren't going to talk about his unreasonable demand for sex? "I'm sorry you had a difficult time this week at work. I know my problems have taken the lead in our conversations, but I care about what you're going through, Peter." Didn't she?

"I appreciate that, Tenille. We have a lot in common and could really help each other."

The only thing she thought they had in common was losing their parents in car accidents as children. They also had a little physical chemistry. But she was exhausted, and he seemed to be offering an olive branch. She certainly didn't want to fight with him.

He stood up and walked over to her. When he reached out his hand, she took it, and they went back to bed together.

Saturday morning, Peter brought her coffee to bed. He was already showered and dressed for work. He told her he would be gone most of the day but would return in time to change into his tux and pick her up for the event.

It felt like things were back to normal for them, and she decided she needed to move on from what had happened last night. She didn't have any experience with sex or relationships, and perhaps she had made a big deal over nothing.

She finished her coffee before heading into the great room of Peter's house. He'd considerately brought in all her things.

He was generous because his house had looked like a showplace until she arrived. Her stuff was everywhere. She quickly got to work and, after three hours, finally had everything put away in the guest room closets and bathroom.

Proud of what she was able to get done, she grabbed a diet coke and sat down for the first time since she'd woken up. Peter's house was shiny and clean again like it was before she'd moved in, and hopefully, her efforts would smooth things over between them.

Tenille closed her eyes before her phone buzzed with a message from Detective Berry asking her to meet with him and Detective DeVries. For a moment, she thought about putting him off until later. It was less than twenty-four hours since the detectives had changed their behavior toward her, and it was hard not to hold a grudge.

But what if they'd discovered something? She wouldn't be able to think about anything else unless she met with them. She called the detective back and made plans to meet at the coffee shop within walking distance from Peter's house.

Tenille could discuss the case and still have extra time to prepare for the charity event that night. She wanted to put in some extra effort for the first real date with Peter and look her best. She quickly changed her clothes and hurried to meet the detectives.

Tenille arrived fifteen minutes early. She reached into her jacket pocket and found her stash of tootsie pops. She felt confident as she opened it before heading inside. She was back to practicing being the brave woman she wanted to be.

Both detectives smiled at her before greeting her. It was such a change from the way they had treated her before that she felt guilty, sort of liking them. They ordered coffee and sat in the back, away from everyone else.

DeVries spoke first. "How much did you know about your uncle's business?"

"I was sixteen. I'm afraid I don't know much. He was a forensic accountant and traveled a great deal."

The detectives looked at each other, and she wondered what they held back. "Tell me," Tenille said barely above a whisper.

Berry studied her before he answered. "Your Uncle Ed's last audit was for a large corporation. He'd uncovered some serious fraud. The FBI has confirmed that they are investigating that same company for fraud and uncovered emails where two of the head managers discussed stopping your uncle and his probe. They'd had two other auditors before, but he was the only one that found the inconsistencies. And the autopsy showed trace evidence of a drug that caused his heart attack. It wasn't from natural causes."

Tenille's eyes filled with tears. This couldn't be happening. "It was a few weeks after my sixteenth birthday. He was at work and had a heart attack. He died before they could get him to the hospital. Uncle Ed was only 59, and we couldn't believe he had a heart condition. He always took care of himself because he said he wanted to be there for us. The coroner insisted that it was his heart, though. I don't understand how he could have made a mistake."

Detective DeVries explained, "The FBI doesn't understand it either. The email threats and payments were made for the contract killing, but there wasn't any evidence that they went through with the crime. Except that your uncle passed away."

"But you said there was trace evidence of something in his system?" Tenille asked.

"Yes, but it isn't enough to convict anyone." Detective Berry lowered his head. "We have to tell you that your aunt was killed the same way."

Tenille couldn't stop the sadness that filled her. She covered her face, and when she lowered her hands, Detective Berry handed her a tissue. His kindness was still surprising, and she couldn't stop herself from asking, "Why do you both suddenly believe me?"

The detectives looked uncomfortable, but finally, Detective Berry handed her back her passport and said, "I'm sorry, Miss Sims, I was too hard on you."

DeVries followed with, "There was an anonymous tip called in that you'd drugged your aunt. The medical examiner said it was true. She was given something that would cause a heart attack in someone with uncontrolled hyperthyroidism. Who else would know that about her? Except for you or a close friend? Next, we went to speak with Mr. Arceneaux, and he went crazy lawyer on us. It looked like you were a poor rich kid who couldn't wait to get her hands on all that money."

Tenille couldn't believe what she was hearing. Someone trying to frame her for her aunt's death was overwhelming.

"But we were wrong," Berry said, and he did look remorseful. "It started sounding more like a Hollywood script than reality. When the feds called with the information they uncovered, we knew the original tip was fake."

Tenille had to interrupt. "I was with Aunt Sue the whole time. We ate all the same foods and drank the same drinks."

"Yes, but you're twenty-two years old, and your heart could probably take the stress," Detective Berry said.

"So what? Did they want to kill me too? Over an audit?"

DeVries admitted, "It seems excessive to us, too, especially since your uncle is gone."

"And they tried to burn down my house. Why?" Tenille couldn't make sense of any of it.

"Most likely to get rid of any evidence," Detective DeVries said.

Tenille immediately thought about the journals. She should have turned them over sooner, but after reading them, the only suspects were her aunt's closest friends. Could one or all of them be capable of murder?

Detective Berry leveled with her. "Look, Miss Sims. We wanted you to know because this monster is still out there and probably trying to get to you."

Tenille stared at Detective Berry. Was she really in danger? She didn't know what else to say or do. Knowing that her aunt and uncle were murdered and that she was in trouble, too, was more than one person should handle. "I was a kid. I don't know anything."

"We know," DeVries said, and he patted her hand. "We are still going through the journals."

The answers had to be in her uncle's journals. She needed to leave the detective work to the professionals so that she could follow her aunt's lead. Thailand looked more appealing, and she would leave town until they figured out more.

"We'll be in touch, okay?" Berry said. "Until then, you be careful."

The detectives walked her out of the coffee shop.

Detective DeVries added, "We've already requested to remove the hold on your bank accounts, but it takes a full business day."

"Thank you," Tenille said and hurried so she could get to Peter as soon as possible.

❧

PETER WASN'T HOME when she got there. She was stunned by the news from the detectives and couldn't stop shaking.

There on the bar was Peter's expensive scotch. She quickly took a shot of it, hoping it would help. The alcohol burned as it went down, but she felt the warmth from it inside.

She wanted to tell Peter everything she'd just learned, but last night's discussion made her think twice. They had plans for the evening, and couldn't she wait to tell him afterward?

Looking at the scotch, she took one more shot, and the shaking seemed to lessen. She could do this.

"You are gorgeous," Peter said when he walked into the house and found her sitting in front of the fireplace wearing the emerald green dress he'd helped her pick out. His smile lit up his eyes.

It only took Peter ten minutes to get dressed, and Tenille was more than a bit jealous since it took her a solid hour and a half.

The extravagantly decorated convention center transported the patrons to a wonderland of flowers and lights. Everyone came dressed to impress, but Peter reminded Tenille that no one compared to her.

He danced with her for most of the night, and they only took breaks to eat or drink. There was also a silent auction, and Peter held Tenille's hand as they perused the items, and he encouraged her to write bids. She couldn't remember ever having a better time. He was attentive and charismatic.

Peter had an incredible time too. After one fast waltz, where everyone stopped to watch them move together and clapped when they finished, he leaned in and told her he loved dancing with her.

He pulled back and stared into her eyes before he kissed her hard on the mouth for everyone to see. Her stomach fluttered for the rest of the night.

Finally, after eleven, he kissed her hand and pulled her toward the door to leave. "Are you finally taking me home, sir, to have your wicked way with me?" she whispered into his ear, and he looked at her like he could devour her on the spot.

They barely made it into his house before peeling off their clothes and having sex in front of the fireplace. It was savage and hot and exactly what they both wanted.

Afterward, Tenille excused herself to shower while Peter poured himself a drink. It had been a grand evening, but Tenille needed to tell Peter everything. He had a business trip planned and wanted her to go with him. But with someone after her, she needed to get out of the country as soon as possible.

With her hair still wet, Tenille threw on a robe before finding Peter in the kitchen. He'd changed his clothes but wasn't wearing pajamas. Instead, he had on slacks and a button-down shirt, and she hoped he wasn't going into the office that late at night. She didn't want to be alone. He grinned devilishly at her. "I see you found my scotch?"

Tenille smiled. He'd poured her a glass with a large square ice cube, and she accepted it sweetly. She would need the alcohol to tell him she couldn't go with him on his trip.

He kissed her on top of her wet hair and winked at her as he picked up his glass. Next, he led her into the great room to sit beside him on the sofa.

"Drink up," he said and clinked his crystal glass with hers. "Here's to an amazing night."

Tenille sipped the scotch at first. The ice didn't help it go down any easier. She took a deep breath before downing it to find her courage.

Peter's eyes were wide when she handed him the empty glass. She felt relaxed and watched as he stood and walked into the other room to set her glass in the sink.

When he returned, he stopped in front of her instead of sitting down. Tenille leaned back to look at Peter's handsome face. The stress and night of dancing had caught up with her. She had to concentrate on what she wanted to say to him.

"I met with the detectives today, Peter."

He nodded but waited for her to explain.

"The good news is that they don't think I'm guilty anymore, and they gave me back my passport. The detectives discovered that my uncle was auditing a large corporation where he found some illegal activity. The owners wanted to cover it up." She couldn't say the word murdered, but Peter understood.

"They believe the same people also gave my aunt the drug and set my house on fire. And that I could be in danger too, Peter. So, I don't think I can go on your business trip to Hawaii."

Tenille hadn't noticed when Peter crouched down before her until he lifted her chin. Had she dozed off? She blinked several times, trying to focus on his attractive face.

He kissed her lips and whispered, "You're safe now."

TENILLE WAS in the most romantic place she had ever been, The Four Seasons Resort in Lanai City, Hawaii, approximately 3,857 miles from her home in Texas. She and Peter had arrived only two days ago, but she was locked inside a giant suite. The phones were removed, and he had armed guards at the door so she couldn't escape.

He'd made it clear that he would never let her go.

When she'd woken up on the plane, she'd known he'd drugged her. It was the same hungover feeling she'd had the day after Christmas when she'd stumbled into the kitchen for coffee. How had she not known that she'd been drugged?

The same men guarding her were on the plane that night. Peter grinned and talked like they were going on vacation to Hawaii. Instead of the fact that he'd drugged and kidnapped her.

She'd slept from Texas to California, where they refueled. They were only two hours from Hawaii when she'd woken, startled over where she was and what had happened.

"Tenille, I told you that I had a business trip after the charity event."

She held her head in her hands and tried to concentrate. "You told me I was safe, but you'd already drugged me."

He warned her to lower her voice.

Tenille became louder and more hysterical. "Why? Are you afraid someone will hear that you took me without my consent?"

Peter shook his head and spoke to her behind clenched teeth. "This is my plane, and these are my people. I'm not afraid of a damn thing. But you won't disrespect me in front of them."

When she tried to argue, he dragged her by the arm to the back of the plane. That was where he explained to her how things would go.

She'd remembered the first time Peter was concise with his directions when the detectives planned to search her home, but she'd thought he was on her side. But Peter Miller played a long game, and she was the prize.

"When we get to the hotel, we will talk, but I won't discuss it on the plane. You will sit next to me, buckle up, and look pretty. I will have the steward bring you some water with electrolytes and some salted pretzels. It should make you feel better." He scolded her as if she were a child. But there was no mistaking the edge in his voice. It wasn't the time to test him.

She swallowed and remembered how scary he seemed to her when she first met him. Then how her deeply rooted manners kept her from driving off that day when she second-guessed having dinner with a stranger. After all, he was handsome and seemingly pleasant.

When the plane landed, he leaned into her and whispered, "Don't forget that I got to you when you didn't even know I was there. I will always be able to get to you, Tenille. But I also know Mel, Carol, and Amelia and can get to them at any time too."

Tenille bit her lip to keep it from trembling. She exited the plane behind him and didn't fight when he reached over and held her hand.

He led her to a black limousine with heavily tinted windows waiting for them. But he talked on the phone the entire way to the hotel. There was no doubt that he was in the shipping business. He shipped illegal weapons to and from different countries, and her heart sunk when she realized he openly discussed his criminal activity in front of her. He had a new group from the Middle East that he would meet there, and that business relationship meant everything to him.

When they arrived at the hotel, two women greeted them and slipped a beautiful flower lei onto Tenille and one made of seashells onto Peter.

Being a VIP had its perks. They didn't have to check in like everyone else but instead were ushered into a VIP lounge where a man walked over and handed Peter keys.

Once behind closed doors, Tenille shrugged away from him. Peter walked over to a fruit basket and picked up a shiny apple. He held it out to her, but she shook her head. He shrugged and took a bite from it.

She stared at him, wary of his behavior. He was unreadable because he had no conscience.

"You can stop looking at me like that, Tenille," he said as he continued eating the apple.

"H-How could you lie to me?" was all she could think to say.

He stopped eating to glare at her. "Watch your tone. I've never lied to you."

"You have from the very start."

He stood up, looked at his watch, and then stalked over to her. She backed up until she was against a wall. He was a breath away, staring into her eyes. "I told you I had serious business in Hawaii, and we needed to go after the charity event. Here we are. Truth."

He wrapped his large hand around one of her wrists. "I told

you that those idiot detectives wouldn't solve the case of your aunt and uncle, and I was right. Truth."

He grabbed her other wrist and lifted her arms above her head before pressing her into the wall. Tenille couldn't stop shaking but stared at him as he slowly revealed himself. "And I told you that you were safe, and you are because I've decided to keep you." He kissed her forcefully before pulling back to say, "Truth again," before rubbing his body against hers. Everywhere he touched her felt like fire licking her skin. Abruptly, he stopped, took a step back, and locked onto her eyes. "Don't make me have to go back on my word, Tenille."

He straightened his clothes and grinned at her. A look she was fast learning was a warning. "I have to go out for a couple of hours. Work."

She didn't move.

He looked her up and down before he said, "Get something to eat, shower, and rest. I think I've explained to you my expectations before, and I'll be back to collect. If you're a good girl, we'll go check out the beach. Maybe take a sunset walk on the shoreline?" He winked at her, turned, and left.

Tenille crumbled to the floor and sobbed.

It took a half-hour before she could move. Her mind was racing as she thought about everything she already knew about Peter. He said things without saying them, and she had to pay closer attention.

Peter had known who she was before she'd met him. He drugged her aunt and uncle, but why? He'd also drugged her, but it didn't have the same effect. Did he know it wouldn't? Of course, he did because he was calculating and driven. He'd said he'd decided to keep her. Had he not planned to do that in the beginning? She remembered what the detective said, "Someone had called in a tip about her." Had Peter set her up initially to take the blame?

The door to the suite opened, and her heart sunk. Was Peter back already? She hadn't showered yet, and he would go mad if she hadn't obeyed him. He'd made that clear.

A small man came in with a tray and looked at her. "Please, I need help," she cried, but he didn't understand her. One of the guards had heard her, though.

"Mr. Miller will be back soon," the guard said. "You need to eat and get ready, as he told you. Mr. Sung is here to unpack your suitcases. He doesn't understand any English." He growled at her. She didn't question him. Would he tell Peter?

She shook as she showered and washed her hair. "Look pretty," was what he'd told her. "I'll be back to collect." There was no mistaking what that meant, and she tried to prepare herself. It was only sex. She'd already had sex with him numerous times. She could get through it to save her life.

Stepping out of the shower, she saw a dress set out for her and makeup on the vanity. She trembled as she got ready. Peter had all the control over the situation, but she was patient. He had watched and listened to her for a long time, but she hadn't known. But now she did, and she would use that against him.

❧

THE NEXT DAY, Peter reminded her no less than eight times how ungrateful she was and how he was a sucker for spoiling her. He hated the tootsie pops she was always eating and threw them away. She hadn't made his coffee the way he wanted, and she hadn't worn the clothes he expected even though he'd picked out every item in her suitcase, including the shoes. The list of things she wasn't went on and on. So, she changed her strategy.

She would be the perfect girlfriend, and Tenille threw everything she had into it. She did all the things he expected and more. She'd figured out he was obsessed with how she looked, and his ego exploded when others stared at her. So, she made the extra effort to have the perfect hair and makeup and a sexy dress with sky-high heels whenever they went out.

The downside was that he could barely keep his hands off her.

Tenille had already finished her hair and makeup for the evening as he explained how valuable the business dinner was to him. "These men are family men. Arms dealers and terrorists, sure, but they also love their wives and children. Their women don't eat at the same table with them, but I need you to disarm them, my beautiful pet," he kissed her neck as he called her his pet—something he'd used recently as an endearment.

"I need you to speak only when spoken to and shine like the gorgeous girl you are," he slipped his hands under her silk robe, and she steadied herself.

Peter was excited about the dinner, and it was telling how important the deal was to him. He leaned back on the bed, watching her as she slipped back into the undergarments he'd removed and added her silk hose.

It had to be why he finally told her his plans and what she'd begged to know. "I think we'll get married while here in Hawaii."

Tenille looked up but tried to act like she wasn't freaking out over the idea.

He walked over to help clip her silk stocking into the garter belt before wrapping his hands around her thigh and pulling her into him.

"We're a foregone conclusion, pet." He sat on the bed and pulled her to stand between his legs. Sitting, he was only a head shorter than her. He looked up into her eyes. "I know. I have disliked you for so long. I mean, ever since the day my alcoholic mother crashed into your parents' car and then plowed into a tree close to our house. The bitch killed your parents and my father. She lied and said my father was driving alone in the car. Idiot cops didn't even put the car at the scene of your parents' accident one county away. It took her five years to drink herself to death. We lost everything. By the time I was old enough to take over my father's company, it was a shell of what it used to be."

"Your mother was the hit-and-run driver?"

He pulled her body into his face and took a deep breath. Telling her this information was getting him hot. He grinned up at her before yanking her down to her knees.

"Bitch thought she'd gotten away with it too. I was thirteen and saw the news about your family. It was the same night and time as my father died. I was there when she used my father's connections to have her wrecked car disassembled and shipped out of the country."

The questioning in Tenille's eyes kept him going. "We lost everything after my father died. He was a great man and taught me he wasn't just building a company but also wealth and a lifestyle. My mother was a beauty queen, and he'd said she was his trophy. But she ruined everything with her drinking. She couldn't hide her sins from me."

Tenille realized that he was telling her all his sins and secrets too. She was more frightened than before. "I'm sorry, Peter. You deserved better."

"I did deserve better." Peter kissed the top of her head but then grabbed her hair to ensure she looked at him. He bared his teeth, and she shivered.

"I spent years watching you inherit everything that I'd lost. My father worked hard to build that company, and my family lived in a big house in Sugarland, too, until he died. Your parents were both teachers. You went from living in a two-bedroom townhome to a mansion in Sugarland with a pool. It wasn't fair."

He tightened his grip on her hair, but she could only stare at him. "You know, killing your uncle was an accident. I was working my ass off to get my college degree and rebuilding the company simultaneously. I was twenty-one and so damn tired. I saw you driving around in that little sports car, and it pissed me off. Why did you deserve to have such an easy life? Back in high school, some of my friends and I used this drug on our dates. It made them easier, but sometimes it would just make them sick. I thought if I just put a little of the drug in his coffee, it would knock him on his ass. Who knew Ed was under stress and his blood pressure was elevated? And Ketamine can cause a heart attack in people with uncontrolled blood pressure. I didn't know. I'm not a pharmacist."

Tenille swallowed back tears as she watched him talk about murdering her uncle without regret.

"I was at his funeral, but you didn't see me. I watched you. You and your aunt were so sad. I felt bad that I'd killed your uncle."

It was apparent to her that he didn't feel bad. He didn't feel anything.

Peter let her hair go and patted her head as if to soothe the pain he'd caused. "I'd decided to leave you alone but saw you walking those two little dogs. Sue bought them for you after the funeral. What were they, a couple of thousand dollars each?" He rolled his eyes. "I wanted them and sent laced cookies to your house."

"The dog biscuits?" Tenille could feel her face burn red, and how dare he call her aunt and uncle by their first names.

"For the record, they weren't dog biscuits. I was using a date rape drug and had planned to knock you both out so I could steal them."

Tenille hated him even more at that moment. "You, bastard, you killed my dogs?"

Peter slapped her hard across the cheek, and she slid across the floor. "I've told you before to watch your mouth. I don't like women that curse."

She tried to close her silk robe as if it would help her pull herself together.

Peter walked over and hauled her to her feet. Lifting her chin so he could see her face, he frowned. "Now see, that will leave a mark if we don't put ice on it." He grabbed her hand to lead her into the other room to the bar.

He picked her up and sat her on the small countertop as he pulled out some ice and placed it in a bag. "Hold this on your cheek," he told her, and she obeyed. Looking around the room, she saw that the guards weren't around. He was getting more lax about security with her.

"I was feeling low after the dogs died. I worked my ass off and had to put cameras in your house so I could watch you and your aunt. But I missed the part where you were going to travel practically nonstop for three years."

He poured himself three fingers of scotch, took a drink, and offered her one. She didn't dare refuse him. He eased her off the countertop and led her back into the bedroom.

"It made my day to see you both finally return for Christmas Eve." He picked out her dress and shoes for the evening and put them on her like his own personal doll. When he zipped her fitted dress, he ran his hand down her backside. She tried not to shiver, but goosebumps covered her skin. He grinned as he stroked her arm.

"It felt like the right time because I was angry about the fifteenth anniversary of losing my dad."

Tenille wanted to scream. It had been fifteen years since she lost her parents too.

"The bottle of Ketamine was old, and I figured it would make you both sick and ruin your Christmas. I laced your Christmas Dinner with it. Then I heard Sue had passed away. I didn't know she had hyperthyroidism, or I wouldn't have done it."

Liar

He put his suit on as he continued talking, "I was quite fond of her. It was like you two had reversed roles, and she was 22, and you were 65."

He held out his arm so she would button the cuffs on his sleeves. He leaned in and whispered, "That was when I came up with the idea to get you arrested for killing them both."

He moved her hair behind her shoulders. "But you were standing there with those big doe eyes as that homeless asshole put his hands on you." He pulled her chin up to look at him. "I don't like anyone touching my things."

She didn't move because he scared her more when he spoke softly. "You were so nervous and sweet at dinner, and I realized it was destiny. You belonged to me."

Peter roughly pulled her body into his. He kissed her hard on the mouth, and she could taste the liquor on his breath. It wasn't a passionate kiss, but there was fire behind it. The all-consuming burn-you-to-the-ground type of fire and it terrified her. He finished with, "Knowing that no one else has had you really did it for me."

She stood stock-still as he stepped away from her to put on his watch, grab his wallet, and put his keys in his pocket. He looked her up and down before handing her a gold bracelet and earrings. Once she put them on, he nodded approvingly.

They were ready for dinner or, as she knew it, showtime.

Peter was excited about the evening. His trophy girlfriend was by his side, and he had picked out the most popular restaurant on the island. When this group saw his perfectly obedient woman, which they claimed didn't exist in America, they would understand who he was and how he conducted business.

However, when he parked the SUV and looked over at Tenille, he grabbed her neck and slammed her head back against the window. She'd twisted her long blonde hair into a ponytail because of the heat. He didn't like it.

"I'm sorry. Please, forgive me," Tenille pleaded as he finally let her go so she could remove the band from her hair.

He clenched his teeth and warned that she would regret it if she embarrassed him that evening. Tenille was mortified when she looked up to see a waitress from the restaurant in the parking lot watching them.

Thankfully, Peter didn't see her. He grabbed Tenille's hand tightly as they walked into the restaurant. The same waitress from outside was standing next to the hostess.

"I've reserved the largest table for Miller," he said, not watching Tenille as she gently wiped underneath her eyes, careful not to smudge her makeup and send Peter into orbit again. The waitress gave her a slight nod, and the concern in her eyes was almost Tenille's undoing.

"Yes, sir. We have your table ready," the hostess said and led them across the room.

Tenille was nervous when the same waitress showed up at their table. "Hi. I'm Nalani. I'll be taking care of you and your guests tonight," she said with a bright smile.

Peter explained how he wanted things, and the waitress gave him her undivided attention. He seemed to calm down as she delivered bread to the table and filled their water glasses.

Ten minutes later, six Middle Eastern men walked in wearing impeccably tailored suits and expensive watches. They dripped of wealth, and Tenille instantly noticed their Italian leather dress shoes. Didn't they know about the heat and humidity in Hawaii?

They were surprisingly cordial and spoke English perfectly but with London accents.

Peter proudly introduced his gorgeous girlfriend, and each of the men spoke to her. Nalani brought more bread and took drink orders. She was extra attentive, and Tenille prayed Peter didn't notice. He was arrogant enough to believe it was for his benefit, but Nalani kept checking on Tenille more than anyone else.

The men discussed where they were from and where they went to college. If she had to guess, Tenille thought they were either in their late twenties or early thirties, close to Peter's age. However, they were all married and had several children already.

They were a powerful group, and that energy surrounded them at dinner. Tenille was nervous she would misstep and kept her head down as much as possible.

When it was time to order dinner, the men waited for Peter to place Tenille's order before any of them. Peter mentioned how it was a family owned business and was on the island for over forty years. The food coming from the kitchen to the other tables looked incredible, and everyone seemed to be excited about the cuisine.

Almost a half-hour later, Nalani came over to tell them that their food would be out soon and when Tenille looked up at her, she motioned toward the ladies' restroom. Tenille suddenly flushed from the fear of getting caught. Had Peter or any of the other men noticed Nalani?

Tenille avoided the waitress' stare and drank from her water glass. The conversation had begun to lag, and Peter began to tell terrible jokes that seemed to get lost in translation with the men. In the middle of his next terrible joke, Tenille stood up. She was a bundle of nerves when all the Middle Eastern men stood too.

She whispered to Peter, "Excuse me, I'm going to the ladies' room."

His expression could have melted steel. He was angry. Maybe because Tenille interrupted his joke, but possibly because she was human and needed the restroom.

Tenille had no idea what went on inside his crazy brain, but she had an opportunity, and if she was going to make it out of there alive, she had to act as normal as possible.

Nodding shyly at all six men standing for her at the table, Tenille smiled as her mouth went completely dry. She smoothed down her blue silk dress and lowered her gaze before turning toward the restrooms.

She casually walked across the opulent room, softly clicking her four-inch heels on the tile floor as if she didn't have a care in the world. The men were still watching her, and she prayed they couldn't see her knees knocking as she shook with fear.

She slowly opened the lavatory door, but once it closed behind her, Nalani wrapped her arms around Tenille and gave her the biggest hug she'd had in a long time.

The waitress handed her a pair of flip-flops and smiled. "They aren't sneakers, but they'll feel better than those spikes you're wearing."

Tenille didn't waste any time ripping off her stilettos and throwing them into the trash. Nalani squeezed her hand, "You don't have to tell me, but was he going to sell you to those scary-looking men?"

Shaking her head, no, Tenille realized she hadn't even thought of that scenario. Peter wasn't done with her yet, but if any of those men had offered him enough money, or if it had guaranteed the arms deal, she would be as good as gone.

Nalani led her, through the kitchen, past the dishwashers, and outside to a pickup truck. There she introduced Tenille to her cousins. Kala and Kai, a young woman and man who were twins, smiled at her.

Kai opened the door for Tenille to get in, and Nalani explained, "I'll deliver the food and refill the drinks at the table. When he notices you're still gone, I'll stall him by saying you're not well but will be out of the restroom soon. Good luck."

Tenille reached for Nalani's arm. "You can't let him know you helped me. Understand?"

The look in Nalani's eyes told her that she did.

"Mahalo," Tenille whispered before she climbed inside the truck between the brother and sister.

Kala drove the truck onto a two-lane road like the devil was after them, and when Tenille thought about Peter, she figured that was fitting. They didn't discuss where they were taking her, and she didn't ask. It didn't matter. In fifteen minutes, Tenille was on a small boat heading away from the town of Lanai and the scariest person she'd ever known.

Nalani waited until the truck was out of sight before heading back inside. Her brothers had delivered food to the table and distracted everyone until she got there to refill drinks.

It took Peter almost fifteen minutes to get suspicious. Nalani offered to check on Peter's girlfriend and went through all the motions of going into the restroom and returning with a worried expression.

He pretended to be understanding, but Nalani knew his type. It was only five minutes more before he threw his napkin down and stalked to the ladies' room himself. Standing outside the door, Peter banged on it loudly. A few tables closer to the bathrooms paused to look at him, but he didn't care.

"Tenille? I'm coming in," he warned before he opened the door. Thankfully, there weren't any other women because he blew his stack, slamming the stall doors.

Nalani had waited on other tables when she saw him heading to the restrooms. She checked on the Middle Eastern men to distract them and be as far away from Peter as possible when he realized his girl was gone.

She heard some yelling in the kitchen and figured he must have stormed into the area of all the dishwashers. Half of them were Nalani's relatives, and the other half she'd gone to school with, so they wouldn't say anything.

Picking up a few empty plates from the table, she looked surprised when Peter stomped toward her. "Where is she?" he snarled, and she knew that she'd saved Tenille's life.

"I'm sorry? Your girlfriend?" Nalani shrugged. "She was throwing up in the restroom. Maybe she went outside to get some air, sir?"

Peter lowered his eyes at the waitress. He checked his pockets to make sure Tenille hadn't lifted his keys. Next, he marched out the front doors with everyone watching him.

Nalani gave the other men a sympathetic look before heading to the kitchen to hideout. She could see the table from the doorway where she stood but hid from the maniac that was sure to come after her again.

Peter yelled and cursed as he headed back to the table. Nalani saw one of the other men try to calm him down, but Peter's face was blood red, and he shoved the man before he picked up the table and flipped it. Everything crashed to the floor.

All the Middle Eastern men, without a word, headed straight for the door. One of them handed the hostess ten one-hundred-dollar bills for the tab, and without another look back, they were gone.

Peter yelled at everyone in the room, demanding that whoever saw Tenille leave come forward and tell him. He'd honestly scared more than one family away.

Before he could do more damage, the police showed up and hauled Peter out to the parking lot. Somehow, he was able to compose himself. "My girl wasn't feeling well and went to the restroom," he said. "I have our car keys. She couldn't have taken the car without me. I'm afraid she might have been drugged and kidnapped."

Nalani thought his explanation sounded too much like something he would be familiar with doing. But she wanted to make her story sound more believable, so she corroborated part of his. "He's right. She was ill, and I went in there to check on her. I gave her some wet napkins. She said she would be out soon, but I got busy with my other tables. I didn't see anything after that, sorry."

As Peter's story began to get some traction with the police officers, Nalani's father walked outside carrying Tenille's shoes. "Found them in the garbage can in the ladies' restroom. They look expensive to me."

The officers frowned as they realized that Peter's girlfriend had left him. "Sorry, dude. That's rough. But we see it with tourists. They come on these big vacations and get into an argument, or one of them runs off with someone else."

Peter stared at Nalani's dad and her. "That is not what happened, and you both know it," he said, pointing an accusatory finger at them.

Nalani's father stared back at Peter without faltering, "Now that's cleared up, there's the matter of damage to our restaurant, Mr. Miller."

The police officers stepped forward and put Peter Miller in handcuffs. They would take him to the police station, where he would most likely pay a fine. It wouldn't keep him away for long, but it gave Tenille enough time to get lost. And when running from the devil, or as she called him, the grim reaper, sometimes a little head start was all one needed.

"This isn't over," Peter said. "It isn't over!" he yelled as the police took him away.

THE END

About the Author

LISA HERRINGTON is a Women's fiction and YA novelist, and blogger. A former medical sales rep, she currently manages the largest Meet-Up writing group in the New Orleans area, The Bayou Writer's Club. She was born and raised in Louisiana, attended college at Ole Miss in Oxford, Mississippi and accepts that in New Orleans we never hide our crazy but instead parade it around on the front porch and give it a cocktail. It's certainly why she has so many stories to tell today. When she's not writing, and spending time with her husband and three children, she spends time reading, watching old movies or planning something new and exciting with her writers' group.

Connect with Lisa, find out about new releases, and get free books at lisaherrington.com

Made in United States
North Haven, CT
23 January 2023

31505245R00173